THE INSPECTOR ZHANG COLLECTION

By Stephen Leather

ALSO BY STEPHEN LEATHER

Pay Off, The Fireman, Hungry Ghost, The Chinaman, The Vets, The Long Shot, The Birthday Girl, The Double Tap, The Solitary Man, The Tunnel Rats, The Bombmaker, The Stretch, Tango One, The Eyewitness, Penalties, Takedown, The Shout, The Bag Carrier, Plausible Deniability, Last Man Standing, Rogue Warrior, The Runner, Breakout, The Hunting, Desperate Measures, Standing Alone, The Chase, Still Standing, Triggers

Spider Shepherd thrillers:
Hard Landing, Soft Target, Cold Kill, Hot Blood, Dead Men, Live Fire, Rough Justice, Fair Game, False Friends, True Colours, White Lies, Black Ops, Dark Forces, Light Touch, Tall Order, Short Range, Slow Burn, Fast Track, Dirty War, Clean Kill

Spider Shepherd: SAS thrillers:
The Sandpit, Moving Targets, Drop Zone, Russian Roulette
Jack Nightingale supernatural thrillers:
Nightfall, Midnight, Nightmare, Nightshade, Lastnight, The Whisper Man, Witch Hunt, The House On Gable Street, San Francisco Night, New York Night, Tennessee Night, New Orleans Night, Las Vegas Night, Rio Grande Night

Table of Contents

1.

INSPECTOR ZHANG GETS HIS WISH

Inspector Zhang's thick-lensed spectacles misted over as he stepped out of the air-conditioned Toyota and into the cloying Singapore night air. He peered up at the luxury five-star hotel, took out a handkerchief and carefully polished his glasses as he waited for Sergeant Lee to join him. They walked into the hotel together and rode up in a mirrored elevator to the sixth floor. The door whispered open and Inspector Zhang stepped out onto a thick scarlet carpet, the colour of fresh blood. "Which way, Sergeant?" he asked. Sergeant Lee was in her mid twenties, with her hair tied up in a bun that made her look older than her twenty-four years. She had only been working with Inspector Zhang for two months and was still anxious to please. She frowned at her notebook, then looked at the two signs on the wall facing them. "Room Six Three Four," she said, and pointed to the left. "This way, Sir."

Inspector Zhang walked slowly down the corridor. He was wearing his second-best grey suit and pale yellow silk tie with light blue squares on it that his wife had given him the previous Christmas and his well-polished shoes glistened under the hallway nights. He had been at home when he had received the call and he had dressed quickly, wanting to be first on the scene. It wasn't every day that a detective got to deal with a murder case in squeaky-clean Singapore.

They reached room Six Three Four and Inspector Zhang knocked on the door. It was opened by a blonde woman in her mid-thirties who glared at him as if he was about to try to sell her life insurance. Inspector Zhang flashed his warrant card. "I am Inspector Zhang of the Singapore Police Force," he said. "I am with the CID at New Bridge Road." He nodded at his companion. "This is Detective Sergeant Lee."

The sergeant took out her warrant card and showed it to the woman who nodded and opened the door wider. "Please come in, we're trying not to alarm our guests," she said.

Inspector Zhang and Sergeant Lee slipped into the room and the woman closed the door. There were four other people in the room – a tall Westerner and a stocky Indian wearing black suits, a pretty young Chinese girl also in a black suit and a white-jacketed waiter. The waiter was standing next to a trolley covered with a white cloth.

The woman who had opened the door offered her hand to the inspector. "I am Geraldine Berghuis," she said, "I am the manager." She was in her thirties with eyebrows plucked so finely that they were just thin lines above her piercing blue eyes. She was wearing an elegant green suit that looked as if it had been made to measure and there was a string of large pearls around her neck. She had several diamond rings on her fingers but her wedding finger was bare. Inspector Zhang shook her hand. Miss Berghuis gestured at a tall, bald man in an expensive suit. "This is Mr. Christopher Mercier, our head of security." Mr. Mercier did not offer his hand, but nodded curtly.

The manager waved her hand at the Indian man and the Chinese woman. "Mr. Ramanan and Miss Xue were on the desk tonight," she said. "They are both assistant managers."

They both nodded at Inspector Zhang and smiled nervously. Ramanan was in his early forties and the girl appeared to be half his age. They both wore silver name badges and had matching neatly-folded handkerchiefs in their top pockets. Inspector Zhang nodded back and then looked at the waiter. "And you are?" Inspector Zhang asked.

"Mr. CK Chau," answered Miss Berghuis. "He delivered Mr. Wilkinson's room service order and discovered the body." The waiter nodded in agreement.

Inspector Zhang looked around the room. "I see no body," he said.

Miss Berghuis pointed at a side door. "Through there," she said. "This is one of our suites, we have a sitting room and a separate bedroom."

"Please be so good as to show me the deceased," said Inspector Zhang.

2

The manager took the two detectives through to a large bedroom. The curtains were drawn and the lights were on. Lying on the king-size bed with his feet hanging over the edge was a naked man. It was a Westerner, Inspector Zhang realised immediately, a big man with a mountainous stomach and a pool of blood that had soaked into the sheet around his head.

"Peter Wilkinson," said Miss Berghuis. "He is an American, and one of our VIP guests. He stays at our hotel once a month. He owns a company which distributes plastic products in the United States and stays in Singapore en route to his factories in China."

Inspector Zhang leant over the bed and peered at the body, nodding thoughtfully. He could see a puncture wound just under the chin and the chest was covered with blood. "One wound," he said. "It appears to have ruptured a vein but not the carotid artery or there would have been much more blood spurting." He looked across at the sergeant. "Carotid blood spray is very distinctive," he said. "I think in this case we have venous bleeding. He would have taken a minute or so to bleed to death, whereas if the artery had been severed death would have been almost instantaneous."

The sergeant nodded and scribbled in her notebook.

"Note the blood over the chest," continued the inspector. "That could have only happened if he was upright so we can therefore deduce that he was standing up when he was stabbed and that he then fell or was pushed back onto the bed." He walked around to look at the bedside table. On it was a wallet and a gold Rolex watch. Inspector Zhang took a ballpoint pen from his inside pocket and used it to flip open the wallet. Inside was a thick wad of notes and half a dozen credit cards, all gold or platinum. "I think we can safely rule out robbery as a motive," he said.

Sergeant Lee scribbled in her notebook.

Inspector Zhang walked back into the sitting room. Miss Berghuis and Sergeant Lee followed him.

"So, what time did you discover the body?" Inspector Zhang asked the waiter.

"About ten o'clock," said the manager, before the waiter could answer. "Mr. Chau called down to reception and we came straight up."

"By we, you mean the front desk staff?"

"Myself, Mr. Mercier, Mr. Ramanan and Miss Xue."

Ramanan and Xue nodded at the inspector but said nothing. Miss Xue looked over at the bedroom door fearfully, as if she expected the dead man to appear at any moment.

Inspector Zhang nodded thoughtfully. "The corridor is covered by CCTV, of course?"

"Of course," said the manager.

"Then I would first like to review the recording," said the inspector.

"Mr. Mercier can take you down to our security room," said Miss Berghuis.

"Excellent," said Inspector Zhang. He looked across at his sergeant. "Sergeant Lee, if you would stay here and take the details of everyone in the room, I will be back shortly. Make sure that nobody leaves and that the crime scene is not disturbed."

"Shall I call in Forensics, Inspector Zhang?" asked the sergeant.

"Later, Sergeant Lee. First things first."

Inspector Zhang and Mercier left the suite and went down in the elevator to the ground floor. Mercier took the inspector behind the front desk and into a small windowless room where there was a desk with a large computer monitor. On the wall behind the desk were another three large monitors each showing the views from twenty different cameras around the hotel.

Mercier sat down and his expensively-manicured fingers played over the keyboard. A view of the corridor on the sixth floor filled the main screen. "What time do you want to look at?" asked Mercier.

"Do we know what time Mr. Wilkinson went to his room?" asked the inspector.

"About half past eight, I think," said Mercier.

"Start at eight twenty and run it on fast forward if that's possible," said Inspector Zhang.

Mercier tapped on the keyboard. The time code at the bottom of the screen showed 8.20 and then the seconds flicked by quickly. The

4

elevator doors opened and a big man and a small Asian woman came out.

"That's him," said Mercier. He pressed a button and the video slowed to its proper speed.

Wilkinson was wearing a dark suit with a Mao collar. His companion was a pretty Asian girl in her twenties with waist-length black hair wearing a tight white mini dress cut low to reveal large breasts. She was holding Wilkinson's hand and laughing at something he had said.

"Freeze that please," said Inspector Zhang as Wilkinson and the girl reached the door to the suite.

Mercier did as he was told and Inspector Zhang peered at the screen. He recognised the woman. "Ah, the lovely Ms. Lulu," said Inspector Zhang.

"You know her?"

"She is an escort for one of the city's more expensive agencies and when she isn't escorting she can be found in one of the bars in Orchard Towers looking for customers." The woman was wearing impossibly high heels but she barely reached Wilkinson's shoulder.

"The Four Floors of Whores?" said Mercier. "She's a prostitute?"

"Come now, Mr. Mercier, as head of security in a five-star hotel you must surely have your share of nocturnal visitors," said Inspector Zhang.

"We have a policy of not allowing visitors in guests' rooms after midnight," said Mercier primly.

"And I'm sure that your guests adhere to that policy," said Inspector Zhang. He looked at the time code on the video. "Ms. Lulu is from Thailand, though she travels to Singapore using a variety of names. Now, from the time code we can see that Mr. Wilkinson and Ms. Lulu arrived at eight thirty. Can you now please advance the video until the time she left the room?"

Mercier tapped a key and the video began to fast-forward. Guests moved back and forth up and down the corridor, hotel staff whizzed by, but the door stayed resolutely closed. Then at nine thirty on the dot the door opened and Ms. Lulu slipped out. Mercier slowed the video to real time and they watched as she tottered down the corridor in her stiletto heels.

"So we can assume that Mr. Wilkinson paid her for one hour," said Inspector Zhang. "Now, when did Mr. Wilkinson order room service?"

"I'm not sure," said Mercier. "We will have to talk to the waiter."

"Then please fast-forward until the waiter arrives with the trolley."

Mercier did as he was told. At five minutes before ten the waiter appeared in the corridor, pushing a trolley. He knocked on the door, then knocked again.

"What is the hotel policy if the guest does not open his door?" asked Inspector Zhang.

"If the 'Do Not Disturb' sign is on then the member of staff will phone through to the room. If it isn't then it's acceptable to use their key."

The waiter knocked again, then used his key card to open the door. Inspector Zhang made a note of the time. It was nine-fifty eight.

"And at what time did the waiter call down to reception to say that he had found Mr. Wilkinson dead on the bed?"

"Just before ten," said Mercier. "You'll have to ask Miss Berghuis. She'll know for sure."

They watched the screen. After a minute or so the waiter appeared at the doorway. He stood there, shaking, his arms folded, then he paced back and forth across the corridor. The time code showed 10.03 when Miss Berghuis appeared, followed by her staff. They hurried into the room.

Mercier pressed a button to freeze the screen and pointed at the time code. "Three minutes past ten," he said. "No one went in or out of the room except for Mr. Wilkinson and his guest. His guest left at nine-thirty and the next time he was seen, he was dead."

Inspector Zhang nodded thoughtfully as he put away his notebook. "So, please, let us go back to the room. I have seen everything that I need to see."

They went back to the sixth floor. Two uniformed police officers had arrived and were standing guard at the door to the suite. They nodded and moved aside to allow the inspector and Mercier inside.

Sergeant Lee was scribbling in her notebook and she looked up as Inspector Zhang walked into the room. "I have everyone's details, Sir," she said.

"Excellent," said the inspector, striding towards the bedroom. "Come with me please, Sergeant Lee. Everyone else please remain where you are. I shall return shortly."

Sergeant Lee followed the inspector into the bedroom and he closed the door behind them and then looked at her, barely able to control his excitement. "Do you know what we have here, Sergeant Lee?"

The sergeant looked at the body on the bed. "A murder, sir?"

Inspector Zhang sighed. "Oh, it's much more than that, Sergeant. What we have here is a locked room mystery."

The sergeant shrugged, but didn't say anything.

"Do you know how long I've waited for a locked room mystery, Sergeant Lee?"

She shrugged again. "No, Sir."

"My whole life," said Inspector Zhang, answering his own question. "We have no unsolved murders in Singapore, and precious few mysteries." He sighed. "At times like this I wish I had a deerstalker hat and a pipe."

"Smoking isn't permitted in public buildings, Inspector," said Sergeant Lee.

"I know that," said Inspector Zhang. "I'm simply saying that a pipe would add to the effect, as would a faithful bloodhound, tugging at its leash."

"And hotels in Singapore do not allow pets, Sir," said Sergeant Lee.

Inspector Zhang sighed mournfully. "You're missing the point," he said. "The point is that we have a dead body in a room that was locked from the inside. A room that no one entered during the time that the victim was murdered. Sergeant Lee, we have a mystery that needs to be solved."

7

"Shall I notify the forensics department, inspector?" asked Sergeant Lee.

"Forensics?" repeated Inspector Zhang. "Have you no soul, Sergeant Lee? This is not a mystery to be solved by science." He tapped the side of his head. "Zis is a matter for ze little grey cells." It wasn't a great Poirot impression, but Inspector Zhang thought it satisfactory. Sergeant Lee just found it confusing and she frowned like a baby about to burst into tears. "Let me look around first, then we'll decide whether or not we need forensics," added Inspector Zhang, in his normal voice.

"Sir, that is not procedure," said Sergeant Lee.

"Indeed it is not, but we shall inform them in due course. However, I would first like to examine the crime scene." He turned to look at the body. "So what do we have?" mused Inspector Zhang. "We have a dead body on a bed. We have a wound, but no weapon. We have a room that was locked from the inside. We have sealed windows and no way in and out other than through a door into a corridor that is constantly monitored by CCTV." He shivered. "Oh, Sergeant Lee, do you not appreciate the beauty of this situation?"

"A man is dead, Inspector Zhang."

"Yes, exactly. He is dead and somewhere there is a killer and it is up to me to find that killer." He looked over her and smiled like a benevolent uncle. "For us to solve," he said, correcting himself. "You will be Watson to my Holmes, Lewis to my Morse."

"Robin to your Batman?" suggested Sergeant Lee.

Inspector Zhang peered at her through his thick-lensed spectacles as he tried to work out if she was mocking him, but she was smiling without guile and so he nodded slowly. "Yes, perhaps," he said. "But without the masks and capes. You know that Batman made his first appearance in Detective Comics way back in 1939?"

"I didn't know that," said the Sergeant, scribbling in her notebook.

"And that he is sometimes referred to as the World's Greatest Detective, which I always considered to be hyperbole."

Sergeant Lee continued to scribble in her notebook. "What are you writing, Sergeant Lee?" he asked.

She blushed. "Nothing," she said, and put her notebook away.

Inspector Zhang nodded slowly and walked slowly around the room. "I assume you are not familiar with the work of John Dickson Carr?" he said.

Sergeant Lee shook her head.

"He was a great American writer who wrote dozens of detective stories and most of them were locked room mysteries. He created a hero called Dr. Gideon Fell, and it was Dr. Fell who solved the crimes."

Sergeant Lee tapped the side of her head. "By using ze little grey cells," she said, in a halfway passable French accent.

Inspector Zhang smiled. "Exactly," he said. "Now, in his book 'The Hollow Man', itself a locked room mystery, John Dickson Carr used Dr. Fell to expound his seven explanations that lead to a locked room murder." He nodded at his Sergeant. "You might want to make a note of them, Sergeant Lee," he said. "Now come with me." They went back into the sitting room. Miss Berghuis was sitting on the sofa next to Mercier. The waiter was standing close to the door as if he was keen to get out of the suite as quickly as possible. The two assistant managers stood by the desk in the corner of the room, looking at each other nervously.

Inspector Zhang walked to the window and stood with his back to it. "So, I have now examined the CCTV footage covering the corridor outside this room, and I have examined the crime scene." Sergeant Lee fumbled for her notebook as Inspector Zhang continued. "The CCTV footage shows that Mr. Wilkinson arrived at his room with a guest at eight-thirty and that his guest, a young woman who is known to the police, left exactly one hour later. What I need to know is when Mr. Wilkinson ordered from room service."

"That will be on the bill, inspector," said Miss Berghuis. She went over to the trolley and picked up a small leather folder and took out a slip of paper. She studied it, and nodded. "The order was placed at nine thirty-six," she said.

"Excellent," said the inspector. "So from that we can assume that Mr. Wilkinson was killed sometime between the placing of the order at nine thirty-six and the arrival of the order at nine fifty-five." He frowned. "That does seem remarkably quick, Miss Berghuis."

The manager smiled. "Inspector, we are a five-star hotel. And Mr. Wilkinson ordered only a club sandwich and a pot of coffee. Hardly a challenge for our chefs."

"Very good," said the inspector, as Miss Berghuis went back to sit on the sofa. "We can therefore rule out Mr. Wilkinson's guest as the killer, as we know for sure that he was still alive at nine thirty-six."

Miss Xue nervously raised her hand. "Actually, Inspector, we know that he was alive after that because he spoke to his wife at about a quarter to ten," she said.

"How so?" asked Inspector Zhang.

"She phoned at nine forty-five," said Miss Xue. "I was on the desk and I was there when the call came through from America. Mrs. Wilkinson was on the phone to her husband for almost five minutes."

"Are you sure?" asked the inspector.

"I am sure that it was his wife, and they spoke for several minutes," she said. "Whether it was for three, four or five minutes I am not sure."

Inspector Zhang nodded. "Then we can assume that it was indeed Mr. Wilkinson that she spoke to," he said. "I cannot believe that a wife could be fooled by an imposter. So we therefore know that Mr. Wilkinson was alive just five minutes before the waiter arrived at his door. Yet we know for a fact that no one entered the room prior to the arrival of the waiter." He drew himself up to his full height of five-feet seven inches and looked in turn at the faces of everyone in the room. "That means that what we have here is what we detectives refer to as a Locked Room Mystery."

He paused for several seconds, nodding wisely before continuing. "As I was explaining to my colleague earlier, there are basically seven explanations as to how a body can be found in a locked room. Explanations provided by the talented mystery writer John Dickson Carr. I think it would be helpful to run through them. The first possibility is that the murder is in fact not a murder, but a series of coincidences or accidents that give the impression that a crime has been committed. A man stumbles and hits his head on a piece of heavy furniture, for instance. Then we have a body, but no weapon and no killer." Inspector Zhang paused to make sure that he had everyone's attention before continuing. "In this case, an accident is unlikely, considering the nature of the wound and the fact that the body is lying down. Plus the blood is only on the bed. If he accidentally stabbed himself on for instance the lamp on the bedside table, we would see blood on it. There is no blood anywhere but the bed, so it is safe to say that it is on the bed that he died."

He turned to look out of the window and linked his fingers behind his back. His spine clicked as he straightened it, and he sighed. "The second explanation is that it is indeed a murder, but a murder in which the victim is compelled to kill himself. Or herself. A mind-altering substance can be used, a gas or a pill, LSD for instance. Mr. Carr suggested that a man might become so bewildered that he could strangle himself with his bare hands, but of course we know that is impossible."

"You think he was drugged?" said Mercier. "Or gassed? How could gas get into the room, we have central air conditioning and the windows are sealed."

"If he was drugged, the Forensics Department would know," said Sergeant Lee. "They could perform tests."

"He did not stab himself to death," said Inspector Zhang quickly. "If he did, the weapon would be in his hands. Or on the bed. There is no knife; therefore he did not kill himself. And I see no evidence that the victim consumed food or drink in this room."

He went over to the mini-bar and opened it. It was full. "You see, nothing has been taken from the mini-bar, and there are no unopened bottles in the room."

He looked over at the room service waiter. "Mr. Wilkinson was dead when you got here? He was dead on the bed and you saw the blood?"

The waiter nodded.

"So he did not consume anything that the waiter brought into the room. We can rule out poison or drugs." He went back to the window. "It is the third explanation that creates some of the most fascinating

11

fictional locked room mysteries," he continued. "That is where it is murder, and the killer uses some sort of mechanical device to carry out the killing. A gun concealed in a phone, for example. Or a knife that springs out of a suitcase. Or a pistol that fires when a clock is wound, or a weight that swings from the ceiling, a chair that exhales a deadly gas when your body warms it." He waved a hand at the bedroom. "In this case we would be looking for some way of stabbing Mr. Wilkinson and making the knife vanish." He smiled at his Sergeant. "What do you think, Sergeant Lee? Do you think there is a mechanical device hidden in the bedroom?"

"It is unlikely," she said quietly, as if she feared giving him the wrong answer.

"I agree," said Inspector Zhang. "It is a hotel room, like any other." The Sergeant smiled with relief.

"It is a suite, one of our best," said the manager.

Inspector Zhang nodded, acknowledging the point. "But nothing in the room has been changed, am I correct? Everything is as it should be?"

"Other than the body on the bed, yes."

"Then we shall move on to the fourth explanation. Suicide."

"Suicide?" repeated the Sergeant. "But if he stabbed himself, where is the weapon?"

"The point of the suicide is to make it look like a murder," said Inspector Zhang. "Either to throw suspicion on someone or to defraud an insurance company. I assume that a wealthy person such as Mr. Wilkinson would have a lot of insurance. Perhaps he has an incurable condition. Cancer perhaps. So he kills himself in such a way that his wife can still claim the insurance."

"Perhaps that's it," said Mercier. "Surely you check to see if he had any policies."

"But where is the weapon he used?" asked the Sergeant. "If Mr. Wilkinson took his own life, where is the knife?"

"But that is the point exactly," said Inspector Zhang. "To make it appear to be a murder and not a suicide, the weapon must disappear. Mr. Carr suggested a knife made of ice. The ice would then melt leaving only water behind. Or a gun could be attached to a length of elastic which would then whip the gun up a chimney or out of a window."

"There are no chimneys and as Mr. Mercier has already pointed out, the windows in our rooms are all sealed," said the manager.

"And I think ice is unlikely as he would have had to carry it in from outside and the Singaporean climate does not lend itself to carrying ice around," said Inspector Zhang. "And if Mr. Wilkinson wanted us to make it look like he had been murdered, I don't think he would have positioned himself on the bed. The floor would be a more likely place. Plus, there is the matter of room service. He spent time with the fragrant Miss Lulu, then ordered a meal. Hardly the actions of a man who was about to take his own life." He folded his arms. "So, that leads me to the fifth type of scenario discussed by Mr. Carr. A murder which derives from illusion or impersonation, where the victim is already dead but the murderer makes it appear that he is still alive."

"How would that work in this case, inspector?" asked Miss Berghuis, frowning.

"If for instance it was the prostitute who killed Mr. Wilkinson and she then arranged for someone else to make the call to room service," said Inspector Zhang. "That would give her an alibi when in fact Mr. Wilkinson was already dead when she left the room."

"Do you think that's what happened?" asked Sergeant Lee.

"That's simply not possible," said Miss Berghuis. "When a call is made to our Room Service section, the number flashes up on the phone. An order would not be accepted if it came from outside the hotel."

Inspector Zhang nodded thoughtfully. "And of course he spoke to his wife after he had ordered from room service so I do not think that Ms. Lulu was the killer. So, that then brings us to number six on Mr. Carr's list. One of the more complicated of his explanations for a locked room murder, and one of the most successful in works of fiction. In such a situation we have a murder which although committed by somebody outside the room nevertheless appears to have been committed by someone inside the room."

Mercier scratched his bald head. "That doesn't make sense," he said.

"Oh Mr. Mercier, it makes perfect sense," said Inspector Zhang. "Take for instance the icicle dagger that Mr. Carr spoke of. Suppose it could be fired through an open window or through a hole drilled into the door. Or a knife thrower in a room opposite the building who throws a knife through an open window but has it tied to a length of string so that he can pull the weapon back. It thus appears that the killer was inside the room when in fact he was outside all the time."

"But the windows are sealed and there are no holes in the door, and besides the main door opens into the sitting room, there is another door off that to the bedroom," said the manager. "The ice dagger would have to turn through ninety degrees and pass through two doors."

Inspector Zhang sighed. "Madam, I am not suggesting for one moment that Mr. Wilkinson was killed by a weapon made from ice."

"Well you are the one who keeps mentioning it," said the manager, flashing him a withering look. "And if the knife didn't melt, where is it?"

"Exactly," said Inspector Zhang. "You have put your finger on the crux of the conundrum. Where is the knife? If indeed it was a knife."

"Do you know?" asked Mercier. "Why are you asking us if you know?"

"I was being rhetorical," said Inspector Zhang. He took off his glasses and began to methodically polish them with his handkerchief. "I am not sure where the murder weapon is, but I have my suspicions. However, let me first finish Mr. Carr's list of explanations with the seventh, which is effectively the exact opposite of the fifth."

Everyone frowned as they tried to remember what the inspector had said was the fifth method. They all looked around, shrugging at each other.

Sergeant Lee walked over to Inspector Zhang and whispered in his ear. "Inspector Zhang, I need to talk to you," she said.

"Sergeant Lee, I am in full flow here," he said. "Can't it wait?"

"No Sir, it can not," said the sergeant.

Inspector Zhang sighed with annoyance then nodded at the door to the bedroom. "This had better be important," he said.

They went through to the bedroom and stood at the foot of the bed. "What is it, Sergeant Lee?" asked the inspector. "You seem concerned."

"Sir, we really should be calling in the Forensic Department," she said. She looked at her watch. "It will soon be midnight."

"Not yet," said Inspector Zhang. "I think we can solve this case without resorting to science."

"But it's procedure, Sir. And we have to follow procedure."

"Sergeant Lee, you know that I speak Japanese, don't you?"

She nodded. "It came in very useful when we were working on the case of the sushi chef who ran amok in his restaurant," she said.

"Exactly," said Inspector Zhang. "But do you know why I studied Japanese?"

The sergeant shook her head.

"There is a famous Japanese writer named Soji Shimada who wrote thirteen locked room mysteries, only one of which – 'The Tokyo Zodiac Murders' – was translated into English. I wanted to read his other stories, which is why I taught myself Japanese."

"I understand, Inspector Zhang."

"This is important to me, Sergeant Lee. This is a mystery that I can solve. I want to prove that to myself." He smiled. "And perhaps to prove to you that even in the third millennium there is a need for real detectives."

"Like Batman?"

"I was thinking more like Sherlock Holmes," said Inspector Zhang. "We have an opportunity here that we may never have again in our lives. In Singapore we are lucky if we have one murder a year."

"Lucky, Sir?"

Inspector Zhang put up his hand. "You are right; lucky is not the right word. Murders are rare in Singapore. Our island state is the most tightly controlled place on the planet; our Government knows everything there is to know about its citizens, so our crime rate is one of the lowest in the world."

"Plus we execute our murderers," said Sergeant Lee. "Which does act as something of a deterrent."

"Exactly. So do you not see how special this case is, Sergeant Lee? Most detectives would give their eye teeth to work on a case such as this, yet all you want to do is to hand it over to the scientists." He looked around as if he feared being overheard. "And what if we have a serial killer, Sergeant Lee?"

"We have only one victim," said the sergeant.

"That we know of," said Inspector Zhang, fighting to stop his voice from trembling. "What if there are more? What if we have on our hands a real live serial killer?" He shuddered. "Can you imagine that, Sergeant Lee?"

The sergeant nodded, but didn't reply.

"You know that Singapore has only ever had one serial killer?" said the inspector.

"Yes, Sir. Adrian Lim."

"Exactly, Sergeant," said the Inspector. Every detective on the island knew of the case, of course. It was taught at the academy. The Toa Payoh Ritual Murders. The killings had taken place in 1981, the year that Inspector Zhang had joined the Singapore Police Force. Adrian Lim, who murdered two children as sacrifices to the Hindu goddess Kali. Lim and his two female accomplices were hanged in 1988.

"But he was caught by forensic evidence," said Sergeant Lee. "Police found a trail of blood leading to the flat."

"Exactly," said Inspector Zhang. "Which is why I want to use deduction to solve this case. All the evidence we need is here, Sergeant Lee. All we have to do is to apply our deductive skills. Do you see that? Do you understand?"

The sergeant nodded slowly. "Yes, Sir, I understand."

He patted her on the back. "Excellent," he said. "Let me now finish my questioning," he said. "And you might give some thought as to what this case will be called, because I am sure that it will become the subject of much discussion so it will need a name."

"A name, Sir?"

"A title. The Locked Hotel Room Murder, for instance. Or The Vanished Knife. Inspector Zhang and The Mystery Of The Disappearing Knife. What do you think?"

"I'm not sure, Sir," said Sergeant Lee.

"Well give it some thought, Sergeant," said Inspector Zhang, as he headed for the door.

Miss Berghuis was deep in conversation with her head of security when Inspector Zhang and Sergeant Lee walked back into the sitting room, but they stopped talking immediately and looked expectantly at the two detectives.

Inspector Zhang walked over to the window and turned to face the hotel staff. "So, to continue, Mr. Carr's seventh and final locked room scenario involves a situation where the victim is assumed to be dead before he or she actually is. That is the reverse of situation number five of course, where the victim is dead, but presumed to be alive."

"So that would mean that Mr. Wilkinson wasn't actually dead when Mr. Chau went into the room?" asked Miss Berghuis.

"He was," said the waiter. "I'm sure he was dead."

"But you're not a doctor, Mr. Chau," said Inspector Zhang, "In the confusion, it might have looked as if he was dead but the actual murder was committed later."

"That's impossible," said Mercier. "He was definitely dead when I got here."

"And you were here soon after the waiter made the call to reception?"

Mercier nodded. "You saw the CCTV footage. Everybody was there within a few minutes at most."

"He was definitely dead," agreed the manager. "You only had to look at the body. At the blood."

"But there was a moment when the waiter was alone with the body," said Inspector Zhang. "When he made the phone call. At that moment he was alone in the room with Mr. Wilkinson, and we have only Mr. Chau's word that Mr. Wilkinson was dead."

"I didn't kill him," said Mr. Chau hurriedly, his eyes darting from side to side.

"I didn't say that you did," said Inspector Zhang. "I merely stated that you were alone with Mr. Wilkinson and you had the opportunity of killing him if he hadn't been dead already. It is one way of solving a locked room mystery. The room is locked, but the person who discovers the body is the killer. He kills the victim then calls for the police." He shrugged. "It happens, but I do not think it happened in this case."

The waiter looked relieved and loosened his shirt collar.

"Besides, if you did kill Mr. Wilkinson, where is the knife?" asked Inspector Zhang.

"Actually Inspector Zhang, we haven't searched anyone yet," said Sergeant Lee.

"And there is no need to search Mr. Chau, Sergeant," said the inspector. "What we need to do now is to go back downstairs to the security office; for it is there that the solution lies."

"All of us?" said the manager. "Surely we don't all need to go?"

"It is the tradition, Madam," said Inspector Zhang. "The detective gathers together the cast of characters and explains the solution to them before unmasking the killer."

The manager laughed, and it was like the harsh bark of an angry dog. "Inspector Zhang, this is not some country house where the butler did it. Just tell us who the killer is."

"It is not a country house, that is true, but a five-star hotel is the closest thing that we have in Singapore," said Inspector Zhang. "Now please humour me and accompany me down to the ground floor."

The inspector led them out of the room and down the corridor to the elevators. He took the first one down with Mercier, the waiter, Miss Berghuis and one of the two uniformed policemen. Sergeant Lee followed in a second elevator with the two assistant managers and the

18

other uniformed policeman. They gathered together outside the security room and Inspector Zhang led them inside. He waved a languid hand at the chair in front of the monitors. "Mr. Mercier, perhaps you would do the honours."

The head of security sat down and ran a hand over his scalp. "We've already looked at the CCTV footage," he said.

"We looked, but did we really see what happened?" asked the inspector. He waited until everyone had gathered behind Mercier's chair before asking him to begin the recording from the point at which Mr. Wilkinson and the prostitute stepped out of the elevator.

"Here we can see Mr. Wilkinson and his guest arriving at eight-thirty," said Inspector Zhang. "Very much alive, obviously."

He watched as Wilkinson and the woman went inside. "She left an hour later. Please skip to that point, Mr. Mercier."

Mercier tapped a key and the video began to fast forward. He slowed to normal speed just before nine-thirty in time to see Ms. Lulu leave the room.

"Now, at this point Mr. Wilkinson ordered his club sandwich and coffee from room service, so again we know that he is still very much alive."

"So who killed him?" asked Miss Berghuis. "If the woman left the room and no one goes in before the waiter, who stabbed him?"

"That is an excellent question, Madam," said Inspector Zhang.

"But can you answer it, inspector?" asked the manager, tersely.

"I think I can," said Inspector Zhang. "The key to solving this mystery lies in understanding that it is not who goes into the room that is important. It is who does not go in."

"That doesn't make any sense at all," said the manager crossly.

"I beg to differ," said Inspector Zhang. "It makes all the sense in the world. It is as Sherlock Holmes himself says in Arthur Conan Doyle's masterpiece The Adventure Of Silver Blaze, it is the fact that the dog did not bark that is significant."

"We do not allow dogs in the hotel," said Mercier. "There are no pets of any kind."

Sergeant Lee looked up from her notebook, smiling, and Inspector Zhang sighed. "I was using the story as an example to show that it is sometimes the absence of an event that is significant, which was the case in the Adventure of Silver Blaze. If I recall correctly it was Inspector Gregory who asks Sherlock Holmes if there is anything about the case that he wants to draw to the policeman's attention. Holmes says yes, to the curious incident of the dog in the night-time. That confuses the inspector who tells Holmes that the dog did nothing in the night-time. To which Holmes replies, "That was the curious incident." Do you understand now, Madam?"

She shook her head impatiently. "No inspector, I am afraid I do not."

"Then, Madam, please allow me to demonstrate," said Inspector Zhang. He put a hand on Mercier's shoulder. "Please, Mr. Mercier, fast-forward now to the point where the waiter arrives with the room service trolley."

"This is a waste of time," said Mercier. "We did this already."

"Please humour me," said the inspector.

Mercier did as he asked and they all watched as the video fast-forwarded to the point where Mr. Chau arrived with his trolley and began knocking on the door.

"Normal speed now, please, Mr. Mercier. The video slowed as they watched the waiter use his key card to enter the room.

"At this point Mr. Chau is discovering the body and calling down to reception." Inspector Zhang waited until the waiter appeared at the door and began pacing up and down. "As you can see, no one enters the room until the hotel staff appear." On the screen Miss Berghuis and her staff appeared and they all hurried into the room. "At this point you phone the police," said the inspector, turning to Miss Berghuis. The manager nodded. Inspector Zhang patted Mercier on the shoulder. "So now fast-forward until my arrival, Mr. Mercier, but not too quickly. And I want everyone to note that no one else enters the room until I arrive with my sergeant."

The door to the room remained closed for twenty minutes until Inspector Zhang and Sergeant Lee stepped out of the elevator.

"Normal speed now please, Mr. Mercier. Thank you."

Mercier pressed a button and the video slowed. Inspector Zhang walked up to the door and knocked on it. It opened and he went inside, followed by his sergeant. The door closed behind them.

"So, now we are inside, talking to you and assessing the situation. We talk, then I go to the bedroom with you, Miss Berghuis, I look at the body, I talk to you, I walk back to the sitting room, and then I walk out with Mr. Mercier." On the screen Inspector Zhang and Mercier walked out of the room and headed for the elevator.

"You can stop it there, Mr. Mercier," said Inspector Zhang, patting him on the shoulder.

The picture froze on the monitor, showing Inspector Zhang and Mercier walking towards the elevator.

"So here is the big question, Mr. Mercier," said Inspector Zhang. "You walk out of the room now, but when exactly did you walk into the room?"

Mercier said nothing.

"You did not arrive with Miss Berghuis."

"He was already in the room when we got there," said the manager. She gasped and put her hand up to her mouth. "My God, he was in there the whole time."

"Apparently so," said Inspector Zhang.

Mercier stood up and tried to get out of the door but the two uniformed policemen blocked his way. Mercier turned to face Inspector Zhang. "This is ridiculous," he said.

"Now Mr. Mercier, I am going to make two predictions, based on what I think happened," said Inspector Zhang. He nodded at Mercier's jacket. "I am certain that you are carrying the murder weapon. You have had no chance to dispose of it so it must still be on your person. And because I do not believe that you planned to kill Mr. Wilkinson, I think that the weapon is actually something quite innocuous. A pen maybe." He registered the look of surprise on Mercier's face and he smiled. "Yes, a pen. But I also think that you have a camera, perhaps even a small video camera. Am I right?"

Mercier didn't answer but he slowly reached into his inside pocket and took out a black Mont Blanc pen. He held it out and Inspector Zhang could see that there was blood on one end. Sergeant Lee stepped forward and held out a clear plastic evidence bag and Mercier dropped the pen into it. Mercier then reached into the left hand pocket of his trousers and took out a slim white video camera, smaller than a pack of cigarettes.

Inspector Zhang took the camera from him. "And Miss Lulu, she is in this with you?"

Mercier looked away but didn't answer.

"She is not involved in the murder of course. She doesn't know that Mr. Wilkinson is dead because he was still alive when she left the room."

Mercier nodded. "She doesn't know."

"Because you never planned to kill Mr. Wilkinson, did you?" said Inspector Zhang.

Mercier rubbed his hands together and shook his head.

"You were there to blackmail Mr. Wilkinson?"

"Blackmail?" said Miss Berghuis.

"It was the only explanation," said Inspector Zhang. "He was in the room when Mr. Wilkinson arrived with Miss Lulu. I am assuming that he wanted to video them in a compromising position with a view to blackmailing him. He was a married man, after all. And divorce in America can be a costly business. The only question is whether Miss Lulu was party to the blackmail, or not."

Mercier nodded. "It was her idea," he said.

"You were her client?"

"Sometimes. Yes. Then she said that she had this rich customer who treated her badly and that she wanted to get back at him. She wanted to hurt him and get money from him. She said she'd split the money with me."

"So she suggested that you hide in the closet and video them together?"

"She had been in his room before and she knew I could easily hide in the closet. She called me when she was on the way back to the hotel and I was in position when they arrived. She made sure that he could never see me. It was easy. But then she was supposed to get him into the shower so that I could slip out, but he wouldn't have it. He said that his wife was due to phone him so he practically threw her out of the room. Then he phoned room service from the sitting room so I couldn't get out, and then his wife called. I was stuck there while he took the call." He ran a hand over his face. He was dripping with sweat. "Then it all went wrong."

"He opened the closet? He found you?"

Mercier nodded. "He shouldn't have, but he did. All his clothes were in the suitcase and his robe was in the bathroom. I don't know why he opened the closet, but he did and he saw me."

"So you killed him?"

Mercier shook his head. "It was an accident."

"You stabbed him in the throat with your pen," said Inspector Zhang.

"He attacked me," said Mercier. "He opened the closet door and saw me and attacked me. We struggled. I had to stop him."

"By driving your pen into his throat?"

Mercier looked at the floor.

"I think not," said Inspector Zhang. "If you stabbed him at the closet, there would be blood there. The only place where there is blood is the bed. Therefore you stabbed him on the bed."

"We were struggling. I pushed him back."

"And then you stabbed him?"

"My pen was in my top pocket. He grabbed it during the struggle and tried to force it into my eye. I pushed it away and it..." He fell silent, unable or unwilling to finish the sentence.

"You stabbed him in the throat?"

Mercier nodded.

"And then rather than leaving the room, you hid in the closet again?"

"I didn't know what else to do. I knew that he had ordered room service so I couldn't risk being seen in the corridor."

"So you waited until the room service waiter discovered the body and while he was phoning the front desk you slipped out of the closet?"

Mercier nodded. "I went through to the next room but there was someone in the corridor so I couldn't leave and I had to pretend that I'd just arrived. It was an accident, Inspector Zhang. I swear."

"That's for a judge to consider," said Inspector Zhang. "There is one more piece of evidence that I require from you, Mr. Mercier. Your handkerchief."

"My handkerchief?"

"I notice that unlike your colleagues you do not have a handkerchief in your pocket," said the inspector. "I therefore assume that you used it to wipe the blood from your hands after you killed Mr. Wilkinson."

Mercier reached into his trouser pocket and pulled out a blood-stained handkerchief. Sergeant Lee held out a plastic evidence bag and Mercier dropped the handkerchief into it.

Inspector Zhang nodded at the two uniformed policemen. "Take him away, please."

The officers handcuffed Mercier and led him out of the room. Inspector Zhang nodded at the two evidence bags that Sergeant Lee was holding, containing the pen and the handkerchief. "You can send them to your friends in Forensics," he said.

"I will," she said.

"I suppose it does prove one thing," said Inspector Zhang. He smiled slyly.

"What is that, Inspector?" asked the Sergeant.

"Why, that the pen is indeed mightier than the sword," he said. He grinned. "There is no need to write that down, Sergeant Lee."

24

2.

INSPECTOR ZHANG AND THE DEAD THAI GANGSTER

Inspector Zhang looked out through the window at the fields far below. There was so much land, he thought, compared with his own Singapore. The near four million population of the island state was crowded into just 253 square miles and there was little in the way of green space. But Thailand had green in abundance, criss-crossed with roads and dotted with small farms, and in the distance, mountains shrouded in mist. He closed his book with a sigh. It would soon be time to land.

"Are you okay, Inspector?" asked Sergeant Lee, removing her headphones. She was twenty four years old, and was wearing her hair long for a change, probably because while they were on the plane they weren't strictly speaking on duty even though they had been sent to Bangkok by the Singapore Police Force.

"Of course," said Inspector Zhang. "Why would I be otherwise?"

"I don't think you like flying," she said. "You did not eat the meal, you have not availed yourself of the in-flight entertainment system, and you seem – distracted."

Inspector Zhang shook his head. "I am fine with flying," he said. "In fact I have a Singapore Airlines frequent flyer card. Two years ago I flew to London with my wife, and the year before that we went to visit relatives of hers in Hong Kong."

"London?" she said. "You went to London?"

"Just for a week," he said. "It was always my dream to visit 221B Baker Street, and to follow the trail of Jack the Ripper."

"Who lives at 221B Baker Street?" asked the Sergeant.

"Why Sherlock Holmes, of course," said Inspector Zhang. "Though I have to say that it was something of a disappointment to discover that in fact there is no 221B and that the only building that comes close is the home of a bank." He shrugged. "But it was fascinating to see where the evil Ripper plied his trade and to follow in his footsteps."

"He was a serial killer in Victorian London, wasn't he?"

"And never caught," said Inspector Zhang. He sighed. "What I would give to be on a case like that; to pit my wits against an adversary of such evil. Can you imagine the thrill of the chase, Sergeant?"

"I'm just glad that I live in Singapore, where we have one of the lowest crime rates in the world."

"For which we are all thankful, of course," said Inspector Zhang. "But it does tend to make a detective's life somewhat dull." He sighed again. "Still, I have my books."

"What have you been reading, Sir?" asked Sergeant Lee.

Inspector Zhang held up the book so that she could see the cover. The Mysterious Affair At Styles by Agatha Christie. "It is one of my favourites," he said. "It is the book that introduces the greatest of all detectives, Hercule Poirot. I never tire of reading it."

"But if you've already read it then you know how it ends," said Sergeant Lee. "There is no mystery."

"The solution is only part of the enjoyment of reading mystery stories," said Inspector Zhang, putting the book into his briefcase. "Agatha Christie wrote thirty novels featuring Poirot and I have read them all several times."

She frowned. "I thought that Sherlock Holmes was the greatest detective, not Poirot."

"There are those who say that, of course," said Inspector Zhang. "But I would say that Sherlock Holmes relied more on physical evidence whereas Hercule Poirot more often than not reached his conclusions by astute questioning." He tapped the side of his head. "By using ze little grey cells," he said, in his best Hercule Poirot impression.

The plane shuddered as the landing gear went down.

"Have you ever travelled abroad for work before, Inspector?" asked Sergeant Lee.

"This is the first time," said Inspector Zhang. He had been asked to fly to Thailand to collect a Singaporean businessman who was being extradited on fraud charges. At first the fraudster had fought his extradition but he had been denied bail and after two weeks in a crowded Thai prison he had practically begged to go home. He was facing seven years in Changi Prison and as bad as Changi was it was a hotel compared with a Thai prison where thirty men to a cell and an open hole in the floor as a toilet were the norm. Inspector Zhang had been told to take an assistant with him and he had experienced no hesitation in choosing Sergeant Lee, though he had felt himself blush a little when he had explained to his wife that the pretty young officer would be accompanying him. Not that there had been any need to blush, Inspector Zhang had been married for thirty years and in all that time he had never even considered being unfaithful. It simply wasn't in his nature. He had fallen in love with his wife on the day that he'd met her and if anything he loved her even more now. He had chosen Sergeant Lee because she was one of the most able detectives on the Force, albeit one of the youngest.

The plane kissed the runway and the air brakes kicked in and Inspector Zhang felt his seat belt cutting into his stomach. The jet turned off the runway and began to taxi towards the terminal, a jagged line of wave-like peaks in the distance.

"And this is your first time in Thailand?" asked Sergeant Lee.

"I've been to Thailand with my wife, but we flew straight to Phuket," he said. "I have never been to Bangkok before."

"It is an amazing city," said Sergeant Lee. "And so big. I read on the internet that more than eight million people live there."

"Twice the population of Singapore," said Inspector Zhang. "But the crime rate here is much, much higher than ours. Every year the city has five thousand murders and at least twenty thousand assaults. In Singapore we are lucky if we have two murders in a month."

Sergeant Lee raised a single eyebrow, a trick that the Inspector had never managed to master. "Lucky, Inspector Zhang?"

"Perhaps lucky is not the right word," admitted Inspector Zhang, though if he was completely honest the inspector would have had to admit that he would have welcomed the opportunity to make more use of his detective skills. In Singapore unsolved murders were a rarity, but he knew that in Bangkok hundreds went unsolved every year.

The plane came to a halt on the taxiway and the captain's voice came over the intercom. "Ladies and gentlemen, I am sorry but there will be a slight delay before we commence disembarkation," he said. "And in the meantime, would Inspector Zhang of the Singapore Police Force please make himself known to a member of the cabin staff."

"That's you," said Sergeant Lee excitedly.

"Yes it is," said Inspector Zhang.

Sergeant Lee waved at a stewardess and pointed at Inspector Zhang. "This is him." She said.

"Inspector Zhang of the Singapore Police Force. And I am his colleague, Sergeant Lee."

The stewardess bent down to put her lips close to his ear and Inspector Zhang caught a whiff of jasmine. "Inspector Zhang, the captain would like a word with you," she said. "Is there a problem?" he asked.

"The captain can explain," she said, and flashed him a professional smile.

Inspector Zhang looked across at Sergeant Lee. "I think you had better come with me," he said. "It can only be a police matter." He pulled his briefcase out from under the seat in front of him, put his book away and then followed the stewardess down the aisle with Sergeant Lee at his heels. There was a male steward wearing a dark grey suit standing at the curtain and he held it back for them to go through the galley to the business class section. Three stewardesses were gathered in the galley, whispering to each other. Inspector Zhang could see from their worried faces that something was very wrong.

"What has happened?" Inspector Zhang asked the steward. He was wearing a badge that identified him as the Chief Purser, Stanley Yip.

"The captain would like to talk to you," said the steward. "He is by the cockpit." He moved a second curtain and motioned for the inspector to go through.

There were thirty seats in the business class section, two seats at each window and a row of two in the middle. A large Indian man wearing a crisp white shirt with black and yellow epaulettes was standing by the toilet at the head of the cabin, talking to a stewardess. He looked up and saw Inspector Zhang and waved for him to join him. "I am Captain Kumar," said the pilot, holding out his hand. He was at least six inches taller than Inspector Zhang with muscular forearms and a thick moustache and jet black hair.

Inspector Zhang shook hands with the pilot and introduced himself and his sergeant. The pilot nodded at the sergeant then turned back to the inspector. He lowered his voice conspiratorially. "We have a problem, Inspector. A passenger has died." The pilot pointed over at the far side of the cabin and for the first time Inspector Zhang noticed a figure covered in a blanket huddled against the fuselage. The window's shutter was down.

"Then it is a doctor you need to pronounce death, not an officer of the law," said Inspector Zhang.

"Oh, there's no doubt that he's dead, Inspector. In fact he has been murdered."

"And you are sure it was murder and not simply a heart attack or a stroke? Has he been examined by a doctor?"

"According to the chief purser he is definitely dead and there is a lot of blood from a wound in his chest."

"Who put the blanket over the victim?" asked Inspector Zhang.

"The chief purser, Mr Yip. He thought it best so as not to upset the passengers. He did it before he informed me."

"The body should always be left uncovered at a crime scene," said Inspector Zhang "Otherwise the scene can be contaminated."

"I think it was probably the first time he had come across a crime scene in the air, but I shall make sure that he knows what to do in future," said the captain.

"I still don't understand why you need my services," said Inspector Zhang. "We are on Thai soil, this is surely a matter for the Thai police."

"It's not as simple as that, Inspector Zhang," said the captain. "I have already spoken to my bosses back in Singapore and they have spoken to the Commissioner of Police and he would like to talk to you." He handed the Inspector a piece of paper on which had been written a Singapore cell phone number. "He said you were to call him immediately." He waved a hand at the door behind him. "You are welcome to use the toilet if you would like some privacy."

Inspector Zhang looked around the cabin. The four cabin attendants were watching him from the galley and there were seven passengers sitting in the first class section all looking at him. "I think you're right," he said. "Please excuse me." He nodded at Sergeant Lee. "Sergeant, please make sure that no further contamination of the crime scene occurs and make sure that everyone remains seated." He handed her his briefcase. "And please put this somewhere for me."

"I will, Sir," said Sergeant Lee as Inspector Zhang pushed open the door to the toilet and stepped inside. He closed the door behind him and looked around. The room had been recently cleaned and smelt of air freshener.

Inspector Zhang took out his cell phone and slowly tapped out the number that the captain had given him. The Commissioner answered on the third ring. Inspector Zhang had never spoken to the Commissioner before, and had only ever seen him at a distance or on television, but there was no mistaking the man's quiet authority on the other end of the line. "I understand that there is a problem on the plane, Inspector Zhang."

"Yes, Sir, there is a body."

"Indeed there is. And from what the captain has said, it is a case of murder."

"I can't confirm that, Sir, as I have not done anything in the way of an investigation. But the pilot tells me that the man is dead and that there is a lot of blood. Sir, we are on Thai soil and as such any investigation should properly be carried out by the Thai police."

The Commissioner sighed. "I wish that life was as simple as that," he said. "There are a number of issues that require resolving before the case is passed over to the Thais, not the least the fact that we need to know exactly where the plane was when the murder was committed. If it was in international air space then it will be a case for us to handle in Singapore. We also need to take into account the nationality of the victim, and the perpetrator."

"The perpetrator?" repeated Inspector Zhang. "Are you suggesting that I solve the crime before allowing the Thai police on board?"

"I am told that you do have a talent for solving mysteries, Inspector Zhang. And from what I have heard, it is a mystery that confronts us."

"But we have no forensic team, I am not even sure of the cause of death."

"If a murder has been committed, the one thing we can be sure of is that the murderer is still on the plane. So long as the doors remained closed, the murderer has nowhere to go."

"So I am to conduct an investigation before anyone can leave the plane?"

"Exactly," said the Commissioner.

"But this is a Boeing 777-200, Sir. There must be more than two hundred people on board." "All the more reason to get started, Inspector Zhang. I have already spoken to my opposite number in the Royal Thai Police Force and he is happy for us to proceed. To be honest, Inspector Zhang, they would be content for you to solve the case and for us to fly the killer home to stand trial in Singapore."

"But if we don't solve the crime then the plane remains a crime scene and will have to stay in Bangkok for the foreseeable future?"

"Exactly," said the Commissioner. "And nobody wants that. The last thing we want is for the world to believe that our national airline was somehow tainted by what has happened. Inspector Zhang, I am assured that you are the man who can handle this smoothly and efficiently."

"I shall do my best, Commissioner," said Inspector Zhang.

"I am sure you will," said the Commissioner, and he ended the call. Inspector Zhang put away his cell phone and stared at his reflection as

31

he drew back his shoulders and took a deep breath. He exhaled slowly, then took out a plastic comb and carefully arranged his hair, then removed his spectacles and polished them with his handkerchief. He was fifty-four years old and had served the Singapore Police Force for almost thirty of those years, but he could count on the fingers of one hand the true murder investigations that he had been involved with. Most murders, especially in Singapore, were committed by relatives or co-workers and generally investigations required little in the way of detecting skills. But what he now faced was a true mystery, a mystery that he had to solve. He put his spectacles back on and tucked the handkerchief back into his pocket. He took another deep breath, then let himself out of the toilet.

"So what is happening?" asked Captain Kumar. "Can we let the passengers off?"

"I am afraid not," said Inspector Zhang. "I have been authorised to carry out an investigation. Until then, the doors remain closed."

"What assistance can I offer you?" asked the pilot.

"I will first examine the body, then I need to speak to the chief purser and to whoever discovered the body." He nodded at Sergeant Lee, who was already taking out her notepad and pen. "Come with me, Sergeant," he said.

He stood in the middle of the cabin and held up his warrant card. "Ladies and Gentlemen, my name is Inspector Zhang of the Singapore Police Force," he said. "As you are no doubt aware there has been an incident on board this flight. I would be grateful if you would all stay in your seats until I have had a chance to examine the scene."

"You can't keep us here against our will!" shouted a Chinese man in a suit sitting at the rear of the cabin. There were thirty seats in the Raffles cabin, but only eight were occupied. The man who had spoken was sitting on the opposite side to where the body was, in a seat next to the window.

"I'm afraid I can," said the Inspector. "You are?"

"Lung Chin-po," said the man. "I have an important meeting to go to." He looked at his watch. "Immigration in Bangkok can take up to an hour, and then there's always heavy traffic. Really, I have to get off this plane now."

"I'm sorry for the inconvenience, but the doors will not be opened until the investigation has been concluded."

A heavyset man in a tweed jacket sitting in the middle of the cabin next to an equally large woman in a pale green trouser suit raised a hand. "I agree with that gentleman," he said in a slow American drawl. "My wife and I are tourists and we've got a limo waiting for us outside. What's happened obviously can't have anything to do with us. We don't know anyone in this part of the world."

Inspector Zhang pushed his spectacles up onto his nose. "Again, I understand how you feel but the sooner I get on with my investigation the sooner we can open the doors and get on our way."

The American groaned and folded his arms as he glared at the Inspector.

"Sergeant Lee, would you get the names, addresses and passport details of all the passengers, and do me a floor plan with seat numbers."

Inspector Zhang walked to the front of the cabin and headed along the bulkhead towards the blanket-covered body. A short man in a black leather jacket and impenetrable sunglasses moved his legs to allow the inspector to squeeze by. Inspector Zhang thanked him and the man nodded.

The pilot followed Inspector Zhang over to the body. It was in seat 11K. Inspector Zhang slowly pulled the pale-blue blanket away. The victim was a Thai man in his thirties, wearing a dark suit with a white shirt and a black tie. The front of the shirt was stained with blood that had pooled and congealed in the man's lap.

"This was how he was found?" asked the Inspector. "With the blood?" "Nothing has been touched," said the captain.

"And who discovered that he was dead?"

"It was one of the flight attendants."

"Could you get her for me, please?" said Inspector Zhang. He leant down over the body, taking a pen and using it to slide the jacket open. There was a small hole in the shirt just below the breastbone and the shirt was peppered with tiny flecks of black. He leant closer and sniffed. Gunshot residue. The man had been shot.

As he straightened up, the pilot returned with a young flight attendant. "This is Sumin," said the pilot. "She was the one who discovered that the passenger was dead."

Inspector Zhang smiled at the flight attendant. "What time did you realise that there was something wrong?" he asked.

"I was checking that passengers had their seatbelts fastened so it was just as we were starting our approach. That would have been about fifteen minutes before we landed."

"And what made you realise that something was wrong?"

"I thought he was asleep," said the flight attendant. "I leaned over to fasten the belt and I moved his jacket. That's when I saw the blood." She shuddered. "There was so much blood."

"What did you do then?" asked the Inspector.

"I went to get the chief purser and he checked for a pulse and when he didn't find one we covered him with a blanket."

"Did you inform the pilot right away?"

"No, Mr Yip said we should wait until we had landed."

"And did you hear anything at all unusual during the flight?"

The flight attendant frowned. "Unusual?"

"A gunshot? A loud bang?"

The stewardess laughed nervously and put a hand up over her mouth. "Of course not," she said. She looked at Captain Kumar. "A gunshot?"

"There was no gunshot," said Captain Kumar. "I was sitting in the cockpit with the first officer just ten feet away, we would have heard a shot if there had been one. As would the rest of the passengers. There was no shot."

"Well I can assure you that there is a bullet hole in the body and gunshot residue on the shirt," said Inspector Zhang. "He was shot and at close range."

"But that's impossible!" said the pilot.

34

"Yes," agreed Inspector Zhang. "It is. Quite impossible." He reached into the dead man's inside pocket and took out a Thai passport. He opened it and compared the picture to the face of the victim. They matched. "Kwanchai Srisai," read Inspector Zhang. "Born in Udon Thani. Thirty-seven years old." He closed the passport, handed it to Sergeant Lee and turned to look at the cabin. "The cabin appears to be almost empty," he said to the pilot. "Have some passengers moved to the rear of the plane?"

The pilot shook his head. "At this time of the year the Raffles Section is rarely full," he said. "The business class fare is quite expensive and the flight from Singapore to Bangkok is short so most of our passengers choose to fly economy."

Inspector Zhang did a quick head count. "Eight passengers in all, including the victim."

The pilot looked across at the flight attendant. "Is that what the manifest says?"

"That is correct," she said. "Eight passengers."

"And during the flight, did any passengers from the economy section come forward to this part of the plane?"

"I don't think so," she said.

"I need to know for certain," said Inspector Zhang.

The flight attendant nodded. "You will need to ask the other members of the cabin crew," she said. "I was busy in the galley for some of the flight and twice I had to clean the toilets and I had to go to the cockpit with coffee for Captain Kumar and the first officer."

"She did," said the captain. "I always have a cup of coffee mid-way through a flight."

"Then I will need to talk to the rest of the cabin crew at some point," said Inspector Zhang. "So tell me, Miss Sumin, was everything okay with Mr. Srisai during the flight?"

"In what way, Inspector?"

"Did anything out the ordinary happen? Before you discovered that he was dead, obviously."

"I don't think so."

"He ate his meal?"

She nodded. "Yes, and he drank a lot of champagne. He was always asking for champagne."

"And he went to the bathroom?"

"Just once. About halfway through the flight, just after I had cleared away his meal things.

"But nothing unusual?"

"No Inspector. Nothing."

Inspector Zhang turned to Sergeant Lee. "So, Sergeant, run through the passengers for me, please."

"As you said, there are seven passengers in addition to the victim," said Sergeant Lee. She turned and pointed to a young Thai girl who was listening to music through headphones, bobbing her head back and forth in time to the music. "The lady in 14A is a Thai student, Tasanee Boontaisong. She studies in Singapore and is returning to see her parents."

Inspector Zhang frowned as he looked at the girl. "I see that there are no rows numbered one to ten and that the front row of the cabin is row 11, he said. "She is in the third row. That would make it row 13, would it not?"

"There is no row 13," said Captain Kumar. "In some cultures the number 13 is considered unlucky."

Sergeant Lee looked up from her notebook. "Clearly on this flight it was number 11 that was unlucky," she said.

Inspector Zhang looked at her sternly but she didn't appear to have been joking, merely stating a fact.

"Two rows behind Miss Boontaisong in 16A is Lung Chin-po, the Singaporean businessman who you spoke to," she continued. "He says he is a friend of the Deputy Commissioner and that he will sue our department if we continue to hold him against his will."

Inspector Zhang chuckled softly. "Well I wish him every success with that," he said.

"Those are the only two passengers sitting on the right hand side," said Sergeant Lee. "Mr. Lung and Miss Boontaisong."

"Port," said Captain Kumar. "That's the port side. Right and left depend on which way you are facing so on planes and boats we say port and starboard. As you face the front, port is on the left and starboard is on the right." He smiled. "It prevents confusion."

"And I am all in favour of preventing confusion," said Inspector Zhang. "So, Sergeant Lee, who is sitting in the middle of the cabin?"

The Sergeant nodded at the man in sunglasses sitting in 11F. He was sitting with his arms folded, staring straight ahead at the bulkhead. "The man there is Mr. Lev Gottesman, from Israel. He is Mr. Srisai's bodyguard. Was, I mean. He was Mr. Srisai's bodyguard."

"And why would Mr. Srisai require the services of a bodyguard?" asked Inspector Zhang.

"I didn't ask," said Sergeant Lee. "I'm sorry. Should I have?"

"I shall question Mr. Gottesman shortly," said the Inspector. "Please continue."

Sergeant Lee pursed her lips and looked at her notebook. "In the row behind Mr. Gottesman, in seat 14A, is Andrew Yates, a British stockbroker who works for a Thai firm. He was attending a meeting in Singapore." Inspector Zhang looked over at a man in his early forties wearing a grey suit. His hair was dyed blond and gel glistened under the cabin lights as he bent down over a Blackberry, texting with both thumbs.

"Directly behind Mr. Yates are Mr. and Mrs. Woodhouse from Seattle in the United States. They are touring South East Asia. They were in Singapore for three days, they have a week in Thailand and then they are due to fly to Vietnam and then on to China."

She nodded at the final passenger, a Thai man sitting at the back of the cabin in seat 16H, adjacent to the aisle. "Mr. Nakprakone is a journalist who works for the Thai Rath newspaper in Bangkok. He is a Thai."

"I have heard of the paper," said Inspector Zhang. "It is one of those sensationalist papers that publishes pictures of accidents and murders on their front pages, I believe."

"Mr. Nakprakone said that it sells more than a million copies every day."

"Sensationalism sells, that is true," sighed Inspector Zhang. "I am personally happier with more dignified newspapers such as our own Straits Times. Did you ask Mr. Nakprakone why he was flying in the business class section?"

"I didn't. Should I have done?"

"It's not a problem," said Inspector Zhang. "So, I assume you asked everyone if they heard or saw anything suspicious during the flight?"

"No one did, Sir."

"And I assume that no one mentioned hearing a gunshot?"

"Definitely not. Besides, Sir, it would be impossible for anyone to get a gun onto a plane. There are stringent security checks at Changi."

The flight attendant who had been talking to the pilot appeared at Inspector Zhang's shoulder "Inspector Zhang, would it be all right to serve drinks and snacks to the passengers?" she asked

"Of course," he said.

The flight attendant smiled and walked to the galley.

"So, first things first," said Inspector Zhang. "We need to know why our victim was murdered. More often than not, if you know why a murder took place you will know who committed it."

"So you want to talk to the bodyguard?"

Inspector Zhang shook his head. "I believe I will get more information from Mr. Nakprakone," he said.

Sergeant Lee scratched her head as Inspector Zhang walked to the rear of the cabin and then cut across seats D and F to get to the Thai man sitting in seat 16H. "Mr. Nakprakone?" he said. The man nodded. Inspector Zhang nodded at the empty seat by the window. "Would you mind if I sat there while I ask you a few questions?"

"Go ahead," said Mr. Nakprakone, and moved his feet to allow the Inspector to squeeze by.

Inspector Zhang sat down and adjusted the creases of his trousers. "I assume that you know that it is Mr. Srisai who has been murdered?"

Mr. Nakprakone nodded.

"I was wondering if you could tell me a little about Mr. Srisai."

Mr. Nakprakone frowned. "Why would you think that I would know anything about him.

"Because you're a journalist and because newspapers don't usually fly their staff around in business class." He smiled and shrugged. "I am in the same position. My boss told me that I had to fly economy. The Singapore Police Force is always trying to reduce costs and I am sure that your newspaper is the same."

Mr. Nakprakone grinned. "That is exactly right," he said, speaking slowly as if he was not entirely comfortable communicating in English.

"So am I right in assuming that you are here in the business class section so that you could talk to him, perhaps even to interview him?"

Mr. Nakprakone nodded. He took a small digital camera from his pocket. "And to also get a photograph."

"Did you talk to him?"

"Only for a very short time. I waited for his bodyguard to go to the toilet and then I asked Khun Srisai for an interview. He refused."

"And did you by any chance get a photograph?"

Mr. Nakprakone switched on the camera and held it out to Inspector Zhang. "Just one," he said.

Inspector Zhang looked at the screen on the back of the camera. Mr. Srisai was in his seat, holding up his hand, an angry look on his face. Inspector Zhang looked at the time code on the bottom of the picture. It had been taken thirty minutes before the plane had landed. "He obviously didn't want to be photographed," he said, handing back the camera.

"Just after I took it the bodyguard came back so I returned to my seat." He put the camera away.

"So tell me, why was Mr. Srisai of such interest to your paper?"

"He is a well known gangster, but he has political aspirations," said the journalist. "There was an attempt on his life in Udon Thani two months ago and he fled to Singapore. But last week his uncle died and he was returning for the funeral."

"Political aspirations?"

"He had been setting up a vote-buying campaign in his home province which could well see him becoming an MP in the next election. But someone put a bomb under his car and killed his driver. And shots were fired at his house at night, killing a maid."

"So he was forced to flee Thailand?"

"We think he was just hiding out while he took care of his enemies."

"Took care?"

Mr. Nakprakone made a gun from his hand and pretended to fire it. "There have been half a dozen killings in his province since he left."

Inspector Zhang nodded thoughtfully. "You think he was taking revenge?"

"I am sure of it. And so was my paper."

"So it is fair to say that a lot of people would want Mr. Srisai dead?"

Mr. Nakprakone nodded.

"You say that his uncle died. What happened?" Two flight attendants began moving down the aisles handing out drinks and snacks.

"He was driving his motorcycle at night and he crashed. He'd been drinking and the other driver fled the scene." He shrugged. "A common enough event in Thailand." He leaned closer to the Inspector. "So he was shot, is that right?"

"It appears so, yes."

"But that is impossible. He was perfectly all right when I spoke to him and there have been no shots. We would have heard or seen something, wouldn't we?"

Inspector Zhang looked forward. All he could see was the back of the seat in front of him. He couldn't see Sergeant Lee or the pilot even though he knew that they were standing at the front of the cabin. "You wouldn't have seen anything sitting here," said Inspector Zhang. "But you would of course have heard a shot, had there been one." He stood up and eased himself into the aisle. "Thank you for your help," he said.

"When can we get off the plane?" asked Mr. Nakprakone.

"As soon as I have ascertained what happened," said the Inspector. He crossed over to the far side of the cabin and walked up the aisle to where Sergeant Lee was standing with the pilot.

"I shall be writing to the Police Commissioner in Singapore," said the American tourist as Inspector Zhang walked by.

"I am acting on the Commissioner's personal instructions," said Inspector Zhang.

"Then you will be hearing from my lawyer," snapped the American.

"I shall look forward to it," said Inspector Zhang. "But in the meantime I have an investigation that requires my undivided attention." He walked away, leaving the American fuming.

Captain Kumar and Sergeant Lee were waiting expectantly by the exit door. "The victim was a Thai gangster," Inspector Zhang said quietly. "He had a lot of enemies."

"That explains the bodyguard," whispered Sergeant Lee. The bodyguard was sitting only a few feet away, reading an in-flight magazine.

"According to the journalist, he spoke to Mr. Srisai about half an hour before the plane landed. So he must have been killed in the time between talking to the journalist and the flight attendant checking that his seat belt was fastened."

"That couldn't have been much more than fifteen minutes," said Captain Kumar, rubbing his chin. He put a hand on Inspector Zhang's shoulder. "I think I should assist my first officer with the paperwork, if that is okay with you."

"Of course, Captain."

"And nobody heard anything?" Inspector Zhang asked Sergeant Lee as Captain Kumar went into the cockpit and closed the door behind him.

"Nothing," she said.

Inspector Zhang frowned. "So how can this be, Sergeant Lee? How can a man die of a gunshot wound in an aeroplane cabin without anyone hearing anything?"

"A silencer, sir?"

Inspector Zhang nodded thoughtfully. "Actually the technical term is suppressor, rather than silencer. And while they do deaden the sound of a gun it would certainly still be loud enough to hear in a confined space such as this."

"Not if everyone was listening through headphones," said the Sergeant.

"A good point, Sergeant." He turned to nod at the passenger in 17D. "But Mr. Yates did not use his headphones; they are still in their sealed plastic bag, so I assume that he was working throughout the flight. Other than the bodyguard, he would have been the closest passenger to the victim. And even if a suppressor was used, we have to ask ourselves how it and the gun were smuggled on board. As you said, there are stringent security screenings at the airport."

"Maybe it was a member of the crew," said the Sergeant. She lowered her voice to a whisper. "What about the captain, Sir? He could have a gun in the cockpit. Or the first officer? Or a member of the cabin crew? Mr. Yip perhaps."

"I had considered the cabin crew, but again it comes down to the fact that the bodyguard did not see Mr. Srisai being attacked."

"Perhaps the bodyguard was not as alert as he claims. He could have been asleep." Sergeant Lee's eyes widened. "The gun," she said. "The gun must still be on the plane."

"One would assume so," said Inspector Zhang.

"We could ask the Thai police to help us find it. They must have dogs that can sniff out guns and explosives at the airport, don't you think?"

"I'm sure they have, but my instructions are to bring the investigation to a conclusion without the involvement of the Royal Thai police."

Sergeant Lee looked crestfallen and Inspector Zhang felt a twinge of guilt at having to dampen her enthusiasm.

"But your idea is a good one, Sergeant Lee," he said. "If there was a gun on the plane, such a dog would be able to find it. But do you know what, Sergeant? I do not believe that the gun is on the plane."

Sergeant Lee frowned as she brushed a lock of hair behind her ear. "So do you now wish to interview the bodyguard?"

"I think I will first talk to Mr. Yates," said Inspector Zhang. He walked down the aisle and stood next to the Westerner, who looked up quizzically from his Blackberry. "Mr. Yates?"

Mr. Yates nodded. "What can I do for you?"

Inspector Zhang pointed at the empty seat. "Do you mind if I sit down and ask you a few questions?"

"Of course, no problem," said Mr. Yates, making room for the Inspector to squeeze by. He put away his Blackberry. "Do you have any idea how long this is going to take, Inspector?" he asked. "I have a meeting to get to."

"I hope not too much longer," said Inspector Zhang as he sat down. "So you are British?"

"Yes, but I haven't been to England for more than fifteen years," said Mr. Yates. "I lived in Hong Kong for a while but I've been based in Bangkok for almost ten years."

"I am a big fan of English writers. Sir Arthur Conan Doyle. Agatha Christie, Dorothy L Sayers, Edgar Wallace."

"I'm not a big reader," said Mr. Yates. "Never have been."

Inspector Zhang's face fell, but he managed to cover his discomfort by removing his spectacles and polishing them with his handkerchief. "So, my Sergeant asked you if you saw or heard anything unusual during the flight?"

"I was working," said Mr. Yates.

"So you didn't hear a shot, for instance?"

"A shot? A gunshot? Of course not." He frowned. "Is that what happened, the guy over there was shot?"

"It appears so, yes."

"That's impossible."

"Yes, I agree. During the flight did you see anyone go over to Mr. Srisai?"

"Who?"

"I'm sorry," said Inspector Zhang. "That is the deceased's name. He is a Thai gentleman. Did you see anyone talking to him during the flight?"

"To be honest I was busy," said Mr. Yates. "I hardly looked up. But there was a Thai man talking to him not long before we landed. They were arguing, I think." He twisted around in his seat and pointed at Mr. Nakprakone. "That guy back there."

"Arguing?"

"There was a flash, I think the man might have taken a photograph, but really I wasn't paying attention." He smiled. "I'm putting together a proposal for a client and it has to be done by close of business today."

"You are a stockbroker?" He put his spectacles back on.

"That's right."

"Have you heard of Mr. Srisai? I gather he is active politically in Thailand."

Mr. Yates shook his head. "I'm more concerned about profit and loss accounts and dividend payments than I am with politics," he said. "The Thai political situation is so messed up that I don't think anyone really understands what's going on. It would make our lives much easier if Thailand was run more like Singapore."

Inspector Zhang nodded in agreement. "I sometimes think that the whole world would be better of if it was run like Singapore," he said.

"So he was a VIP, was he?"

"Apparently."

"That explains the run-in with security he had at Changi, then. Thai VIPs expect kid gloves treatment wherever they go."

"What happened?" asked Inspector Zhang.

"I don't know, really. He was behind me at the security check and the arch thing beeped when he went through. They wanted to search him but he was arguing."

"Arguing about what?"

"I've no idea. I just collected my briefcase and walked away. But he was shouting about something or other."

Inspector Zhang thanked him and then stood up and rejoined Sergeant Lee at the front of the cabin. "Is everything okay, Sir?" she asked.

"Everything is satisfactory," said the Inspector.

The door to the cockpit opened and Captain Kumar came out with Mr. Yip. The pilot smiled apologetically. "I know that you said that we wouldn't be allowing anyone off the plane until your investigation has been completed, but Mr. Yip tells me that the economy class passengers are starting to get restless," he said. "We've turned the engines off and we haven't connected to an ancillary power source yet which means that our air-conditioning isn't on. Here in Raffles Class it isn't a problem but economy is almost full and it's getting hot back there."

Inspector Zhang nodded thoughtfully. "I think we have almost concluded our investigation," he said.

"We have?" said Sergeant Lee, surprised.

Inspector Zhang smiled at the chief purser. "Mr. Yip, members of your cabin crew would have been in the galley throughout the flight, yes?"

Mr. Yip nodded. "Of course."

"Then I need you to confirm with them that at no point did any of the economy passengers move through the galley to the front cabin."

"They wouldn't have been allowed to," said Mr. Yip. "Not even to use the toilet. We insist that economy class passengers remain in the economy cabin."

"I understand, but I would like you to confirm that for me," said the Inspector.

Mr. Yip nodded and hurried back to the galley.

"Captain Kumar, would it be possible for the passengers to disembark from the rear of the plane?"

"It wouldn't be a problem, though we would have to bring out a stairway," said the pilot. "If the economy passengers are getting off then we should be allowed to get off with them," said Mr. Woodhouse from his seat in the middle of the cabin.

"I'm afraid that's not possible," said Inspector Zhang.

Mr. Woodhouse waved a blue passport in the air. "I'm an American citizen," he said. "You can't keep us prisoners like this."

"That's right," agreed his wife.

"We're just tourists, this is nothing to do with us," said Mr. Woodhouse.

"Exactly!" said his wife.

"I am sorry for the inconvenience," said Inspector Zhang.

"Being sorry doesn't cut it," said the American. "This isn't fair. You're saying that if we had flown economy you'd let us off, but because we bought business class tickets you're keeping us prisoner." He jabbed a thick finger at the Inspector. "I demand that the American Ambassador is informed of this immediately."

"Immediately!" echoed Mrs. Woodhouse.

"Please Mr. Woodhouse, Mrs. Woodhouse, just bear with us," said Inspector Zhang calmly. "This will all be resolved shortly."

Mr. Yip came back down the aisle. "I have spoken to all the cabin crew and I have their assurance that no passengers left the economy cabin throughout the flight."

"In that case, Captain, I have no objection to you allowing the Economy passengers to disembark from the rear of the plane."

"I'm going too," said the Chinese businessman. He stood up and opened the locker above his head and pulled out a Louis Vuitton briefcase.

"I am afraid I must ask you to remain in your seat for a little while longer, Mr. Lung," said Inspector Zhang.

Mr. Lung turned to look at the Inspector, his upper lip curled back in a snarl. "No," he said. "I've been here long enough. This is Thailand. You've no jurisdiction here. You do not have the authority to keep me on this plane."

"You might well be right, Mr. Lung," said the Inspector. "But of one thing I am sure, immediately you step out of this plane the Thai police will have the authority to arrest you and I will make sure that they do just that. And I am also sure that you would not appreciate the inside of a Thai prison, because that is where you will be held until this investigation is complete."

"This is an outrage," snapped the businessman, but he went back to his seat.

"I agree," said Inspector Zhang. "Murder is an outrage. Which is why I want to solve this murder as quickly as possible. Once the perpetrator has been apprehended we can all leave the plane."

The bodyguard was sitting in his seat, staring at the bulkhead. He didn't look up as Inspector Zhang sat down next to him in seat 11D. "You are Mr. Lev Gottesman," he said.

The man nodded but said nothing.

"From Israel?"

"From Tel Aviv."

"And you were employed by Mr. Srisai, as a bodyguard?"

The man turned his head slowly until Inspector Zhang could see his own reflection in the impenetrable lenses of the man's sunglasses. "Is that some sort of a wisecrack?" he said, his voice a hoarse whisper.

"I am merely trying to ascertain the facts in this case," said Inspector Zhang.

The man's lips formed a tight line and then he nodded slowly. "Yes, I was hired to be his bodyguard. And yes, the fact that he's dead means I did not do a good job." He folded his arms and stared at the bulkhead again.

"Mr. Gottesman, I would like you to remove your sunglasses please."

"Why?"

"Because I like to see a man's eyes when he is talking to me. The eyes, after all, are the windows to the soul."

The Israeli took off his glasses, folded them, and put them into the inside pocket of his leather jacket.

"Thank you," said Inspector Zhang. "And if you would be so good as to give me your passport." The bodyguard reached into his pocket and handed the Inspector a blue passport.

"How long have you been in Mr. Srisai"s employ?"

"About eight weeks."

"And your predecessor was killed?"

The Israeli nodded. "There was a car bomb. The bodyguard was driving. Bodyguards should never drive. Drivers drive and bodyguards take care of security. Mr. Srisai did not take his own safety seriously enough."

"Your predecessor was Thai?"

The Israeli nodded again. "They are not well trained, the Thais. They think that any soldier or cop can be a bodyguard, but the skills are different."

"And your skills, where do they come from? You were a soldier?"

The bodyguard sneered. "All Israelis are soldiers. Our country is surrounded by enemies.

"More than a soldier then? Mossad? Did you use to work for the Israeli intelligence service?"

The Israeli nodded but said nothing. Inspector Zhang flicked through the passport.

"So you are a professional," said Inspector Zhang. "As a professional, what do you think happened?"

"He died. I failed. And as for being a professional, I doubt that anyone will employ me again after this." Sergeant Lee appeared at Inspector Zhang's side, taking notes. "And you saw nothing?" asked the Inspector.

The bodyguard turned to stare at Inspector Zhang with eyes that were a blue so pale they were almost grey. "If I had seen anything, do you think I would have allowed it to happen?" he said

"Obviously not. And equally, you heard nothing?"

"Of course I heard nothing."

"So what do you think happened, Mr. Gottesman? Who killed your client?"

"He had many enemies."

"So I gather. But are any of those enemies on this plane?"

"He didn't see any while we were waiting to board."

"But you would have been in the VIP lounge, would you not? So you wouldn't have seen

everyone."

"True," said the Israeli. "But the only people in the forward cabin are those with business class tickets. It couldn't have been any one from the rear of the plane, could it?"

"I agree," said Inspector Zhang. "Now when was the last time you saw him alive?"

"I went to the toilet shortly before landing. I came back to find that journalist pestering Mr. Srisai. Then I read a magazine, then the flight attendant came around to tell us to fasten our seat belts and when she checked Mr. Srisai she realised something was wrong. She fetched the guy in the suit and he said he was dead and covered him with a blanket."

"You didn't check for yourself?"

"They told me to stay in my seat. They said there was nothing I could do." Inspector Zhang nodded thoughtfully. "Was he an easy man to work for?" The bodyguard shrugged. "He liked to do things his own way."

"So he was difficult?"

"I wouldn't say difficult."

"There was an argument at security back at the airport, I'm told."

"It was nothing. A misunderstanding."

"About what?"

"The metal detector beeped. They searched him. I think it was his watch that set it off. He wears a big gold Rolex."

"And there was an argument?"

"He didn't want to be stopped. Men like Mr. Srisai, they are used to getting their own way.

"And while you were in Singapore, where did you stay?"

"We moved from hotel to hotel, changing every few days. Last night we stayed at the Sheraton."

"Because Mr. Srisai was concerned for his safety?"

The bodyguard nodded. "He said there were people who still wanted him dead, even though he had left Thailand."

"But nothing happened during the flight to give you any cause for concern?"

"That's right. I was stunned when they said he was dead. I don't know how it could have happened."

Inspector Zhang handed the bodyguard his passport. "You say that you have only worked for Mr. Srisai for two months."

"That's correct."

"But I see from the visas in your passport that you only arrived from Israel two months ago." The bodyguard put away the passport. "That's right. I was hired over the phone and flew out to take up the position."

"But you had never met before then?"

The bodyguard shook his head. "A friend of Mr. Srisai recommended me. We spoke on the phone and agreed terms and I flew straight out to Thailand. Shortly after I arrived shots were fired at his house and a maid was killed so he decided to fly to Singapore."

Inspector Zhang smiled. "Well, thank you for your time," he said. He stood up and patted Sergeant Lee on the arm. "Come with me," he said and took her through the galley and into the economy cabin which

50

was almost empty. The cabin crew were shepherding the few remaining passengers out of the door at the rear of the plane. "I think it best we speak here so that the passengers cannot hear us," he said. "So what do you think, Sergeant?"

She shrugged and opened her notebook. "I don't know, Sir, I just don't know. We have an impossible situation, a crime that could not have happened and yet clearly has happened."

"Very succinctly put, Sergeant," said Inspector Zhang.

"We know that the victim couldn't have been shot on the plane. That would have been impossible."

"That is true," said Inspector Zhang.

"But if he had been shot before he boarded, why was there no blood? And how could a man with a bullet in his chest get on to the plane, eat his meal and go to the toilet? That would be impossible, too."

"Again, that is true," agreed the Inspector.

"So it's impossible," said Sergeant Lee, flicking through her notebook. "The only solutions are impossible ones."

Inspector Zhang held up his hand. "Then at this point we must consider the words of Sherlock Holmes in The Adventure of the Beryl Coronet, by Sir Arthur Conan Doyle. For in that book the great detective lays down one of the great truths of detection – once you eliminate the impossible, whatever remains, no matter how improbable, must be the truth."

Sergeant Lee frowned. "But how does that help us if everything is impossible?"

"No, Sergeant. Everything cannot be impossible, because we have a victim and we have a crime scene and we also have a murderer that we have yet to identify. What we have to do is to eliminate the impossible, and that we have done. We know that he was killed on the plane. That is certain because he was alive for most of the flight. So it was impossible for him to have been killed before boarding. But we are equally certain that it was impossible for him to have been shot while he was sitting in the cabin."

"Exactly," said Sergeant Lee. "It's impossible. The whole thing is impossible." She snapped her notebook shut in frustration.

Inspector Zhang smiled. "Not necessarily," he said quietly. "We have eliminated the impossible, so we are left with the truth. If he was not shot on the plane, then he must have been shot before he boarded. That is the only possibility."

"Okay," said the Sergeant hesitantly.

"And if he did not die before boarding, then he must have been murdered on the plane."

The Sergeant shrugged.

"So the only possible explanation is that he was shot before he boarded and was murdered on the plane." Inspector Zhang pushed his spectacles up his nose. "I know that those two statements appear to be mutually exclusive, but it is the only possible explanation." He took out his cell phone. "I must use my phone," he said, and headed towards the rear of the plane.

The pilot came up to Sergeant Lee and they both watched as Inspector Zhang talked into his cell phone, his hand cupped around his mouth. "Is he always like this?" asked Captain Kumar.

"Like what?" asked Sergeant Lee.

"Secretive," said the pilot. "As if he doesn't want anyone else to know what's going on."

"I think Inspector Zhang does not like to be wrong," she said. "So until he is sure, he holds his own counsel."

"Do you think he knows who the killer is?"

"If anyone does, it is Inspector Zhang," she said.

They waited until Inspector Zhang had finished, but when he did put the phone away he turned his back on them and headed out of the door at the back of the plane.

"Now where is he going?" asked Captain Kumar.

"I have absolutely no idea," said Sergeant Lee.

After a few minutes the Inspector returned, followed by two brown-uniformed Thai policemen with large handguns in holsters and gleaming black boots.

"Is everything all right, Inspector?" asked the pilot.

"Everything is perfect," said Inspector Zhang. "I am now in a position to hand the perpetrator of the crime over to the Thai authorities." He strode past them and headed towards the front of the plane. Captain Kumar and Sergeant Lee fell into step behind the two Thai police officers.

Inspector Zhang stopped at the front of the cabin and looked down at the bodyguard, who was sipping a glass of orange juice. "So, Mr. Gottesman, I now understand everything," he said.

The Israeli shrugged.

"The confrontation at the security checkpoint at Changi Airport was nothing to do with your client's watch, was it?"

"It was his watch; it set off the alarm," said the bodyguard.

"No, Mr. Gottesman, it was not his watch. And you should know that I have only just finished talking to the head of security at the airport."

The bodyguard slowly put down his glass of orange juice.

"Your client was wearing a bullet-proof vest under his shirt and he was told by security staff that he could not wear it on the plane, isn't that the case, Mr. Gottesman?"

The Israeli said nothing and his face remained a blank mask.

"They made him remove the bullet-proof jacket and check it in to the hold," said Inspector Zhang.

"If that happened, I didn't see it. I'd already left the security area."

"Nonsense, you are a professional bodyguard, your job requires you to stay with him at all times. No bodyguard would leave his client's side. And I also spoke to the hotel where Mr. Srisai stayed. There were reports of a shot this morning. A gunshot. At the hotel."

The bodyguard shrugged carelessly. "That's news to me," he said.

Inspector Zhang's eyes hardened. "It is time to stop lying, Mr. Gottesman."

"I'm not lying. Why would I lie?"

Inspector Zhang pointed a finger at the bodyguard's face. "I know everything, Mr. Gottesman, so lying is futile. You were with Mr. Srisai when he was shot. The chief of security at the hotel told me as much."

"So?"

"So I need you to explain the circumstances of the shooting to me."

The bodyguard sighed and folded his arms. "We left the hotel. We were heading to the car. Out of nowhere this guy appeared with a gun. He shot Mr. Srisai in the chest and ran off."

"Which is when you realised that your client was wearing a bullet-proof vest under his shirt."

The bodyguard nodded.

"And that came as a surprise to you, did it not?"

"He hadn't told me he was wearing a vest, if that's what you mean."

"The vest that saved his life."

The bodyguard nodded but didn't say anything.

"Can you explain to me why the police were not called?"

"Mr. Srisai said not to. The shooter ran off. Then we heard a motorbike. He got clean away. He'd been wearing a mask, so we didn't know what he looked like. Mr. Srisai said he just wanted to get out of Singapore."

"And he wasn't hurt?"

"Not a scratch. He fell back when he was shot but he wasn't hurt."

"And you went straight to the airport?"

"He didn't want to miss his flight."

"And he didn't wait to change his clothes?"

"That's right. He said we were to get into the car and go. He was worried that the police would be involved and they wouldn't allow him to leave the country."

Inspector Zhang turned to look at Sergeant Lee. "Which explains why there was a bullet hole in the shirt and gunpowder residue."

Sergeant Lee nodded and scribbled in her notebook. Then she stopped writing and frowned.

"But if he was wearing a bullet proof vest, how did he die?" she asked.

Inspector Zhang looked at the bodyguard. Beads of sweat had formed on the Israeli's forehead and he was licking his lips nervously. "My Sergeant raises a moot point, doesn't she, Mr. Gottesman?"

"This is nothing to do with me," said the bodyguard.

"Oh, it is everything to do with you," said Inspector Zhang. "You are a professional, trained by the Mossad. You are the best of the best, are you not?"

"That's what they say," said the Israeli.

"So perhaps you can explain how an assassin got so close to your client that he was able to shoot him in the chest?"

"He took us by surprise," said the bodyguard.

"And how did the assassin know where your client was?"

The bodyguard didn't reply.

"You were moving from hotel to hotel. And I am assuming that Mr. Srisai did not broadcast the fact that he was flying back to Bangkok today."

The bodyguard's lips had tightened into a thin, impenetrable line.

"Someone must have told the assassin where and when to strike. And that someone can only be you."

"You can't prove that," said the bodyguard quietly.

Inspector Zhang nodded slowly. "You are probably right," he said.

"So why are we wasting our time here?"

"Because it is what happened on board this plane that concerns me, Mr. Gottesman. Mr. Srisai was not injured in the attack outside the hotel. But he is now dead. And you killed him."

The bodyguard shook his head. "You can't possibly prove that. And anyway, why would I want to kill my client?"

Inspector Zhang shrugged. "I am fairly sure that I can prove it," he said. "And so far as motive goes, I think it is probably one of the oldest motives in the world. Money. I think you were paid to kill Mr. Srisai."

"Ridiculous," snapped the Bodyguard.

"I think that when Mr. Srisai's former bodyguard was killed, someone close to Mr. Srisai used the opportunity to introduce you. That person was an enemy that Mr. Srisai thought was a friend. And that someone paid you not to guard Mr. Srisai, but to arrange his assassination. But your first plan failed because unbeknown to you Mr. Srisai was wearing a bullet-proof vest."

"All this is hypothetical," said the bodyguard. "You have no proof."

"When Mr. Srisai passed through the security check he was told to remove his vest. Which gave you an idea, didn't it? You realised that if you could somehow deal him a killing blow through the bullet-hole in his shirt, then you would have everybody looking at an impossible murder. And I have no doubt that when you got off the plane you would be on the first flight out of the country." He turned to look at Sergeant Lee. "Israel never extradites its own citizens," he said. "Once back on Israeli soil he would be safe."

"But why kill him on the plane?" asked Sergeant Lee. "Why not wait?"

"Because Mr. Srisai was not a stupid man. He would have come to the same conclusion that I reached - namely that Mr. Gottesman was the only person who could have set up this morning's assassination attempt. And I am sure that he was planning retribution on his return to Thailand." He looked over the top of his spectacles at the sweating bodyguard. "I'm right, aren't I, Mr. Gottesman. You knew that as soon as you arrived in Thailand Mr. Srisai would enact his revenge and have you killed?"

"I'm saying nothing," said the bodyguard. "You have no proof. No witnesses. You have nothing but a theory. A ridiculous theory."

"That may be so," said Inspector Zhang. "But you have the proof, don't you? On your person?"

The bodyguard's eyes narrowed and he glared at the Inspector with undisguised hatred.

"It would of course be impossible for you or anyone to bring a gun on board. And equally impossible to bring a knife. Except for a very special knife, of course. The sort of knife that someone trained by Mossad would be very familiar with." He paused, and the briefest flicker of a smile crossed his lips before he continued. "A Kevlar knife, perhaps. Or one made from carbon fibre. A knife that can pass through any security check without triggering the alarms."

"Pure guesswork," sneered the bodyguard.

Inspector Zhang shook his head. "Educated guesswork," he said. "I know for a fact that you killed Mr. Srisai because you were the last person to see him alive. You went over to him after the journalist went back to his seat and you must have killed him then. You went to the toilet to prepare your weapon and when you came back you leant over Mr. Srisai and stabbed him through the hole that had been left by the bullet that had struck his vest earlier in the day. You probably put one hand over his mouth to stifle any sound he might have made. With your skills I have no doubt that you would know how to kill him instantly.

The bodyguard looked up at Captain Kumar. "Do I have to listen to this nonsense?" he asked

"I am afraid you do," said the pilot.

"I know you have the knife on your person, Mr. Gottesman, because you have been sitting in that seat ever since Mr. Srisai was killed," said Inspector Zhang. He held out his hand. "You can either give it to me or these Thai police officers can take it from you. It is your choice."

The bodyguard stared at Inspector Zhang for several seconds, then he slowly bent down and slipped his hand into his left trouser leg before pulling out a black carbon fibre stiletto knife. He held it, with the tip pointing at Inspector Zhang's chest, then he sighed and reversed the weapon and gave it to him.

Inspector Zhang took the knife between his thumb and finger. There was congealed blood on the blade. Sergeant Lee already had a clear plastic bag open for him and he dropped the knife into it.

Inspector Zhang stood up and the two Thai policemen pulled the bodyguard to his feet. He put up no resistance as they led him away.

"So the Thai police will take over the case?" asked Sergeant Lee.

"The victim was Thai, the murderer is Israeli. The crime was committed in Thai airspace. I think it best the Thais handle it."

"And the Commissioner will be satisfied with that?"

Inspector Zhang smiled. "I think so far as the plane is allowed to fly back to Singapore, the Commissioner will be happy," he said.

Sergeant Lee closed her notebook and put it away. "You solved an impossible mystery, Inspector Zhang."

"Yes, I did," agreed the Inspector. "But the real mystery is who recommended Mr. Gottesman in the first place, and I fear that is one mystery that will never be solved.

"Perhaps you could help the Thai Police with the investigation."

Inspector Zhang's smile widened. "What a wonderful idea, Sergeant. I shall offer them my services."

3.

INSPECTOR ZHANG AND THE FALLING WOMAN

Mrs. Zhang slipped her hand inside her husband's as they walked together away from the seafood restaurant. "That was a lovely evening," she said. "Thank you so much."

Inspector Zhang smiled and gently squeezed her delicate hand. "It isn't over yet," he said. "It isn't every day that I get to celebrate thirty years of marriage to the most wonderful girl in Singapore."

Mrs. Zhang giggled. "I've not been a girl for a long time," she said.

"You will always be my girl," said Inspector Zhang.

Mrs. Zhang stopped walking and turned to face him. She put her arms around his neck and stood on tiptoe to kiss him on the lips. "I will love you until my last breath, and beyond," she said.

"That's probably the lobster and the champagne talking," said Inspector Zhang.

Mrs. Zhang laughed. "It was very good lobster," she admitted. She released her grip on his neck and slid her hand into his again.

The restaurant that Inspector Zhang had taken his wife to was on a quay overlooking the Singapore River, with cute little tables and candles in old wine bottles and a chef who cooked the best lobster in the city. The chef was known to have a predilection for the ladyboys of Orchard Towers but his culinary skills were such that everyone turned a blind eye to his weakness.

As they walked slowly towards where he had left his car, they saw a group of three Indian men looking up at a ten-storey apartment block. One of them was pointing up at the top of the building. Inspector Zhang craned his neck to see what they were looking at and gasped when he saw a Chinese woman standing on the roof of the block, holding onto a railing.

"I'm jumping!" the woman shouted. The wind whipped her black dress around her legs. "I'm going to jump!"

"Oh my goodness," said Mrs. Zhang, covering her mouth with her hand.

Inspector Zhang walked towards the building, reaching for his mobile phone. He called headquarters, explained the situation and asked for a negotiating unit to be despatched. He put his phone away, cupped his hands around his mouth and shouted up at the woman. "This is the police, please go back inside, Madam!"

The three Indians looked over at Inspector Zhang. "Are you really with the police?" said the youngest of the group, a teenager wearing combat trousers and a T-shirt with a Nike swoosh across the front.

"I am Inspector Zhang of the CID, based at New Bridge Road," he said. "Can you please move away, if she does fall it could be dangerous."

"For her, sure," laughed the Indian.

Inspector Zhang was about to scold the teenager for his insensitivity but before he could so the woman shouted again. "I'm going to jump!" she yelled.

Inspector Zhang cupped his hands around his mouth. "Please stay where you are!" he shouted. "We can talk about this."

"I'm going to jump!" screamed the woman. "Don't try to stop me!"

"What's your name?" shouted Inspector Zhang.

The woman shouted something but the wind whipped away her words.

"What did she say?" asked Inspector Zhang's wife.

"I didn't hear," he said. He cupped his hands around his mouth and shouted up at the woman again. "What is your name?"

"Celia!" shouted the woman..

"Okay Celia, please step away from the edge. I will come up and talk to you."

"I'm going to jump!"

60

More passers-by were stopping to look up at the building and cars were stopping in the road, drivers trying to see what was going on. Inspector Zhang waved at the cars to keep moving but no one paid him any attention. Suddenly he heard screams and he turned around just as the Chinese woman slammed into the ground with a sickening thud. Blood splattered across the pavement. The spectators scattered and one of the Indian men began to wail.

"Please, would everyone move back," said Inspector Zhang, holding up his warrant card. "I need everybody to get away from the body now."

Inspector Zhang went over to his wife who was staring at the body, her eyes wide. He put his arm around her. "You have to go home, my dear," he said.

Mrs. Zhang frowned. "Aren't you coming?"

"I'm the first officer on the scene," he said, putting his arm around her slim waist. "I have to stay. I'm sorry."

Mrs. Zhang nodded. She knew what it meant to be married to a policeman, especially one who was as conscientious as her husband. "I'll wait up for you," she said and stood on tiptoe to kiss him on the cheek.

"You'd better," said Inspector Zhang, giving her his car keys. As Mrs. Zhang headed towards the car Inspector Zhang used his mobile phone to contact headquarters to report the death and to cancel the negotiating team. The operator promised to despatch an ambulance immediately.

Inspector Zhang ended the call and phoned Sergeant Lee. She was at home and he asked her to come to the scene as soon as possible.

A small crowd was gathering around the body and Inspector Zhang went over and asked them to move back. "There is nothing to see," he said, even though he knew that wasn't true. There was something to see - a dead body. During his career as a policeman, Inspector Zhang had seen many dead bodies but most people were rarely confronted by death and when they were they tended to stop and stare in morbid fascination.

The woman was lying face down, one leg twisted awkwardly, one arm under her body, and a pool of blood was slowly spreading around her head. He didn't need to check for signs of life. Her dress had ridden up her legs exposing her thighs and Inspector Zhang tenderly pulled it down.

As he straightened up, a patrol car arrived and two uniformed policemen got out. Inspector Zhang showed them his warrant card, explained what had happened, and asked them to help keep the onlookers away. There were now more than fifty people pressing around trying to get a look at the body.

Sergeant Lee arrived just ten minutes after Inspector Zhang had called her. She was wearing a dark blue suit and had her hair clipped up at the back. "I'm sorry to bring you in so late but I was the first on the scene," said Inspector Zhang.

"But you're not on duty tonight," said Sergeant Lee.

"An inspector of the Singapore Police Force is always on duty," said Inspector Zhang.

"But isn't it your thirtieth wedding anniversary tonight?" asked Sergeant Lee, walking over to the body with the inspector.

"My wife understands," said Inspector Zhang.

"Did she jump?" asked the Sergeant, leaning over the body and taking out her notebook.

"She was calling out saying that she was going to jump and I was trying to talk to her but..." He shrugged. "Sometimes there is nothing that can be done to stop them."

Sergeant Lee looked up at the building and shuddered.

"This is your first suicide?" asked the inspector.

Sergeant Lee nodded solemnly.

"It is not uncommon in Singapore," said Inspector Zhang. "We have an average of four hundred a year, more during times of economic crisis."

"I don't understand why anyone would kill themselves," she said. "Especially a young woman."

"It's usually because of money, or an affair of the heart. But our suicide rate is still well below that of Japan, Hong Kong and South Korea."

"I suppose because our lives are better here in Singapore," said the sergeant.

"Do you know which country in the world has the highest rate of suicides?" asked the inspector. Sergeant Lee shook her head. "Lithuania, followed by Russia," said Inspector Zhang. "Their suicide rates are four times ours." He looked down at the body. "And like you, I can never understand why anyone would want to take their own life."

"I don't see a bag or a wallet," said Sergeant Lee.

"That's not unusual," said Inspector Zhang. "Suicides generally take off their glasses and leave their belongings behind. A man, for instance, will often take out his wallet, keys and spare change and place it on the ground before jumping." He shrugged. "I don't know why, but that's what they do."

An ambulance pulled up in front of the building and two paramedics climbed out. Inspector Zhang went over to speak to them, then returned to Sergeant Lee and told her to accompany him into the building.

The glass-doors were locked and there was no one sitting behind the counter at reception. "They probably only have the desk manned during the day," said the inspector.

There was a stainless steel panel set into the wall with forty numbered buttons and a speaker grille. At the top of the panel was a small camera set behind thick glass. Inspector Zhang pressed button number one. After a few seconds a man asked him in Chinese who he was and what he wanted. Inspector Zhang held up his warrant card and replied in Mandarin, telling the man who he was and that he required him to open the door. The lock buzzed and Sergeant Lee pushed the door open. Inspector Zhang thanked the man and put away his warrant card.

He followed Sergeant Lee into the marbled foyer and looked around. "No CCTV," he said. "That's a pity." There were two elevators and he pressed the button to summon one.

63

"Some residents find them intrusive," said Sergeant Lee. "They wanted to install them inside our building, but too many people objected."

"If you do nothing wrong, you have nothing to fear from CCTV," said Inspector Zhang.

"Some people prefer to keep their privacy, I suppose," said the sergeant.

The elevator arrived and they took it up to the tenth floor. There they found a door that led outside. It opened onto a stone-flagged roof where there was a small white-painted gazebo and several wooden benches. There was a barbecue area and a dozen tall palms in earthenware tubs.

Sergeant Lee pointed at a Louis Vuitton handbag on one of the benches. "There, Sir," she said.

Inspector Zhang went over to the railing to look down at the street below while Sergeant Lee examined the bag. She took out a wallet and flipped it open. Inside were half a dozen credit cards and her NRIC, the card carried by every Singaporean. The card was pink, showing that she was a citizen. Cards carried by permanent residents were blue.

"Celia Wong," said Sergeant Lee, reading the card. "Married. Twenty-seven years old."

"So young," said Inspector Zhang, staring down at the pavement far below. The crowds had moved on and there was no sign that a woman had died there. There would be blood on the pavement still, thought Inspector Zhang, but he couldn't see the red stain from the roof.

"I'm twenty-four," said Sergeant Lee.

"I meant so young to kill herself," said the inspector. "She had her whole life in front of her. Why would she want to end it?"

Sergeant Lee shrugged, not knowing what to say.

"Where does she live?" asked the inspector.

"A building in Yio Chu Kang," she said. "I know the building. It's a Housing and Development Board block."

"Are you sure?" asked the inspector, turning to face her.

Sergeant Lee nodded. "I was there on a case last year," she said. "Shall I phone the husband?"

"Definitely not," said Inspector Zhang. "News like this has to be broken in person, and in a sympathetic manner. Do you have your car?"

"I do, inspector."

"Then you shall drive," said Inspector Zhang. "My wife has taken my car."

It took Sergeant Lee twenty minutes to drive to Yio Chu Kang. Inspector Zhang was pleasantly surprised at her driving skills, she was neither too slow nor two fast and she made good use of her rear view mirror and side mirrors. She parked confidently in a space only a few feet wider than her Honda Civic.

They climbed out and looked up at the building. Inspector Zhang realised that his sergeant was right, it was an HDB block, cheap housing provided by the Government for those on low incomes.

They walked over to the main entrance. The intercom system was old and showing signs of wear with several buttons missing. Sergeant Lee pressed the button for Mr. Wong's apartment and there was a buzzing noise. A few seconds later a man asked who was there.

Sergeant Lee put her face close to the intercom. "This is Sergeant Lee of the Singapore Police Force," she said. "I am with Inspector Zhang. We are with the CID at New Bridge Road."

"It's late, what do you want?"

"Are you Mr. Wong?" asked Sergeant Lee.

"Yes."

"And your wife is Celia Wong?"

"Is my wife all right? Has something happened?"

"We'd like to come in and talk to you, Mr. Wong. It would be easier if we could talk to you face to face."

The door buzzed and Sergeant Lee pushed it open. They walked to the elevator and went up to the sixth floor. Wong already had the door to his apartment open. He was wearing a black silk dressing gown and red pyjamas with gold dragons on them. "What's wrong?" he asked. "Is my wife all right? I've been phoning her all night but she isn't answering her phone."

"Can we come in please?" asked Inspector Zhang.

Mr. Wong opened the door wide and let them into his apartment. He was in his mid-thirties, tall with a neatly-trimmed goatee beard. The inspector and Sergeant Lee walked through to a sitting room that was barely large enough to hold two sofas and a circular dining table. The window was wide open and a soft breeze blew in from outside. There was a small LCD television on a rosewood table showing a football match, the sound muted. "Look, tell me what's going on," said Wong.

"I'm afraid we have some bad news for you, Mr. Wong," said Inspector Zhang. "It might be best if you sat down."

Mr. Wong did as the inspector asked and sat down on an overstuffed sofa. Sergeant Lee sat on a rosewood chair but Inspector Zhang remained standing. "Where is your wife, Mr. Wong?" asked Inspector Zhang. "Where did she go?"

"She said she was going out to see a friend, but that was hours ago."

"Who is the friend?"

"I don't know. She didn't say. She just said that she would be back in two hours but that was ages ago. Look, has something happened? Is she in trouble?"

"Your wife died earlier tonight, Mr. Wong. I am so sorry."

Mr. Wong's eyes narrowed and then he looked across at Sergeant Lee. "She what?" he asked, but the sergeant said nothing. Sergeant Lee looked at Inspector Zhang. He was the superior officer so it was up to him to do the talking.

"She fell from a building," said Inspector Zhang. "I am so sorry for your loss."

Mr. Wong shook his head. "No, there's some mistake," he said. "My wife went to a restaurant. She was having dinner." He frowned. "What building?"

"An apartment building in River Valley."

"Then there's definitely been a mistake, my wife wouldn't have any reason to go to River Valley."

"Where did your wife say she was going, Mr. Wong?" asked Inspector Zhang.

"I don't know. She didn't say which restaurant."

"Then how do you know she wasn't going to River Valley?"

"Because she doesn't have any friends there. If she did, I'd know."

"Mr. Wong, we found your wife's handbag." He took Mrs. Wong's NRI card from his pocket and gave it to Mr. Wong. Mr. Wong stared at it, his lower lip trembling.

"Mr. Wong, I'm sorry but I have to ask. Was your wife upset about something?"

Mr. Wong continued to stare at the card.

"Mr. Wong, was your wife upset about something?" repeated the inspector.

Mr. Wong looked up, frowning. "Upset?"

"We think she deliberately jumped off the building. But there was no note."

"My wife did not kill herself. Why would you say that?"

"It wasn't an accident," said Inspector Zhang.

"How can you possibly know that? You said she didn't leave a note. Suicides always leave notes, don't they?"

"Not always." Inspector Zhang took a deep breath. "Mr. Wong, I know that your wife killed herself because I was there," he said.

"You were there?"

"In River Valley. I saw her jump."

A tear ran down Mr. Wong's left cheek.

"I'm sorry, Mr. Wong, there is no doubt. It is your wife."

Another tear trickled down Mr. Wong's face, then he hunched forward and buried his face in his hands. He began to sob quietly.

Sergeant Lee looked over at Inspector Zhang. He forced a smile. Sergeant Lee got up and went to sit on the sofa next to Mr. Wong. She put her arm around him. Inspector Zhang sighed, but didn't say anything. It was not procedure to offer physical comfort to the recently bereaved, but Sergeant Lee was young and relatively inexperienced and a woman. He made a mental note to mention it to her later.

"We're very sorry," whispered Sergeant Lee.

Mr. Wong cried for several minutes, then he suddenly got up off the sofa and rushed to the kitchen. He reappeared shortly afterwards, dabbing at his face with a piece of kitchen towel. "Is it okay for me to have a drink?" he asked Inspector Zhang.

"Of course," said Inspector Zhang.

Mr. Wong went over to a cupboard, poured himself a large measure of brandy and sat down again. He took a long drink, his hands trembling. "What happens now?" he asked.

"At some point you will have to go to the Forensic Medicine Department to identify the body, but that is a formality. It is definitely her, I am afraid. Then you need to contact a funeral director to make arrangements."

Mr. Wong nodded at the inspector and dabbed at his eyes again.

"Mr. Wong, I know this is painful for you, but I do have some questions for you," said Inspector Zhang. "Was your wife troubled in any way?"

"She was having problems at work," said Mr. Wong. "She works for an import-export business and they were about to downsize. She was worried she might lose her job."

"And where do you work, Mr. Wong?"

"At the airport. I work in the baggage handling department."

"And were you and your wife having any problems?"

"What are you suggesting?" said Mr. Wong. "Are you saying that you think my wife killed herself because of me?"

Inspector Zhang held up his hands. "Absolutely not, Mr. Wong, but it would be helpful if we knew what her state of mind was when she was on the roof."

"Why? She's dead. That's the end of it. She killed herself, why do you need to know what she was thinking? Will knowing bring her back?" He sniffed and wiped his eyes.

Inspector Zhang grimaced. "It's my job, I'm sorry. It's just..." He left the sentence unfinished.

"What?" said Mr. Wong.

Inspector Zhang shifted uncomfortably from foot to foot. "The thing is Mr. Wong, people either want to kill themselves, or they don't. Those that do tend to just do it. They write a note, usually, and then they do what they have to do. But there are others for whom suicide is a cry for help, they want attention, they want to be noticed, they want to talk."

"So?"

"So your wife is unusual in that she did both. She was talking, she was shouting that she wanted to jump, and then she did. That is a rarity. Once they start to talk, they usually continue. That is why we have negotiating teams who are trained to deal with a person in crisis." He shrugged. "Anyway, I shall not intrude on your grief any longer. Someone from the Forensic Medicine Department will call you to arrange a viewing."

"A viewing?"

"To identify the body. That has to be done by a relative."

Mr. Wong didn't get up and Inspector Zhang and Sergeant Lee saw themselves out.

"Would you like to know something, Sergeant Lee?" asked the inspector, as they walked out of the building.

"Of course," said the sergeant.

"I never trust a man with a goatee beard," he said. "I'm not sure why, but there is something inherently deceitful about a man who spends an inordinate amount of time shaping his facial hair, don't you think?"

Sergeant Lee frowned. "I've never given it much thought," she said.

"You should, Sergeant," said the inspector.

Sergeant Lee took out her notebook and scribbled in it.

Inspector Zhang was at his desk at exactly nine o'clock the following day. He sat down and logged on to his terminal and checked his email. There was nothing of any importance. He flicked through his copy of the Straits Times. The story of Celia Wong's suicide was on page seven, a mere three paragraphs that looked as if they had come straight from the police blotter. His telephone rang and he picked it up. "Inspector Zhang? This is Dr. Choi from the Forensic Medicine Division."

"Dr. Choi. How are you?" Inspector Zhang had known Maggie Choi for almost fifteen years but she always used his title when she addressed him and he always returned the courtesy. She was in her late thirties, a slightly overweight lady with a moon face and like Inspector Zhang hampered by poor eyesight.

"I am fine, Inspector Zhang, thank you for asking. I am calling about the body that you sent to us last night."

"Ah yes. Celia Wong."

"That's correct. Twenty-seven year old Chinese female. I'm calling to notify you about the cause of death."

"I don't think there's much doubt about that, Dr. Choi," said Inspector Zhang. "I was there when she fell."

"Oh, her injuries were catastrophic, there is no question of that," said the doctor. "But they weren't the cause of death. They were post-mortem."

"That's interesting," said the inspector, sitting up straight.

"Drowning was the cause of death."

"Drowning?" repeated Inspector Zhang, unable to believe his ears.

"Her lungs were full of water."

As Inspector Zhang took down the details in his notebook, Sergeant Lee arrived, carrying a cup of Starbucks coffee. Inspector Zhang put down the phone and blinked at his sergeant. "Sergeant Lee, we have ourselves a mystery," he said.

"A mystery?" repeated Sergeant Lee.

"An impossible mystery," said Inspector Zhang, "and they are the best." He took off his spectacles and leant back in his chair as he polished the lenses with his handkerchief. "An impossible mystery is just that, a mystery where something impossible has happened. In this case, Mrs. Wong jumped from the building but the fall did not kill her."

"It didn't?"

"According to the Forensic Medicine Department, Mrs. Wong drowned."

"But that's impossible."

"Exactly," said Inspector Zhang. "That is why I said we have an impossible mystery." He put his glasses on and steepled his fingers over his stomach. "The impossible mystery was a feature of the golden age of detective fiction, where an amateur sleuth or professional investigator would be called in to examine a crime which had been committed in an impossible manner. Some of the best were written by Agatha Christie, Ellery Queen and the great John Dickson Carr. And we mustn't forget Sir Arthur Conan Doyle, of course, and his immortal Sherlock Holmes. And now, Sergeant Lee, you and I have a real life impossible mystery to solve."

"So you now suspect foul play?" asked Sergeant Lee.

"How could it not be?" asked Inspector Zhang.

"But Mrs. Wong told you that she was going to kill herself, and then she did."

"You think that she managed to drown herself as she fell? That is very unlikely. Impossible in fact." He stood up. "First we must return to the scene of the crime, because that is what I think we have now. A crime."

Inspector Zhang drove them to River Valley and parked in a multi-storey car park. This time there was a doorman on duty and he buzzed them in. His name was Mr. Lau and he told the detectives that he worked from eight o'clock in the morning until six o'clock in the evening. He was in his sixties, a small man with a bald head and a mole the size of a small coin on his chin. Inspector Zhang showed him a photocopy of Mrs. Wong's identity card. "Has this lady ever visited anyone in the building?"

Mr. Lau licked his lower lip as he studied the photocopy, then he shook his head. "I don't think so," he said.

"And there's no CCTV in the building?"

"The residents didn't want it," he said. "People like their privacy."

"It would make our job easier if every building had CCTV," said Inspector Zhang.

"I suppose you'd like them inside people's homes, too," said Mr. Lau.

"That might be going too far," said Inspector Zhang, putting the photocopy into his pocket. "Do you have a list of the occupants of the building?"

Mr. Lau bent down and pulled a clipboard from underneath the counter. The top sheet was a list of all the apartments, the names of the occupants and contact numbers. Inspector Zhang studied the list. "Can I have a copy of this?"

"It's the only copy I have," said Mr. Lau. "But there's a photocopier in the office, I can make a copy for you."

Inspector Zhang smiled. "That would be very helpful, thank you."

Mr. Lau went into the office and returned with a photocopied sheet that he handed to the inspector.

"We'll be on the roof for a while," said Inspector Zhang. "Can you tell me, is the door to the roof ever locked?"

"It's supposed to be," said Mr. Lau. "All the residents have keys, but often it gets left open."

"So anyone could gain access?"

"I suppose so, yes."

"Do you happen to know if it was locked last night?"

Mr. Lau shook his head. "I was up three days ago and it was locked then, but I haven't checked since. It's a relaxation area for the residents; they can have barbecues up there if they want. It's a pleasant place to sit, when it isn't too hot. There's a nice breeze up there, from the river."

Inspector Zhang thanked him and then went up in the elevator to the tenth floor with Sergeant Lee. They went out onto the roof and over to the section of the railing that Mrs. Wong had fallen from. Inspector Zhang looked down at the street below. "She was here when she was shouting," he said. "She was standing here, leaning against the railing." He pointed down to the pavement far below. "I was there with my wife. And four other people, all of us looking up. I tried to talk to her but all I could do was shout. I am not sure if she even heard me. She carried on shouting and more people stopped to look at her."

"It was definitely her?"

"It was the same dress, that I'm sure of. Was it the same woman? How could it not be, Sergeant Lee? I saw her fall. I saw her hit the ground. We found her handbag up here with her ID card." Inspector Zhang sighed. "So how did she manage to drown between here and the ground?"

"It's a mystery," said Sergeant Lee.

Inspector Zhang beamed. "Yes," he said. "It is."

"Can you solve it, Inspector Zhang?"

"I hope so," said the inspector. "I really do." He turned away from the railing. "We have to ask ourselves why she came here," he said. "When it appeared to be suicide, where she was didn't matter because she could have chosen any tall building. But if she didn't kill herself, there must have been a reason why she came to this particular one."

Sergeant Lee nodded. "She came to see someone?"

"I think so," said the inspector.

"Should we speak to the apartment owners?"

Inspector Zhang scratched his chin. The building was ten stories high with four apartments on each floor. It would only take a few hours to knock on all the doors. But if the killer lived in one of the apartments, visiting them would only tip them off that the police were on the case. "Let's go and look at her belongings first," he said. "That might make things clearer."

During Inspector Zhang's time with the Singapore Police Force, the Forensic Medicine Division had evolved from the Centre for Forensic Medicine and before that the Department of Forensic Medicine. It was a case of a rose by any other name, Inspector Zhang knew, because its role hadn't changed – it provided forensic expertise to the State Coroner and technical support to the police. They drove to Outram Road and parked close to Block 9 of the Health Sciences Authority, which housed the mortuary.

They showed their warrant cards to a bored security guard and went through to an office where Dr. Choi was waiting. "Good morning, Inspector Zhang," she said. She smiled showing perfect white teeth.

"Good morning, Dr. Choi." He waved a hand at his sergeant. "This is Sergeant Lee. She is assisting me on this case."

A white-coated assistant came in carrying a large cardboard box which he placed on a stainless steel table. "These are Mrs. Wong's personal effects and clothing," said Dr. Choi. "Do you want to look at the body?"

"I don't think so," said Inspector Zhang. "But you can answer one question for me. The water in Mrs. Wong's lungs, was it sea water?"

Dr. Choi shook her head. "It was definitely not salt water," she said. "There were no traces of salt. It was plain water." She looked at her watch. "I have an autopsy that has to be done before lunch," she said. "Please just leave the box here when you've finished and I'll collect it."

Sergeant Lee opened the box as Dr. Choi left the room. She took out the Louis Vuitton handbag and placed it on the table, followed by the dead woman's dress, shoes and underwear. She started to open the handbag, but Inspector Zhang stopped her with a wave of her hand.

"The clothing first," he said. "Do you notice anything?"

"A dress. Shoes. Bra. Pants." Sergeant Lee shrugged. "Nothing out of the ordinary."

Inspector Zhang smiled. "The dress is Karen Millen, is it not?"

Sergeant Lee examined the label. "It is," she said. "You have a good eye for fashion, inspector."

"Karen Millen is one of my wife's favourite labels. Though she usually only shops there during the sales. It is an expensive brand."

"I like Karen Millen myself, but you are right, they are expensive."

"And the underwear," said Inspector Zhang. "I am less of an expert on underwear, but it also looks expensive."

Sergeant Lee examined the bra and pants. "Yes, it is of good quality," she said. "Real silk."

Inspector Zhang nodded. "Do you think they are the sort of items that would be purchased by a woman who lived in an HDB block?"

"Possibly not," said Sergeant Lee.

"But the shoes, what about the shoes?"

Sergeant Lee picked up one of the shoes. "Poor quality," she said. "Probably made in China."

"And the bag. A Louis Vuitton copy. I thought that strange, that she was happy to pay for a Karen Millen dress but then had a fake handbag. And her shoes were not of good quality. The shoes and the bag fitted with the HDB apartment, but not the Karen Millen dress."

"And the underwear," said Sergeant Lee.

"I wasn't aware of the underwear at the time," said Inspector Zhang. He gestured at the handbag. "Let's see what she has in her bag."

Sergeant Lee unzipped the bag and took out a Nokia mobile phone, various items of make up, her wallet, some breath mints, a set of keys and a Parker pen.

Inspector Zhang picked up the keys. "There is no keycard, I see. To get into the main door."

"So someone must have buzzed her in," said Sergeant Lee.

"Perhaps," said Inspector Zhang.

"Inspector Zhang, I am confused. Do you think that Mrs. Wong killed herself? Or do you think she was murdered?"

"She could not have drowned herself and then thrown herself off the roof," said Inspector Zhang. "And it would of course be impossible for to her to have drowned after she jumped. There is therefore only one possibility remaining. She drowned and then someone else threw her off the roof."

"But why would anyone do that?" asked Sergeant Lee.

"A very good question, Sergeant," said Inspector Zhang. "For if we know why the crime was committed, we will certainly know who did it. For now, I think we should go and see Mr. Wong."

He picked up Mrs. Wong's mobile phone and scrolled through for her husband's mobile phone number. He was just about to press the call button when Sergeant Lee put her hand on his. "That might not be a good idea, Inspector," she said. "He might think that it was his wife calling."

Inspector Zhang realised that she was right, and used his own phone to call Mr. Wong. When Mr. Wong answered, Inspector Zhang arranged to go around and see him early that evening.

"Can't you tell me what it is over the phone?" Mr. Wong asked.

"Interviews are always better conducted face to face," said Inspector Zhang, and he ended the call.

Inspector Zhang and Sergeant Lee arrived at Mr. Wong's apartment at six o'clock and he was clearly not happy to see them. "What is it you want?" he asked as they sat down on the sofa. "This is a very upsetting time for me; the last thing I want is to be answering more questions."

"We have had some more information regarding the death of your wife," said Inspector Zhang. "It might be that you are correct when you say that your wife didn't kill herself."

"What are you saying, inspector?"

"I need to ask you some questions about what you were doing last night."

"I was here," said Wong. "You know I was here. You were in my apartment."

"But before that. What time did you come home?"

"I came home after work. My wife was here and she said she was going out for dinner with a friend. I cooked for myself and I watched some television. When she didn't come back by ten o'clock I called her cell phone but she didn't answer."

"Can anyone confirm that?"

Mr. Wong frowned. "Why do I need anyone to confirm anything?"

"It's simply procedure, Mr. Wong."

Mr. Wong sighed. "As it so happens, I went to talk to my neighbour at about ten o'clock. His television was on loud and it was disturbing me. I asked him to turn the volume down."

"His name?"

"Mr. Diswani."

"Thank you," said Inspector Zhang. "And one more thing. I noticed yesterday that you have a plaster on your hand."

Wong held up his right hand. There was a flesh-coloured sticking plaster on his little finger. "I cut myself."

"Do you mind telling me how?"

"When I was cooking. It's just a small cut. It's nothing."

Inspector Zhang nodded thoughtfully.

"Why are you asking me these questions?" said Wong.

"We're trying to find out what happened to your wife."

"You said she fell from a building."

"That's true," said Inspector Zhang. "But it now appears that something happened to her before she came off the roof."

"What do you mean?" said Wong quickly.

"I'm afraid I can't go into details at this stage, but we are now sure that Mrs. Wong didn't kill herself." He patted his stomach. "Could I impose on you to use your bathroom," he said. "My stomach isn't so good today."

Wong pointed down a corridor. "Along there, first door on the right," he said.

Inspector Zhang thanked him and walked along to the bathroom. When he got back to the sitting room, Sergeant Lee was sitting on the sofa next to Wong. They were looking through a photograph album. There were tears in Wong's eyes.

"We'll leave you now, Mr. Wong," said the inspector. "And once again I'm sorry for your loss."

Wong sniffed. "What will happen now, inspector?"

"Our investigation will continue," said Inspector Zhang.

Mr. Wong showed them out. Inspector Zhang smiled at Sergeant Lee as the door closed on them. "I never trust a man who cries easily," he said.

"He's just lost his wife," said Sergeant Lee. "Wouldn't you cry if you lost your wife?"

Inspector Zhang considered the question for several seconds, then he nodded slowly. "I would grieve. I would be sadder than I have ever been in my life. But I'm not sure that I would cry. Grief is not about tears; grief is a state of mind." He took off his glasses and polished them with his handkerchief. "But perhaps you are right. Perhaps I am too critical of Mr. Wong."

"Perhaps it is the goatee," said Sergeant Lee.

Inspector Zhang smiled and walked down the corridor, stopping at the apartment next to Mr. Wong's. He knocked on the door. It was opened by an elderly Indian man.

"Mr. Diswani?" said Inspector Zhang. He held out his warrant card. "I am Inspector Zhang from New Bridge Road police station."

Mr. Diswani blinked at the warrant card and then nodded. "I am Mr. Diswani," he said,

"Did Mr. Wong have occasion to talk to you about the volume of your television set last night?"

Mr. Diswani's jaw dropped. "He called the police about that? I told him, it was no louder than usual but he pointed his finger at me and called me terrible names."

"And what time was this?"

"About ten o'clock," said Mr. Diswani. "And I turned the volume down immediately, but then I could barely hear it. Come in for yourself and listen. I don't understand why he was so angry."

"It isn't a problem," said Inspector Zhang, putting away his warrant card. "You enjoy the rest of your evening."

Mr. Diswani closed the door, muttering to himself. Inspector Zhang and Sergeant Lee walked to the elevator and went down to the ground floor. "So what do you think, Sergeant Lee?" asked the inspector as they headed for their car.

Sergeant Lee sighed. "It is confusing," she said.

"Yes, it is," agreed the inspector. "Let us suppose that she was murdered, that she was dead before she hit the ground. So the question we have to ask, Sergeant Lee, is why the murderer felt that they had to kill Mrs. Wong twice."

"Overkill," said Sergeant Lee as Inspector Zhang unlocked the front passenger door and climbed in. Sergeant Lee got into the driving seat and closed the door. "Perhaps the killer wanted to make sure that she was dead," she said.

"There are easier ways to do that," said Inspector Zhang, settling back into his seat. "Besides, I think it would be obvious that she was already dead so there would be no need to make sure." He sighed and took off his spectacles. "I think I am getting a headache," he said, massaging his temples

"I have aspirin in my bag," said the sergeant.

"We can wait until we're back in the office," said Inspector Zhang. "Aspirins are best taken with water." He put his spectacles back on. "Water," he said. "I'd forgotten, the water."

"Water?" repeated Sergeant Lee.

Inspector Zhang turned to look at her. "Celia Wong drowned, but her clothes were dry when she went off the building. How could that be if she had only just drowned?"

Sergeant Lee frowned but said nothing.

"How does someone drown without their clothes getting wet?" whispered Inspector Zhang to himself. "Now that is a mystery." He folded his arms. "I think we need to take a closer look at the list that the security guard gave us."

They drove back to New Bridge Road police station. Inspector Zhang had left the list in his desk and he took it out while Sergeant Lee fetched him a glass of water so that he could take his aspirin.

"What are you looking for, Sir?" she asked when she returned with his water.

Inspector Zhang swallowed a white tablet and washed it down and then tapped the list. "Mrs. Wong must have gone to that particular building for a reason," he said.

"You think she went there to see someone? A man?"

Inspector Zhang smiled. "I certainly think she went to see someone, but I think it much more likely that it was a woman she was calling on." He passed her the list. "There are only three single women living in the building. We shall go around first thing in the morning."

Inspector Zhang and Sergeant Lee arrived at the River Valley apartment block at eight o'clock on the dot. Mr. Lau was already at his desk and he buzzed them in.

Inspector Zhang showed Mr. Lau the list of tenants. "I see there are three single women living in the block," he said.

"That's right," said Mr. Lau. "This is mainly a family building; the apartments are all quite spacious."

"Would you happen to know if any of these women are Chinese, between twenty-five and thirty-five years old, with shoulder-length hair. A little taller than my sergeant here."

"Why yes," said Mr. Lau. "That describes Miss Yu perfectly. She lives on the ninth floor. Shirley Yu."

Inspector Zhang took back the list. "Excellent," he said. "We shall go up and talk to her. Just one more thing, Mr. Lau. Do you happen to know if she works in the airport."

Mr. Lau nodded. "Yes, she does."

Inspector Zhang smiled to himself and walked to the elevators. Sergeant Lee followed. They rode up to the tenth floor in silence.

Inspector Zhang knocked on the door to Miss Yu's apartment. A pretty Chinese woman in a dark business suit opened the door.

"Miss Yu?" asked Inspector Zhang.

"Yes," she said. "What do you want?"

Inspector Zhang showed her his warrant card and identified himself, then introduced Sergeant Lee. Miss Yu looked at her watch. "I'm going to work," she said.

"The airport?"

"That's right. What is this about?"

"We're asking residents about the girl who died the other day," said Inspector Zhang. "Can we come in?"

"I really am in a hurry," she said.

"It is important, and we won't take up too much of your time."

Miss Yu sighed and let them in. The apartment was large with a balcony overlooking the river. The furniture was Italian and there was a huge television dominating one wall. "You have a lovely home, Miss Yu," said Inspector Zhang.

"Thank you."

"And you live here alone?"

Miss Yu nodded and looked pointedly at her watch again.

"What is it you do at the airport?" asked Inspector Zhang. "It must pay well for you to be able to avoid a beautiful apartment such as this."

"My parents bought it for me," said Miss Yu tersely. "You said this was about the girl who killed herself?"

"Yes, were you in the building when it happened?"

"What time was that?"

"Just before ten o'clock."

Miss Yu nodded. "I was at home, yes."

"Alone?"

"Of course, alone."

"And did Mrs. Wong press the buzzer for your flat?"

"Mrs. Wong? Who is Mrs. Wong?"

"I'm sorry," said Inspector Zhang. "She is the lady who died."

"Why do you think she pressed my buzzer?"

"She needed to get access to the roof and she didn't have a keycard so someone must have admitted her," said Inspector Zhang.

"No one pressed my buzzer all night. I got home from work, I cooked myself dinner, I watched television and I was in bed by eleven."

Sergeant Lee scribbled in her notebook. "I wonder if I might ask you a favour, Miss Yu?" said Inspector Zhang.

"A favour?" She looked at her watch impatiently.

"My wife and I are thinking of moving to this area, would you mind showing me around?"

"You want me to give you a tour of my apartment?"

"That's so kind of you," said Inspector Zhang, heading for a door at the far end of the sitting room. "Is this the bedroom?"

"One of the bedrooms," said Miss Yu, hurrying after him. "Inspector Zhang, I really have to go to work."

Inspector Zhang nodded appreciatively at the spacious bedroom. There was a king size bed and a sofa against one wall, and another large balcony. There were sliding mirrored doors at the far end of the room and Inspector Zhang slid them back. "A walk-in closet," he said. "That's what my wife really wants, a closet that she can walk into."

"Please, Inspector..." said Miss Yu. "Really, I have to go."

Inspector Zhang stepped into the closet and ran his hand along a line of dresses. He pulled out a black dress and looked at the label. "Karen Millen," he said. "I was telling Sergeant Lee that my wife is a big fan of Karen Millen's designs." He put the dress back on the rail and pulled out another one. "I see you have a lot of her dresses. And that you like black. My wife prefers red."

"Inspector Zhang, I really don't see what the content of my closet has to do with you."

82

The inspector walked out of the closet and went into the bathroom. The walls and floors were lined with marble and there was a large bath in the centre of the room, big enough for two people. "Is that a Jacuzzi?" asked Inspector Zhang. "My wife has always wanted a Jacuzzi."

"Yes, it's a Jacuzzi. Please, Inspector Zhang, I have to go to work."

"I expect it's a wonderful way to relax, after a hard day at work," said Inspector Zhang.

There was a white cabinet to the left of the sink and Inspector Zhang went over and opened it. It was full of medical supplies and he pulled out a pack of sticking plasters.

"I really must protest at this intrusion into my privacy," said Miss Yu. "I am going to have to ask you to leave."

Inspector Zhang put the pack of plasters back into the cabinet and closed the door. "I think we've seen all that we need, Miss Yu."

"I'm glad to hear that," said Miss Yu, folding her arms. "I really do have to get to work."

"There is just one more thing," said the inspector. He lowered his chin and looked at her over the top of his spectacles. "I am arresting you for the murder of Mrs. Celia Wong."

Miss Yu's jaw dropped, and Sergeant Lee looked equally astonished.

They drove Miss Yu to CID headquarters at New Bridge Road, processed her, and then drove out to the airport where they met up with two uniformed policemen.

They found Mr. Wong sitting at a computer in the baggage handling control room. He saw them walk into the room and got up from his seat. "What's wrong?" he asked.

"We're here to arrest you for the murder of your wife," said Inspector Zhang.

"Nonsense," said Mr. Wong. "I was at home when she died."

"No, you were at home when she fell from the roof," said Inspector Zhang. "Your mistress Shirley Yu pushed her off the roof after first standing on the edge and pretending to be her. She wore a similar

Karen Millen dress and at that distance no one could see her face. Then she pushed your wife's body off. But you were in Miss Yu's apartment earlier. And that is where you killed your wife. You drowned her in the bath."

"Sheer fantasy," said Mr. Wong.

"I'm afraid we have Miss Yu in custody already, and she has told us everything."

Mr. Wong's shoulders slumped. His legs started to shake and he sat down heavily. "It was an accident," he said. "I didn't mean to kill her."

"Your wife found out that you were having an affair?" said Inspector Zhang.

"She must have done. She must have found the key and copied it, and then followed me to the apartment."

"And she used the key to let herself in?"

Wong nodded. "Shirley and I were in the bath. Together. Celia burst in with a knife."

"She was angry?"

Wong laughed sharply. "She was like a woman possessed. I'd never seen her so angry. She came at Shirley with the knife, trying to stab her. I tried to take the knife from her and she cut me." He held up his hand. "The blood just seemed to make her crazier. She kept trying to stab me, saying that I'd ruined her life and that she was going to kill me."

"So you pushed her under the water?"

Wong shook his head. "I didn't mean to kill her, but it was the only way I could stop her. She fell into the bath and I knelt on her and tried to pull the knife away but she kept struggling. Then suddenly she went still."

"And Miss Yu, what was she doing while this was going on?"

"She was hysterical," said Wong. She was sitting on the floor, crying and shaking. It wasn't her fault, inspector. Shirley didn't do anything wrong."

"She covered up a murder, Mr. Wong," said Inspector Zhang quietly.

"We had no choice," said Mr. Wong.

"And the key? The key that your wife used to let herself into the apartment. You took it?"

"She must have been planning it for ages because she had made a copy of the key I used. And last night I couldn't find my keycard to get into the building. Celia had taken it. She followed me to the building and then used the keycard to get in and the key to get into the apartment."

"And after she was dead, you took the key and the keycard?"

"I knew that if you found them you would find the apartment," said Mr. Wong. "I didn't mean to kill her, Inspector Zhang."

"But you did," said Sergeant Lee.

"It was an accident," said Mr. Wong.

"But throwing her off the building wasn't," said Inspector Zhang. "That was quite deliberate."

"I had to give myself an alibi," said Mr. Wong. He put his head in his hands. "I didn't want to do it, and neither did Shirley. But we knew that if my wife's body was found then I'd be the obvious suspect." He looked up at the inspector. "It's true, isn't it? Most murders are committed by family members?"

"Or work colleagues. Or neighbours. Yes, that is true. It is very rare for someone to be killed by a stranger."

"That was what I told Shirley. If you found my wife and I didn't have an alibi then I would be the obvious suspect. But if she died when I was in my apartment, then I would be in the clear."

"Your mistress and your wife are not dissimilar in appearance, which enabled the deception," said the inspector.

Mr. Wong nodded. "That was what gave me the idea," he said. "We removed the clothes she was wearing and then we dried her hair and redressed her in one of Shirley's dresses. Shirley changed into a similar dress and then we carried my wife to the roof. Then I went home. I made some phone calls and then I knocked on the door of the flat next door and asked Mr. Diswani to turn down the volume of their television set." Mr. Wong smiled. "I caused quite a scene."

"You wanted the neighbour to remember you, so that he would confirm your alibi."

Mr. Wong nodded. "It worked, didn't it?"

"That part of your plan did, yes," said Inspector Zhang. "Once you had established your alibi, your mistress stood on the edge of the roof to attract the attention of passers-by."

"She was so high up, no one would know that it wasn't my wife. Then she tipped Celia's body over and went back to her apartment."

"It was a very good plan," said Inspector Zhang. "But not good enough." He nodded at the two uniformed policemen. "Take him away," he said.

One of the policemen handcuffed Mr. Wong and he was led out of the front door.

"What will happen to them, do you think?" asked the sergeant.

"That is up to a jury," said Inspector Zhang. "But I don't think that any jury will believe that drowning is a valid means of self-defence. Drowning takes time. He must have held her under the water long after his wife had let go of the knife." He shuddered. "But as I said, that is not our concern."

He walked towards the door and they went down together to a waiting police car.

"When did you first suspect the husband, Inspector Zhang?" asked Sergeant Lee, following Inspector Zhang into the car.

"The second time we saw him," said the inspector. "When I asked him about the cut on his hand he had a sticking plaster, remember?

"He said that he had cut himself when he was cooking."

"Yes, that's what he said. But he was right-handed and his cut was on his right hand. I couldn't help wonder how someone right-handed could cut themselves on the right hand."

"He could have done that picking up the knife, or if the knife had slipped."

Inspector Zhang nodded and pushed his spectacles further up on his nose. "But it was the plaster, rather than the wound, that was the real clue that something was amiss."

"The plaster?" repeated Sergeant Lee. "It was a regular sticking plaster, I thought."

"Yes it was," said the inspector. "It was a small flesh-coloured plaster, nothing out of the ordinary about it. But when I went to the bathroom, I looked in the first aid cupboard and the plasters there were the transparent kind. A different brand completely."

"Ah," said Sergeant Lee.

"So it seemed obvious to me that if the plaster had come from somewhere else, then there was every possibility that he was lying about the circumstances that had led to him receiving the wound. And lies, I always say, are like cockroaches. For every one that you see, there are ten that are hidden."

"And when you checked the first aid cabinet in Miss Yu's bathroom, you saw the same brand of plaster that Mr. Wong had used."

"Exactly. Which meant that he must have been in her apartment when he was injured."

Sergeant Lee nodded and scribbled in her notebook.

"What are you writing?" asked the inspector.

"I write down everything you tell me, Inspector Zhang. So that I won't forget."

"Perhaps one day you will write about my cases, become my Dr. Watson."

Sergeant Lee smiled. "That would be an honour, Inspector Zhang, because you are most certainly my Sherlock Holmes."

Inspector Zhang beamed with pride but said nothing.

4.

INSPECTOR ZHANG AND THE HOTEL GUEST

Inspector Zhang removed his spectacles and polished them with a large red handkerchief as he waited for the Indian receptionist to finish her phone call. It was a hot day, even for tropical Singapore, and he was already regretting the five minute walk the Clarke Quay MRT station to the Best Western Hotel in Carpenter Street. His wife had borrowed his car to visit one of her relatives in Malaysia, his sergeant's car was being serviced, and there were no cars available in the office pool so he had no option other than to use the mass transit system. The receptionist put down the receiver, flashed him a professional smile, and asked him how she could help. "My name is Inspector Zhang of the Singapore Police Force," he said. "I am with the CID at New Bridge Road." He nodded at his companion, a twenty-four-year old Chinese woman in a pale green suit with her hair tied up in a neat bun. "This is my colleague, Sergeant Lee." Sergeant Lee smiled and held out her warrant card. "I believe it was the manager who called us," said Inspector Zhang, putting away his wallet. "About a body."

The receptionist gasped. "A body? Here? Are you sure?"

"Can I speak to the manager? I am told he is a Mr Leutzinger."

The receptionist hurried away to a back room and reappeared with a tall, cadaverous man in a black suit. He shook hands solemnly with Inspector Zhang. The manager's nails were beautifully manicured and glistened as if they had been given a coat of varnish. "I am afraid you have been misinformed, Inspector. We didn't report a body. What we reported to the police was that we had somebody in the hotel. A man who has lost his memory. He has no idea who he is but he is very much alive."

"And why do you require the services of the police?" said Inspector Zhang, frowning.

"Because he has no money. No identification. And no idea who he is or where he is supposed to be."

Inspector Zhang nodded thoughtfully. "Very well," he said. "Where is this gentleman?"

"Upstairs, in room 302."

"But if he has checked in he must have shown his passport or ID card. And you would have checked his credit card."

"That's the problem, Inspector Zhang. It's not his room. But he has the keycard."

"So who did book the room?"

"A Mrs Petrova. From Russia. She has been out all day."

"But this man in the room now, he had the correct keycard for the room?"

The manager nodded. "He let himself in and the chambermaid found him there when she went in to clean the room. It's all a bit of a mystery, I'm afraid."

A smile spread across Inspector Zhang's face. There was nothing that Inspector Zhang liked more than a mystery, but in low-crime Singapore they were few and far between. "Indeed it is," he said. "Let us go and talk to the gentleman."

They went up in the lift together, then along the corridor to room 302. The manager knocked gently on the door. It was opened by a Westerner in a dark blue suit, his tie loose around his neck. He was holding a damp towel to the back of his head. He was in his forties, with jet-black hair and a neatly-trimmed greying moustache.

Inspector Zhang introduced himself and Sergeant Lee as the man sat down on the bed and dabbed at his head with the towel.

"Are you hurt?" asked Inspector Zhang.

"I have a bump on the back of my head," said the man. He showed the towel to the inspector. "There's no blood, so I don't think It's too bad."

"We said that he should see a doctor but he insisted that he was all right," said the manager.

There was a chair in front of a dressing table and Inspector Zhang moved it so that he could sit down opposite the man. "I am told you do not know who you are," he said.

The man nodded. "I can't remember anything. Not a thing."

"You sound English. From the south of England perhaps, but I am not very good at accents. Are you from England?"

The man shrugged. "I don't know."

"I think you are. You are definitely not American, Australian or South African."

"I'm sorry, Really I can't help you." He dabbed at the back of his head with the wet towel. "I don't know where I'm from. Everything before I set foot in this hotel is a blank."

"And you have no wallet? No identification?"

The man shrugged again. "I think I might have been robbed," he said.

"That seems highly likely," said Inspector Zhang. "You are dressed like a businessman but I don't see a briefcase?"

"If I had one, it was probably stolen."

"No mobile phone?"

The man shook his head.

"And you have no idea if you live in Singapore or if you are a visitor?"

"I'm sorry. This is crazy, isn't it?"

"It is unfortunate," said Inspector Zhang. "But it does happen. A blow to the head can cause temporary amnesia."

"If he arrived at the airport immigration will have his photograph," said Sergeant Lee.

"My colleague is correct," Inspector Zhang said to the man on the bed. "And of course if you are a citizen or a permanent resident your fingerprint and photograph will be on your National Registration

Identity Card, so one way or another we will be able to find out who you are sooner rather than later."

"That's good to hear."

"From my first impression I would say that you live in Singapore, either as a citizen or a permanent resident. And I would say that you are either married, so I'm sure that your wife is looking for you."

"Why do you think that?"" asked the man.

Inspector Zhang spoke to the man in rapid Mandarin, but it was clear from the blank look on his face that he didn't understand.

"And as you don't understand Mandarin. I would think that the person you live with is not Chinese. Probably a Westerner like yourself."

The manager stared incredulously at Inspector Zhang. "Inspector, I can clearly see that he is not wearing a wedding band, so why would you think that he is married?"

"He is not wearing a wedding band now, but you can see that the skin is paler around the base of the wedding finger, so he does normally wear a ring," said the inspector. "But it was more his suit that suggests he is living with someone."

"My suit?" said the man.

"Do you like cats?" asked Inspector Zhang.

"Cats?"

"Felines. Are you a cat person or a dog person? People tend to favour one or the other. Myself, I prefer dogs though unfortunately they are not allowed in my building."

The man ran a hand through his hair. "Dogs, I think." He nodded thoughtfully. "Yes, dogs."

"But your wife, she is a cat person, I'm sure."

The man shook his head, bemused. "How can you possibly know that," he said.

"Because you have white cat hairs on the legs of your trousers, as if a cat has been rubbing itself against your legs. But there are no similar hairs on your jacket. In my experience cat lovers pick up their pets so from that I deduce that you are not a cat lover but probably live with someone who is. The pale skin on your wedding fingers suggests a wife."

The man looked at his hand. "They must have taken my wedding ring when I was mugged," he said. "And my watch." He held out his left arm. "They've taken my watch, too."

"What about your spectacles?"

"My spectacles?" said the man. "I'm not wearing spectacles."

"But you have the small indentations either side of your nose that suggests you do have problems with your vision."

The man reached up with his left hand and rubbed the bridge of his nose. "Everything is a bit blurry, I thought it was the bang on my head."

"Do you have a packet of cigarettes on you?" asked Inspector Zhang.

The man frowned. "Do you think I smoke?"

"There are faint nicotine stains between your first and second finger on your right hand," said Inspector Zhang. "I would tend to think that you have given up recently. This is a no smoking room so if you are still smoking then that would suggest you were not staying here."

"I went through all my pockets and there were no cigarettes and no lighter." He smiled. "But now that we are talking about cigarettes, I do feel like having one."

"Then I think I am right, you are a smoker who has recently given up the habit," said Inspector Zhang. "Now tell me, what is the first thing you do remember?"

"I was outside the hotel," said the man. "I went through my pockets and found the keycard. It was in the little folder that had the room number so I came to see if there was anything here that would jog my memory."

"And there isn't?"

The man waved his hand around the room. "There's nothing here, as you can see."

Inspector Zhang looked over at the manager. "The guest who checked in had no luggage?"

"Apparently not," said Mr Chung.

"Would that be unusual?"

"Not if the guest was here for business. Sometimes guests check in first thing in the morning and then check out that evening. We are very well located for the business district."

"And Mrs Petrova was a regular guest?"

"I will have to check," said the manager.

"What am I going to do?" asked the man.

"If you would please wait here," said Inspector Zhang. "If we do not solve this mystery shortly then we will take you to New Bridge Road station." He nodded at Sergeant Lee. "If you do remember anything then please tell my sergeant straight away."

Inspector Zhang went down to the ground floor with the manager to reception. There he tapped on a computer and peered at the screen. "It's the first time that Mrs Petrova has stayed here," he said.

"And she paid by credit card?"

"Yes, just for the one night."

"And was a Russian?"

The manager nodded. "She showed a Russian driving licence as her ID."

"Can you show me the CCTV footage?" asked Inspector Zhang.

The manager took him through a side door into a windowless office. There was a desk on which there was a computer and a leatherbound diary, and against one wall a bookcase filled with neatly-labelled files.

On a table in one corner was a computer monitor on which were half a dozen views from CCTV cameras located around the hotel. The manager sat down in front of the computer and reached for the mouse. "What would you like to see, Inspector?" he asked.

"Mrs Petrova checking in," said Inspector Zhang, sitting down next to the manager and adjusting the creases of his trousers.

The manager clicked on a menu and after a few seconds they were looking at a view of the reception desk where the Indian receptionist was handing a keycard to a blonde woman wearing impenetrable sunglasses and a floppy hat.

"It's difficult to see her face," said Inspector Zhang.

"It is a hot day and fair skin burns easily," said the manager.

The woman walked to the lifts. She was wearing a blue and white dress and had a Louis Vuitton shoulder bag. It seemed to Inspector Zhang that she deliberately kept her head turned away from the CCTV camera.

"And what time did the gentleman arrive?" asked Inspector Zhang.

The manager peered at the time code at the bottom of the screen. It said 10.35am. "About two hours later."

"Be so good as to show me," requested the inspector.

The manager clicked the mouse and a fresh picture filled the screen, this from a camera covering the lifts. The man came into view through the main entrance and walked over to the lift.

"That's interesting," said the inspector.

"What?" asked the manager, turning around in his chair.

"He doesn't appear to be hurt. And if he had just been attacked, why didn't he go to the receptionist? Why didn't he ask for her to call the police?"

"Perhaps he was confused. Perhaps he didn't realise that he had been attacked. He has amnesia. Perhaps he forgot everything."

"Also I don't see him holding the keycard," said Inspector Zhang. "He said that he found the keycard in his pocket and that's why he went up to the room." He rubbed his chin thoughtfully. "So tell me, do you have CCTV cameras inside the lifts?"

"Of course," said the manager. He clicked on the mouse, scrolled down a menu and after a few seconds a CCTV picture of the man entering the lift filled the screen. The man reached out with his right hand to press the button for the third floor and then stood facing one of the mirrored walls and tidied his hair with both hands.

"That's interesting," said Inspector Zhang.

"What is?" asked the manager.

"Can you freeze the picture where he is arranging his hair?"

The manager clicked the mouse, then the picture froze.

"You're looking to see if there is a wound?" asked the manager.

"There would be nothing to see," said Inspector Zhang. "There is no blood, just a bump. No, Mr Leutzinger, I am admiring the watch on his wrist. It appears to be a very expensive Rolex."

"But his watch was stolen. Along with his wallet and everything else."

"Exactly," said Inspector Zhang.

The manager frowned. "So you think he was lying about the mugging?"

"Oh no," said Inspector Zhang. "That's not what he's lying about." He stood up. "Let's go back upstairs and I'll explain everything," he said.

They went back up to the third floor where the man was still sitting on the bed and dabbing the towel on the back of his head.

Inspector Zhang sat down opposite the man and looked at him solemnly." It is time to tell the truth," he said. "If you continue to lie then you will be in even more trouble than you are already in."

The man looked confused. "What are you talking about?"

"I am talking about the fact that you were not attacked outside. In fact you were attacked here, in this room. By Mrs Petrova though I doubt that is her real name. But I am sure that you came here to see her and that she, with or without an accomplice, robbed you."

"I told you, I can't remember anything. " He looked across at Sergeant Lee as if hoping that she would agree with him but she looked back at him impassively.

"Let me tell you what I think happened," said Inspector Zhang. "I think you came here specifically to meet Mrs Petrova. It was your first meeting and I think that perhaps you met her on the internet. In a chat room perhaps. Or one of those social networking sites that are so popular."

"Nonsense," said the man.

A smile spread slowly across the inspector's face. "But how can you say that if you've truly lost your memory?" he said. "If you really have no memory of what happened before you were attacked, then surely anything is possible."

The man swallowed nervously but said nothing.

"Well then let us consider the evidence," continued Inspector Zhang. "In my experience muggers do not take men's wedding rings. Women's jewellery, of course. And diamond rings. But generally not wedding bands. And they certainly don't bother stealing spectacles. I therefore assume that you removed the ring and the spectacles yourself. Now why would a man do that?" He turned to look at his sergeant. "What do you think, Sergeant Lee?"

She looked up from her notebook, in which she had been scribbling furiously. "The glasses to make himself more attractive, the ring because he wanted to appear unmarried?" she said.

Inspector Zhang nodded approvingly. "And did you notice that he dyes his hair? It was unnaturally black for a man of his age and you could see where the roots are grey. He is a man who takes pride in his appearance, who likes to look good for the ladies." He turned back to the man. "Isn't that so?"

The man's shoulders slumped. He dropped the towel on the bed and sat with his head in his hands. "I've been a fool," he said.

"Yes, you have," agreed the inspector. "But now is the time to tell the truth. What is your name?"

"Fisher," the man mumbled. "Sebastian Fisher."

"And you live in Singapore?"

The man nodded but didn't look up. "I'm a stockbroker. I sell stocks and shares."

"And your office is nearby?"

The man nodded.

"And you came here to meet Mrs Petrova?"

"She said she was here on business and wanted to meet me. She said she was in an unhappy marriage and that she…." He sighed. "I was a fool."

"Mrs Petrova will not be her real name, of course. She knocked you unconscious and robbed you?"

"It wasn't her. I was looking at her when I was hit. When I came around they'd taken my money, my wallet, my watch. Everything. I was sitting on the bed when the chambermaid came in. She asked me what I was doing in the room and I panicked."

"You could have simply told the truth," said Inspector Zhang.

"And tell everybody why I'd gone to her room? And why I wasn't wearing my wedding ring. What possible reason could I give for being there? Then I saw the keycard on the bedside table and I said that I'd let myself in because I'd lost my memory and found the card in my pocket."

"Your wedding ring and your spectacles are in your office?"

Fisher nodded.

"I think we will find that Mrs Petrova and her accomplice have been doing this elsewhere," said Inspector Zhang. "Street muggings are rare in Singapore, but inviting their victim to a hotel makes everything much easier. I have no doubt we will discover that the credit card she used was not hers. I assume you told her you were well off?"

"I wanted to make a good impression," said Mr Fisher. "I know, I was stupid."

Inspector Zhang took off his glasses and polished them with his handkerchief. "So tell me, Mr Fisher," he said. "Your wife is the cat-lover in your house, was I correct?"

Mr Fisher nodded sadly. "She loves those cats more than she loves me," he said, putting his head in his hands. "That's part of the problem."

"And you do smoke?"

"I've told my wife that I've given up, but yes, I do sneak out for a cigarette. I feel like a prisoner sometimes." He looked up at Inspector Zhang. "Does my wife have to know about this?"

"All I need from you is a statement about the robbery," said Inspector Zhang. "I am prepared to overlook your memory lapse. As to what you do or don't tell your wife, that is completely up to you." He replaced his spectacles. "But speaking as a man who has been married for thirty years I can tell you that it's best never to try to keep a secret from a wife. They tend to find out the truth about everything, eventually."

"A bit like yourself, Inspector Zhang, " said Sergeant Lee, and the inspector beamed happily.

5.

INSPECTOR ZHANG AND THE DISAPPEARING DRUGS

Inspector Zhang smiled fondly at his wife as she placed his kaya toast in front of him. Kaya could be bought in a bottle in any supermarket but Mrs. Zhang made it herself, slow cooking coconut milk, eggs, sugar vanilla and a hint of pandan leaves, using a recipe that had been handed down from her grandmother. She spread it on a slice of wholemeal toast with a little butter and served it with a soft-boiled egg, just the way he liked it. "You make the best kaya toast in Singapore," he said.

"You can buy it in McDonald's these days," she said.

"You can buy many things in McDonald's but nothing they sell comes close to your cooking," said Inspector Zhang.

"Such sweet talk," she said, blushing prettily and sitting down opposite him. She poured more coffee into his cup.

Inspector Zhang took a bite out of his toast and sighed with contentment. "I would have married you for this toast alone," he said.

Mrs. Zhang giggled and put her hand over her mouth. She'd done that on the first date, more than thirty years earlier and it was one of the many things he loved about her.

His mobile phone rang and he sighed. It was in the pocket of his suit jacket, hanging on the back of the sofa.

"I'll get it," said his wife. "You finish your breakfast."

She went over to the sofa, retrieved his phone, and took the call. She pulled a face and took the phone over to him. "It is the Senior Assistant Commissioner," she said. "He wants to speak to you."

Inspector Zhang swallowed and took the phone from her. "This is Inspector Zhang," he said.

"Inspector, I am sorry to bother you so early, but I need to see you this morning," said the Senior Assistant Commissioner. "Can you come to office at the start of your shift today?"

"Of course, Sir," said Inspector Zhang. "Can you tell me what it is in connection with?"

"It is of a highly confidential nature, Inspector. I shall explain when I see you."

The line went dead and Inspector Zhang frowned at the phone.

"He sounds different," said Mrs. Zhang. "Not like the man we used to know."

"He is Senior Assistant Commissioner now," said Inspector Zhang. "He is a very important man."

"He is your friend."

Mr. Zhang put the phone down next to his plate. "We haven't been friends for a long time," he said.

"I don't think he remembered me," said Mrs. Zhang.

"It has been a long time since we socialised. More than twenty years."

"Twenty-five," she said. "We had a celebratory drink, do you remember, when he was promoted to sergeant."

"Was that twenty-five years ago?" mused Inspector Zhang. "You know, I think you are right." He looked at his watch, finished his coffee, and picked up his phone.

Mrs. Zhang helped him on with his jacket, then kissed him on the cheek. "I shall cook you fish head bee hoon tonight," she said.

"You spoil me," said Inspector Zhang, but he was already looking forward to his favourite dish.

He drove to police headquarters at New Phoenix Park. The block that housed the police was next to a twin block occupied by the Ministry of Home Affairs. The Senior Assistant Commissioner's office was on the sixth floor, a corner office with a huge desk and a wall full of framed commendations.

Inspector Zhang had to wait for fifteen minutes on a hard chair until a secretary showed him into the Senior Assistant Commissioner's office. The Senior Assistant Commissioner seemed much older than the last time that Inspector Zhang had seen him. As he sat down Inspector Zhang tried to remember when he'd last seen the Senior Assistant Commissioner and decided that it had been almost five years when they'd both attended the funeral of a former Deputy Commissioner. The five years had not been kind to the Senior Assistant Commissioner. His hair was thinning and he'd put on weight and there was an unhealthy pallor to his skin.

There was a cup of tea in front of the Senior Assistant Commissioner and he stirred it thoughtfully as he looked at Inspector Zhang. "Was that May-ling I spoke to this morning? Your wife?"

"Yes it was," said Inspector Zhang.

"How long have you been married now?"

"Thirty years."

"That is a long time," said the Senior Assistant Commissioner.

"It feels like only yesterday," said Inspector Zhang.

"You are a lucky man," said the Senior Assistant Commissioner. "May-ling was a beautiful woman." He sipped his tea.

"She still is," said Inspector Zhang. "The most beautiful woman in Singapore. And the best cook."

"I am divorced," said the Senior Assistant Commissioner., putting down his cup.

"I am sorry to hear that," said Inspector Zhang.

The Senior Assistant Commissioner shrugged. "This job puts a strain on relationships. The hours. The nature of the work." He sighed. "Anyway, I did not ask you here to complain. I asked you here because I have a problem. A problem of a sensitive nature."

"You can of course rely on my discretion," said Inspector Zhang.

The Senior Assistant Commissioner frowned and then nodded slowly, "Yes, I know that, Inspector Zhang. You are one of the most conscientious officers on the force. Not a blemish on your record. Not a single black mark." He sat back in his executive chair. "And you have the reputation of being a detective who can solve mysteries."

Inspector Zhang smiled but said nothing. He could see that the Senior Assistant Commissioner was troubled, and he had learned over the years that people said most when they were not interrupted.

"I have a case which could be considered as a mystery. A mystery that..." The Senior Assistant Commissioner shrugged. "Well, frankly Inspector Zhang, it has stumped me." He sighed and placed his hands face down on his highly-polished desk. "Have you come across Inspector Kwok. Inspector Sally Kwok."

"I don't believe so," said Inspector Zhang.

"She is something of a high-flyer, marked for great things," said the Senior Assistant Commissioner. "She is currently on attachment with the Drugs Squad. I personally assigned her what should have been a very straight-forward drugs case but somehow it has turned into a..." He shrugged and sighed. "A mystery. That is the only word for it. A mystery." He stood up and walked around behind his chair and leant his arms on the back. It was, Inspector Zhang realised, a very defensive posture.

"A Customs team discovered a consignment of heroin in a container that had arrived at the port," said the Senior Assistant Commissioner. "It was a chance thing, a drugs dog was on the way to a job when he walked by a container that had just come off a ship and he indicated that there were drugs inside. The container was opened and a hundred kilos of Burmese heroin was discovered in cardboard boxes. Ten boxes, each of ten kilos. The street value in Singapore would be about thirteen million US dollars. It was a huge haul. We had the heroin but we wanted to catch the men who had imported it. That is when I called in Inspector Kwok."

Inspector Zhang nodded but said nothing. It was indeed a big haul, and the Senior Assistant Commissioner must have had a reason for giving such a big case to a mere inspector.

"The container had been hired by an import-export company who were acting on behalf of customers who were bringing in goods from Thailand, but who didn't need a complete forty-foot container," continued the Senior Assistant Commissioner. "Basically the import-export company paid for the container and then found customers who wanted to bring in goods. It was a mixed consignment. Along with the boxes of drugs there was furniture, soft goods, toys, and foodstuffs. The container was to be taken to the warehouse of the import-export company where it would be opened and the goods delivered to the various customers. The plan was for Inspector Kwok's team to follow the boxes of drugs to the customer who had paid for them. It should have been a simple enough case but that's not how it worked out."

The Senior Assistant Commissioner sighed. "It wasn't the first time that the customer had taken delivery of boxes in a container from Thailand," he said. "They were in fact a regular customer. But the customer never actually met anyone from the import-export company. All charges were paid for in Thailand, by a company that apparently does not exist. Or at least does not exist now. The shipping costs were paid in full from Thailand along with instructions of what to do with the consignment. Basically the boxes were to be taken to a delivery address and left there."

He walked around his chair, sat down, and poured himself a glass of water from a bottle. He didn't offer any to Inspector Zhang, and slowly sipped some before continuing.

"The delivery address was never the same, but it was always an apartment in a block in the Geylang area. The delivery men would take the boxes to the apartment and would find a key under the mat outside the door. They would unlock the door, place the boxes in the apartment, then relock the door, put the key back under the mat, and leave. They had apparently done that four times over the past year. The consignment we found was the fifth."

He took another sip of water.

"So, Inspector Kwok liaised with the delivery company and obtained the address from them. She then arranged for our technical department to install CCTV cameras in the hallway of the apartment building and for human surveillance outside the building. Her team then monitored the delivery of the drugs and watched on CCTV as the delivery men went inside the apartment, delivered the boxes, and then left. The men arrived at the apartment, retrieved the key, and took the boxes inside. A few minutes later they left, locked the door, and put the key back under the mat. Inspector Kwok and her team then settled down to wait for the drugs to be collected." He sighed. "Seven days they waited. Round-the-clock surveillance, three teams of four. I personally signed off on the budget."

The Senior Assistant Commissioner picked up a pen and tapped it on the desk. "On the seventh day she called me and said that she thought something had gone wrong, that perhaps the criminals had discovered that the apartment was under surveillance. I gave her permission to abort the operation and to enter the apartment." He put down the pen and interlinked his fingers. "Inspector Kwok did so and discovered that the drugs had vanished. The apartment was empty." He sighed again. "So you see, Inspector Zhang, we have a mystery. I believe it is what crime writers call a closed room mystery."

"A locked room mystery, yes," said Inspector Zhang. "It is a staple of crime fiction."

"And I gather that you are something of an expert in the field," said the Senior Assistant Commissioner.

"Hardly an expert, Sir," said Inspector Zhang, feeling his cheeks redden at the compliment.

"There's no need for modesty, Inspector," said the Senior Assistant Commissioner. "Everyone knows of your success in solving the murder of the American businessman found in his locked hotel room. I need you to apply your expertise to this case. I need you to find the missing drugs and apprehend the criminals."

"I should be most happy to assist," said Inspector Zhang.

"I have asked Inspector Kwok to meet with you at the apartment," said the Senior Assistant Commissioner. "Hopefully you will be able to cast some light on the situation." He handed Inspector Zhang a piece of paper on which was written an address in Geylang.

"I shall certainly do my best," said Inspector Zhang.

The Senior Assistant Commissioner leaned back in his chair. "Answer me a question," he said.

"If I can."

"Why are you still an inspector? Why did you never move through the ranks. You were one of the cleverest at the Academy. Everyone said that you were destined for great things within the force."

Inspector Zhang shrugged. "I am happy being a detective," he said. "I am not a good manager. And I am not suited for politics. You need to be good at both to reach the top."

"You are happy as an inspector?"

"Very."

The Senior Assistant Commissioner sighed. "It is certainly much harder the higher one climbs," he said. "There are some days when I wish I was back handling cases and solving crimes."

"There is a feeling of satisfaction from cracking a case, that is certainly true," said Inspector Zhang.

"But then I think of the salary, and the pension, and the respect," said the Senior Assistant Commissioner. "I could never give that up." He waved at the door. "Anyway, thank you for agreeing to help, and as I said, I will be relying on your discretion."

Inspector Zhang drove back to New Bridge Road where Sergeant Lee was waiting for him in the CID office. She was wearing a pale blue suit and had her hair clipped up with a large navy blue clip. He explained that they had to postpone their current investigations as the Senior Assistant Commissioner's assignment took precedence.

He decided to let the sergeant drive as that would give him time to think. Inspector Zhang did not enjoy driving and generally found it stressful, even in rule-conscious Singapore. He settled back in his seat as Sergeant Lee drove out of the car park. "So do you know Inspector Sally Kwok?" he asked as they headed towards Geylang.

"We were at the Academy together," she said.

Inspector Zhang looked across at her, surprised. "Is she your age?"

"A year younger, I think."

"She has done very well to make inspector at twenty-three," said Inspector Zhang. "I myself was not promoted until I was thirty-five."

"She is what they call a high-flyer, Sir."

"But twenty-three? You are an able detective, Sergeant Lee, Your record is second to none. But you are still a sergeant."

"Yes, Sir," said Sergeant Lee. "I am aware of that."

"What I mean, Sergeant Lee, is that Miss Kwok must be an exceptional police officer to have been promoted so quickly."

"One would assume so," said Sergeant Lee.

"Was her ability discernable at the academy?"

"Not her ability, no," said Sergeant Lee. "But I think we all knew that she was destined for great things."

"You intrigue me, Sergeant Lee," said Inspector Zhang, taking off his spectacles and polishing them.

"I don't mean to," she said.

"I sense that there is something you are not telling me."

Sergeant Lee flashed him a tight smile and she made a left turn. "I'm not one to gossip, Inspector."

"I am very well aware of that," said Inspector Zhang. "Your discretion is one of your many excellent qualities. But as I have been told to assist Inspector Kwok, anything you can tell me that might help me would be greatly appreciated. And be kept in total confidence, of course."

Sergeant Lee pursed her lips for several seconds as if she was having trouble reaching a decision, then she nodded slowly. "Inspector Kwok is very pretty," she said. "She has something of a hypnotic effect on men."

Inspector Zhang smiled. "Hypnotic?"

"In the way that a cobra can hypnotise a rabbit before striking," she said.

Inspector Zhang chuckled as he put his spectacles back on. "And do you think that perhaps the Senior Assistant Commissioner is of the rabbit persuasion?"

106

"Inspector, I couldn't possibly say such a thing," she said, her cheeks reddening.

"Sergeant Lee, I was joking," said Inspector Zhang. "It's just that the thought had occurred to me that if she was such a good police officer that she was promoted to inspector at twenty-three, how did she manage to misplace a hundred kilos of Burmese heroin?"

Sergeant Lee pulled up in front of a ten-storey apartment block. There was a black Lexus already parked there and next to it a young woman in a belted raincoat that looked like something that Philip Marlow might have worn in a Raymond Chandler novel. It was a wonderful coat, thought Inspector Zhang as he climbed out of Sergeant Lee's car. A real detective's coat.

"Inspector Zhang?" said the woman.

"Indeed," said Inspector Zhang. "You are Inspector Kwok?"

She flashed him a wonderful smile. "Thank you so much for coming," she said, hurrying over to him. "This is a nightmare, an absolute nightmare."

She was very pretty, and looked younger than twenty-three. Her hair was shoulder length, black and glistening, her cheekbones were as sharp as razors, her skin as flawless as a porcelain figurine. She held out her right hand, the nails perfectly manicured and painted blood red. Inspector Zhang had a sudden impulse to take the hand and kiss the back of it in the style of Hercule Poirot but he resisted the urge and shook it instead. "I am here to be of service," he said. He turned to introduce his Sergeant. "And this is Sergeant Lee."

Inspector Kwok nodded curtly at Sergeant Lee and gave her the faintest of smiles, before turning back to Inspector Zhang. "The apartment is on the eighth floor," he said. "A very auspicious number."

"Not always," said Sergeant Lee, her voice little more than a whisper and Inspector Zhang doubted that Inspector Kwok had heard but he nevertheless gave the sergeant a stern look.

Inspector Kwok took them over to the entrance to the building and tapped a four-digit code into the keypad. The lock clicked and she pushed open the door. There was a reception desk but it was unmanned. "There is a security guard at night but not during the day," said Inspector Kwok. There were two elevators and one was already on the ground floor, its door open. They rode up together to the eighth floor.

"Actually, Inspector Kwok, we were at the Academy together," said Sergeant Lee.

"Really?" said Inspector Kwok, her face a blank mask. "There were a great many entrants that year, I seem to remember. So, Inspector Zhang, you solved the case of the body in the five star hotel, didn't you?"

"I did," said Inspector Zhang.

"I must say that I do not like mysteries," said Inspector Kwok. "I like there to be clear physical evidence that proves how a crime was committed and who committed it."

"Often one has to be able to read the evidence," said Inspector Zhang. "It is a question of spotting the clues and understanding their significance. That is what I enjoy about a mystery. "

"And you did not use any forensic evidence, is that correct?"

"Sometimes forensic evidence is not necessary," said Inspector Zhang. "Sometimes we detectives rely too much on technology and not enough on ze little grey cells."

Inspector Kwok frowned and was just about to ask him what he meant when the lift stopped and the doors opened. She stepped out and Inspector Zhang and Sergeant Lee followed her. As the lift doors closed behind them, Inspector Kwok pointed up at a smoke detector in the ceiling. "This is our surveillance camera," she said. "It feeds a signal down to an empty apartment on the second floor. It was on twenty-four hours a day and we digitally recorded everything." She pointed at a door just six feet away from the camera. "And this is the apartment. Number eight-four-two."

The number was on a small plastic sign at eye height. Below it was a small security viewer so that anyone inside could see who was at the door before opening it. There was a single lock below a round steel doorknob.

On the floor was a rubber matt with the word WELCOME on it in large black capital letters.

"And the key was under the mat, I am told," said Inspector Zhang.

"Exactly," said Inspector Kwok. She took a brass key from her pocket and showed it to him.

"Please place it in the position it was on the day that the drugs were delivered," said Inspector Zhang.

Inspector Kwok knelt down, lifted a corner of the mat and placed the key on the floor. Then she let the mat fall back into place and straightened up. "Just like that," she said.

"Now, show me exactly what happened," said Inspector Zhang.

Sergeant Lee took out her notebook and began taking notes.

"The two men from the delivery company came up in the lift with the boxes," said Inspector Kwok. "I was down on the second floor with the Drugs Squad team. They arrived on this floor and one of the men moved the mat to get the key, and unlocked the door."

"And how were they carrying the boxes. There were ten cardboard boxes, were there not?"

Inspector Zhang nodded. "Ten boxes, each containing ten kilos. Each kilo was wrapped in plastic. So there were ten packages in each box, and ten boxes. The men had five boxes each, stacked on a trolley. One of the two-wheeled trolleys that porters use."

"And they drove the boxes here from where?"

"From the company's bonded warehouse, inside the container port."

"And of course you examined the drugs in the warehouse?"

"Of course."

"So the men brought the drugs up to the eighth floor. What happened then?"

"They unlocked the door and took the trolley inside. They put the drugs in the middle of the room and then left."

"Did you see them do that?"

"What do you mean?" she asked.

Inspector Zhang pointed at the smoke detector. "The camera allows for coverage of the hallway, but if the door is closed you would not be able to see inside the apartment. Did they close the door when they went inside or leave it open."

"They closed it," she said.

"And there is no surveillance camera inside the apartment?"

"No, Inspector Zhang. There is not."

"That is a pity," said Inspector Zhang. "So what happened next?"

"The two men were inside for two minutes. They reappeared with their trolleys and went back downstairs. We then waited for the drugs to be collected. But no one came."

"You waited for a week, I gather?"

"Yes. A week. And then I spoke to the Senior Assistant Commissioner who said that we should go in and check and when we went in, the drugs had gone."

Inspector Zhang waved at the door. "If you would be so good as to open the door," he said. "Exactly as you did then."

Inspector Kwok nodded, bent down and retrieved the key and inserted it into the lock. "The lock and the key are new," she said. "It is a security lock and has to be turned twice to lock and unlock." She turned the key twice and opened the door, then pointed to a metal strip that ran around the doorframe. "You can see that the door has been reinforced, too."

Inspector Zhang studied the metal reinforcing and nodded. "They wanted to make sure that the apartment was secure," he said. "Not surprising when you think about the value of a hundred kilos of heroin."

Inspector Kwok stood to the side to allow Inspector Zhang in first. He stepped over the threshold. It was a small apartment, a square room about fifteen feet by twelve feet, with a sliding window that led out onto a small balcony that overlooked another apartment block. There were two doors to his left, and one to the right. There was an old Toshiba television set on a black sideboard, a plastic sofa and a wooden coffee table with circular stains dotted over it and cigarette burn marks around the edge.

Between the two doors to his left was a teak veneer storage unit with Chinese figurines on one shelf and Chinese books on another. There were two glass doors in the unit, behind one was a collection of earthenware teapots and behind the other was a half-empty bottle of Chivas Regal whisky.

One of the doors led to a small kitchen with an old rattling refrigerator and a grease-encrusted stove. Inspector Zhang opened the refrigerator. It was empty. A cockroach scuttled from underneath the stove, got half way across the tiled floor, then turned around and went back the way it had come.

The other door led to a small shower room with a washbasin and toilet. There was no toilet paper, Inspector Zhang noticed, and no soap or shampoo.

The door on the other side of the sitting room led to a bedroom with a double bed with a white-painted headboard, a matching side table and a large wooden wardrobe. Inspector Zhang opened the wardrobe, but there were only half a dozen wire coat hangers inside.

"The apartment was just like this when you entered?" he asked.

"Exactly," said Inspector Kwok.

Inspector Zhang knelt down carefully and peered under the bed. Another cockroach scuttled away and disappeared under the skirting board.

"We looked everywhere," said Inspector Kwok.

"I'm sure you did," said Inspector Zhang.

"But as you can see, it is a small apartment and there are no hiding places."

Inspector Zhang tapped the floor with his foot. The bedroom floor was tiled, as was the sitting room, bathroom and kitchen. It was the same pale green tiles in all the rooms.

"How long were the men in the apartment?" he asked.

"Two minutes. Three at most. They left the boxes and then they took the trolleys back to the van."

Inspector Zhang nodded thoughtfully. He looked up at the ceiling. It was plaster, painted white.

He went over to the bedroom window and opened it. He peered out. Down below was a car park. There were no ledges or balconies, and no external pipework that would have allowed someone to have climbed out.

"We had a car down there with two undercover police officers," said Inspector Kwok. "They had the rear of the building under constant surveillance."

Inspector Zhang craned his neck to look upwards.

"If anyone had lowered the drugs up or down through the window, we would have seen it," Inspector Kwok said.

"One would hope so," said Inspector Zhang.

He pulled his head back in and looked over at Sergeant Lee., who was standing at the bedroom door, taking notes. "What do you think, Sergeant?"

Sergeant Lee looked up from her notebook. "It is a mystery, Inspector Zhang," she said.

"Indeed it is. Do you have any thoughts on how we might solve it?"

She frowned thoughtfully. "The drugs were brought into the apartment and they are clearly not here now," she said. "They must therefore have been removed. The question is how were they removed? If they were not lowered out through the bedroom window, then perhaps through the sitting room. There is a balcony there."

Inspector Zhang went through to the sitting room and opened the sliding glass door that led to a small balcony where there was an air-conditioning unit and three large ceramic plant pots which were filled with soil and the remains of long-dead flowers.

"We had the front of the building under observation, obviously," said Inspector Kwok. "During the time we had the building under surveillance no one appeared on the balcony."

Inspector Zhang examined the plant pots. They were each over two feet high with paintings of feeding cranes and bamboo on the side. They were of poor quality and the glaze was cracking.

Inspector Zhang tipped one of the plant pots on its side, then up-ended it and with a grunt lifted it up. Soil spilled out over the balcony.

He did the same with the other two plant pots. They both contained nothing but soil. Inspector Zhang stared down at the dirt thoughtfully. "So, the drugs are not on the balcony and they did not leave by the windows." he said quietly. "There are therefore only two possibilities. Either they are still in the apartment but so well hidden that we cannot see them, or they were removed by some other route."

"But how is that possible?" asked Inspector Kwok. "We have searched everywhere."

Inspector Zhang walked through to the kitchen. There was a broom leaning behind the door and he picked it up. He turned it upside down and methodically tapped the handle against each of the tiles on the floor. They all made a dull thudding sound as he hit them. He did the same in the shower room, and then repeated the process in the sitting room and the bedroom. Every tile sounded the same.

"Inspector Zhang, we checked the floor," said Inspector Kwok. "And the ceiling. Both are completely solid."

"I'm sure you did," said Inspector Zhang. "But there is no harm in my checking for myself."

He walked around the apartment, tapping the ceiling at regular intervals. He checked the kitchen, the shower room, the sitting room and the bedroom. There was no difference in sound anywhere, no indication that there were any trapdoors or hidden compartments. The ceiling was as solid as the floor.

Inspector Zhang gave the broom to Sergeant Lee and she returned it to the kitchen.

"Did you speak to the occupants of the apartments on either side of this one?" Inspector Zhang asked Inspector Kwok.

"Of course. There is an old couple to the left. He is a retired schoolteacher and his wife is bed-ridden. Their bedroom is next to the kitchen and bathroom of this apartment. To the right is a young Indian girl with two young children. Her husband is a construction worker in Dubai. She only leaves the house to go shopping or to occasionally take the children to the park. We checked her side of the party wall and there is no way anyone could have gotten through."

Inspector Zhang stood in the middle of the sitting room, looking around. "So, we are sure that the drugs did not pass through the walls, or through the floor or the ceiling, or go out of the windows."

"That is correct, Inspector Zhang."

"And you saw the ten boxes being brought in? Each box would be how big, exactly?"

Inspector Kwok used her hands to demonstrate the size of the box. About fifty centimetres wide, twenty-five centimetres long, a foot wide, and twenty-five centimetres tall.

Inspector Zhang rubbed his chin. "And you have checked the sofa and the television?"

"Of course." She moved the sofa so that he could see a long cut that had been made in the material at the back. "We took the television apart and the refrigerator. And the shower cubicle. And the bed. There is nowhere in the apartment where a hundred kilos of heroin could be hidden."

Sergeant Lee came out of the kitchen. "What about the drains, Inspector Zhang?" she asked.

"The drains?" said Inspector Zhang, frowning.

"What if they unpacked the drugs and somehow dropped them down the drain? In the shower room or the kitchen."

"Throw them away, you mean?"

"No, Inspector, I meant they could have wrapped the drugs in something waterproof and then sent it down the pipes to an accomplice down below. The accomplice could have intercepted the drugs before they reached the sewage system."

Inspector Zhang nodded approvingly. "Why, Sergeant, I had no idea that you were so resourceful. What an intriguing idea."

"Do you think it's possible?"

"Sadly, no," said Inspector Zhang. "The heroin was packed in one kilo packages, and they would not fit down the pipes in either the kitchen or the bathroom. Someone would have had to have repackaged all the heroin which would have taken hours and we know that there

114

was no one else in the apartment." He looked across at Inspector Kwok. "Is that not the case?" he asked.

"There was no one inside, we are sure of that," said Inspector Kwok.

"But can you be sure?" asked Sergeant Lee. "Your men did not enter the apartment with the delivery men. There could have been someone hiding in the bedroom. They could have waited until the delivery men left and then repackaged the drugs and flushed them down the waste pipes to be collected by an accomplice downstairs."

Inspector Kwok's lips tightened in annoyance. "We had the apartment under constant surveillance and no one left the premises. There was no one there when we entered. Therefore we are certain that the apartment was empty all the time we had it under surveillance."

"What about the recording of the CCTV footage?" asked Inspector Zhang. "Where is that?"

"We have taken it to New Phoenix Park," said Inspector Kwok. "We wanted our technicians to check that there was nothing wrong."

"What did you think might be wrong?"

Inspector Kwok shrugged. "The Senior Assistant Commissioner thought that perhaps the camera had been interfered with. That perhaps someone had blocked the camera somehow while they removed the drugs."

"And what did the technicians find?"

"That the CCTV footage was fine. The simple fact is that no one entered or left the apartment while we had it under surveillance."

"Then let us go and examine it ourselves," said Inspector Zhang.

They left the apartment and Inspector Kwok locked the door and pocketed the key. They rode down in the lift together and walked through reception. "Before we go to New Phoenix Park, I'd like to see where your surveillance teams were," said Inspector Zhang.

Inspector Kwok took them around to the back of the apartment block to the car park and showed them where the surveillance team had been parked. Inspector Zhang looked up at the building. They had a clear view of the bedroom windows. There was no way that the drugs could have been moved through the windows without being seen from the car.

They then walked to the front of the building. Inspector Kwok pointed at the apartment block across the road. "We were able to use an apartment over there," she said. "I had two men in a bedroom on the fourth floor with a clear view of the balcony."

"Can we go inside?" asked Inspector Zhang.

"It is just an apartment," said Inspector Kwok. "It is owned by a prison officer who was happy to assist the police."

"I would just like to see what the view is like. If it's no trouble."

Inspector Kwok nodded and took them across the road. There was an intercom by the entrance and she pressed the button for the apartment on the fourth floor and after a couple of minutes she went back to Inspector Zhang and Sergeant Lee. "The husband is at work but his wife is home and she's happy for us to go up," she said.

"Excellent," said Inspector Zhang.

They went up to the fourth floor and the prison officer's wife already had the door open for them. She was Indian in a bright blue sari and she offered them tea which Inspector Zhang politely declined. "We only want a quick look through your window, madam, then we shall be on our way," he said.

Inspector Kwok pointed at a door. "We used that bedroom," she said. "We had two men in there at all times, working in eight-hour shifts," she said. The prison officer's wife opened the door and smiled for them to go through. It was a small room with a single bed and a small built-in wardrobe and dressing table. There were no personal effects so Inspector Zhang assumed it was a spare bedroom.

There was a single window overlooking the apartment block opposite. Because the apartment they were in was on the fourth floor and the apartment where the drugs had been kept was on the eighth floor, it was impossible to see inside. In fact all that could be seen was the balcony. "One cannot see inside the apartment from here," said Inspector Zhang.

"No, but they had a clear view of the balcony. And no one went onto the balcony throughout the surveillance."

Inspector Zhang went up to the window and stood so close to it that his breath fogged on the glass.

"I do not wish to cast aspersions on your team, but you are sure that they were never away from their post?"

"They are professionals, Inspector Zhang. And they kept logs every fifteen minutes."

Inspector Zhang nodded thoughtfully. "Very well," he said. He turned around to face her. "Now it is time for me to look at the surveillance footage," he said.

Inspector Kwok drove her Lexus to the New Phoenix Park headquarters. Inspector Zhang and Sergeant Lee followed her. "That is a very nice car," said Inspector Zhang.

"Very expensive," said Sergeant Lee.

"I did not see a wedding ring on her finger."

"No, she isn't married," said Sergeant Lee. "Are you wondering how an inspector can afford a Lexus?"

"Like you said, it is an expensive car," said Inspector Zhang. "Is she from a wealthy family?"

"No, her father is a waiter, I think. And her mother works in a department store."

Inspector Zhang folded his arms. "And is there gossip, Sergeant Lee?"

"There is always gossip," said the sergeant. "This is Singapore. Shopping and gossiping are our main occupations."

"And what is the gossip concerning Inspector Kwok?"

"I really couldn't say, Inspector," she said. "She is a colleague and I am pleased for her."

"Pleased for her?"

"Pleased at her rapid advancement. It is good to see a woman progressing through the ranks so quickly."

Inspector Zhang looked across at her but couldn't tell if she was being sarcastic or not. He folded his arms and they drove the rest of the way in silence.

They walked into the building together and Inspector Kwok took them up to a meeting room on the second floor where there were several desktop computers and a large flat screen monitor on one wall. There was a technician waiting for them, a young woman in a pale green trouser suit, and she stood up as they walked in.

The technician arranged three chairs so that they could sit facing the monitor and then she sat down at one of the computers.

"What is it you would like to see, exactly?" asked Inspector Kwok. "We have seven days of surveillance video and in most of it nothing is happening."

"When the drugs arrive, and then later when you and your team went inside," said Inspector Zhang.

The technician nodded and tapped away on her computer keyboard. An image filled the monitor. The corridor outside the apartment. The apartment number was clearly visible on the door.

"You can't see the lift but you will see the men come into view," said Inspector Kwok. As she finished the sentence two men appeared on the screen, pushing trolleys. There were five boxes on each trolley. The older of the two was a Chinese man in his late fifties, grey haired and with a tired face. He was wearing blue overalls with the name of the company on his chest, as was his companion, a chubby Indian man in his early twenties.

The Chinese man stood his trolley by the door and bent down to take the key from under the mat. Inspector Zhang read the time code on the bottom of the screen. It was just after ten-thirty in the morning. Sergeant Lee was scribbling in her notebook and as he looked across at her she nodded at him, letting him know that she was making a note of the time. The man unlocked the door and pushed in his trolley, followed by the Indian. Then the door closed.

"They went inside and left the boxes in the sitting room, next to the sofa," said Inspector Kwok.

The door remained closed for just under three minutes, then the two men reappeared with empty trolleys. The Chinese man relocked the door and put the key back under the mat, then the two men pushed their trolleys towards the lift.

"The door then remained locked for seven days," said Inspector Kwok. "No one went in or out before me, seven days later."

"And the room was under constant surveillance?"

"I was there eighteen hours a day and there were always at least two detectives in the observation room," said Inspector Kwok. "And once we discovered that the apartment was empty I myself watched every second of the video, albeit speeded up, of course."

Inspector Zhang rubbed his chin thoughtfully. "And the two men who delivered the drugs. Who are they?"

"The owner of the company, Mr. Yin. It was Mr. Yin who opened the door. And one of his workers. A Mr. Chandra."

"And was there anyone else from the company involved?"

"There was a driver, but he stayed outside with the van."

"Very well. Can we now jump ahead to when you and your team entered the apartment."

The technician tapped on her keyboard again and the picture jumped. According to the time code they had advanced almost seven days. Inspector Kwok walked to the door, followed by two male detectives and two uniformed officers. She bent down, picked up the key and slotted it into the lock. She seemed to have trouble with the lock and she stepped aside to let one of the uniformed officers try. "I didn't realise it was a security lock," she said. "It had to be turned twice."

The uniformed officer also had trouble with the lock, but eventually he opened the door and stepped aside to allow Inspector Kwok to go in. "And that was it," said Inspector Kwok. "The drugs had gone. The apartment was empty. And during the seven days that we had the apartment under observation no one went in or came out."

"And you have no idea where the drugs are, or how they were removed from the apartment."

"It is a mystery," said Inspector Kwok.

"But a mystery that we shall solve, Inspector Kwok."

"Are you sure?" she asked.

"Inspector Zhang is an expert at solving mysteries," said Sergeant Lee, looking up from her notebook. "It is what he does best."

"Thank you, Sergeant Lee," he said.

"So what shall we do?" asked Inspector Kwok. "How do we begin this investigation? Where do we start?"

"First I would like to talk to the owner of the company that delivered the boxes. Mr. Yin, you said his name is."

"Yes, Mr. Yin. His company is based at the container port."

"Then we should go and see him there," said Inspector Zhang. "Perhaps we should all go in the same car. It might make things easier."

"Absolutely," said Inspector Kwok.

They walked out of the building together into the fierce Singaporean sun.

"We should use the Lexus, it is more spacious than my sergeant's vehicle," said Inspector Zhang.

"Exactly what I was going to suggest," said Inspector Kwok, taking out her keys. Inspector Zhang climbed into the front passenger seat and Sergeant Lee got into the back.

Inspector Kwok was an assured driver and it didn't take her long to get them to the container port. They showed their warrant cards to two security guards and headed for the bonded warehouse.

There were containers piled high wherever they looked in a multitude of colours, though all were one of two sizes – twenty feet long or forty feet. Even in metric Singapore, containers were still measured in feet.

In the distance there was a line of massive container ships with huge cranes swinging containers back and forth above them. There was a near-constant stream of loaded trucks heading towards the exit.

"Did you know that half of the world's annual supply of crude oil goes through Singapore?" said Inspector Zhang. "And a fifth of the world's shipping containers. More than a billion tonnes of goods go through here every year."

"Singapore is one of the wonders of the world," agreed Inspector Kwok. "We have achieved so much and yet we are a mere city state of just over five million people."

"I do sometimes wonder how many of these containers have drugs inside," mused Inspector Zhang. "There are so many of them that there isn't time to check even a small percentage."

"We were lucky with the Burmese heroin," said Inspector Kwok.

"Up to a point," said Sergeant Lee from the back of the car. Inspector Zhang turned to look at her and she smiled politely.

They pulled up in front of the warehouse. A man in a rumpled dark blue suit came out and greeted Inspector Kwok as she climbed out of the Lexus. It was the Chinese man from the video. Mr. Yin. Inspector Kwok introduced him to Inspector Zhang and Sergeant Lee and he solemnly shook hands with them both before taking them inside. The warehouse was filled with boxes and crates and two fork-lift trucks were ferrying more crates from a truck parked in a goods bay. One of the fork-lift drivers was the Indian from the surveillance video.

There was a small office in the corner and Mr. Yin took them inside. A secretary with badly-permed hair was putting files into a cabinet and Mr. Yin asked her to prepare tea for his guests.

Mr. Yin sat down behind his desk and the three detectives sat on high-backed wooden chairs facing him. "We want to thank you again for all your co-operation, Mr. Yin," said Inspector Zhang.

"I am always happy to help the Singapore Police Force," he said. "I am vehemently anti-drugs. I have two children myself and we must make sure that our youngsters are protected."

"Indeed," said Inspector Zhang.

"Do you have children, Inspector?" asked Mr. Yin.

"I do not," said Inspector Zhang. "But I am as concerned as you about the perils of drugs. As is our government. Which is why we execute drugs smugglers in Singapore."

"Which is as it should be," said Mr. Yin. He interlinked his fingers. "So how can I help you today?"

"We have a problem at the apartment where the drugs were left," said Inspector Zhang. "We seem to have mislaid them."

Mr. Yin's forehead creased into a frown. "Mislaid?" he said.

"They have vanished," said Inspector Zhang. "Into thin air it appears."

"But that's impossible."

"I quite agree," said Inspector Zhang.

The secretary appeared with a tray of tea things. She poured them each a small cup of jasmine tea and then went back to her files. Inspector Zhang inhaled the perfumed fragrance and then sipped his tea.

"Now I gather that you had made similar deliveries before," said Inspector Zhang.

"Not me personally," said Mr. Yin. "But our company has."

"Why did you handle the delivery yourself on this occasion?"

"We thought it would be safer to have as few people involved as possible," said Inspector Kwok. "Mr. Yin owns the company so he offered to help rather than send one of his delivery staff."

"So Inspector Kwok had explained to you that there was heroin in the boxes?"

Mr. Yin nodded. "So you can imagine how horrified I was," he said. "To have my company used in that manner, by drug smugglers. How dare they? I run a reputable business, Inspector Zhang, we pay our taxes, we obey the rules and regulations and believe me in this business there are more rules than you can shake a stick at."

"I am sure there are," said Inspector Zhang. "Now please tell me, this was the first time that you had delivered boxes to this particular apartment?"

"It was a different apartment for each delivery," said Mr. Yin. "But always in Geylang."

"And what did you think they contained?"

"It was always industrial coatings. In powder form."

"And is it normal to deliver industrial coatings to an apartment?"

"A lot of small businesses are run from home," said Mr. Yin. "And this was a relatively small delivery."

"And always the same arrangement for the deliveries? The key under the mat?"

Mr. Yin nodded. "We were emailed instructions each time. We were given an address and told to leave the boxes inside."

"Isn't that unusual?" asked Inspector Zhang.

"As I said, delivering small consignments to apartments is not unusual," said Mr. Yin.

"But leaving keys under mats. Is that not unusual?"

"I suppose so," said Mr. Yin. "Though we often leave deliveries with neighbours."

"Even so…"

"You have to understand, Inspector Zhang. We handle dozens of deliveries every day, from single boxes to full containers. This was a relatively small job for us, the paperwork was all in order and they were a regular customer who also paid promptly. We had no reason to suspect that something untoward was going on."

"I understand that," said Inspector Zhang.

"Obviously if we had known…"   Mr. Yin shrugged and left the sentence unfinished.

"I am sure," said Inspector Zhang. He looked at his wristwatch. "I wonder if I might ask you for just a little more co-operation, Mr. Yin."

"Of course. Anything."

"Would you mind coming back to the apartment so that we can run through what happened?"

"I don't understand." Mr. Yin looked over at Inspector Zhang. "I thought you just needed my help to deliver the boxes."

"It will not take very long," said Inspector Zhang. "We can drive you there. We have a Lexus."

"If it's absolutely necessary, I suppose I could spare the time," said Mr. Yin, reluctantly. "But I am very busy. This is our busy time of the year."

"We will not take too much of your time, Mr. Yin," said Inspector Zhang. He stood up and waved at the door. "The sooner we leave, the sooner we'll be finished."

They went outside and this time Inspector Zhang got into the back of the car with Sergeant Lee while Mr. Yin climbed into the front with Inspector Kwok. They drove back to Geylang in silence. Inspector Kwok parked the car and they walked together into the apartment block.

"This is the way you came on that day?" asked Inspector Zhang.

Mr. Yin nodded. "Yes. We had trolleys. One trolley each."

"And on each trolley there were five boxes?"

"Yes."

Inspector Kwok opened the door and they went through to reception and up to the eighth floor.

"So you and your assistant arrived here and pushed the trolleys to the apartment?"

Mr. Yin nodded. "I went through all this with Inspector Kwok."

They walked to the door of the apartment. "Do you have the key, Inspector?" asked Inspector Zhang. Inspector Kwok produced the brass key and Inspector Zhang nodded at the mat. "If you would be so good as to put it where it was that day."

Inspector Kwok put the key under the mat and then stood up.

"Now, proceed exactly as you did on that day, Mr. Yin."

"But I don't have the trolley so it cannot be the same."

"Please do as best you can," said Inspector Zhang. He stood back and folded his arms.

Mr. Yin sighed, then bent down and retrieved the key. He inserted it into the lock and turned it twice anti-clockwise to open the door. He took out the key, pushed open the door and walked into the apartment.

The three detectives followed him.

"And then you closed the door?"

"Yes. I did."

"So please do that now."

Mr. Yin closed the door.

"And where did you leave the boxes?"

Mr. Yin pointed at the side of the sofa. "There," he said.

"And then you left the apartment?"

"Yes," said Mr. Yin. "Is that all you need from me?"

"Just bear with me a little while longer, Mr. Yin," said Inspector Zhang. He walked around the sitting room, deep in thought.

"Inspector Zhang, I really think we have imposed on Mr. Yin's public spiritedness quite enough," said Inspector Kwok. "He has a business to run."

"Soon," said Inspector Zhang. "We are almost there."

He walked into the bedroom and Sergeant Lee followed him. "Inspector Zhang, what are you looking for? We know that the drugs are not in the apartment."

Inspector Zhang smiled. "I am not looking for the heroin, Sergeant Lee. I am looking for the boxes, and that is quite a different matter."

"The boxes?"

"Yes, the boxes. They are key to this." He smiled. "If you will forgive the pun."

"Pun? What pun?" Sergeant Lee frowned in confusion.

Inspector Zhang sighed as he looked around the bedroom. "The bed was examined, of course. That only leaves the wardrobe."

"The wardrobe is empty, Inspector Zhang," said Sergeant Lee. She opened the doors to show him. "Coat hangers and dust, nothing else."

"Mr. Yin, come in here please," called Inspector Zhang.

Mr. Yin walked into the bedroom. He looked annoyed. "I really must protest," he said. "I have a business to run."

"Would you be so kind as to help me move the wardrobe," said Inspector Zhang.

"You want me to do what?"

"The wardrobe. Just help me move it."

"Why?"

"Because I suspect there is something beneath it." He smiled. "I can hardly ask the ladies, can I?"

He took hold of the left side of the wardrobe and waited until a reluctant Mr. Yin took hold of the right hand side. They both lifted and moved the wardrobe forward a couple of feet. Sergeant Lee gasped when she saw what had been hidden by the wardrobe. Flattened cardboard boxes. She bent down and picked them up. There were ten of them. "The boxes," she said.

"Yes," said Inspector Zhang. "The boxes."

"But how can that be?" asked Inspector Kwok.

Inspector Zhang let go of the wardrobe and looked over at Mr. Yin. "Why don't you explain, Mr. Yin?"

"I don't know what you mean."

"Yes you do, Mr. Yin. The drugs were never in the boxes. Not by the time you brought them up to the apartment. They might well have been in the boxes at the warehouse but at some point between there and here you and your assistant took the drugs out and it was empty boxes that you brought into the apartment."

"Nonsense," said Mr. Yin.

"There is no other explanation," said Inspector Zhang. "You and he were the only people to enter the apartment. It can only have been you."

"You cannot prove anything," said Mr. Yin.

"I think I can," said Inspector Zhang. He pointed at the collapsed boxes. "When you and your assistant entered the apartment neither of you were wearing gloves. Therefore if you did indeed conceal the boxes under the wardrobe, your fingerprints and DNA will be on the cardboard."

Mr. Yin glared at Inspector Zhang for several seconds, then his shoulders slumped. "I have been a fool," he said.

"I agree," said Inspector Zhang. "When you were approached by Inspector Kwok you realised that she was providing you with a golden opportunity to cover your crime. You were the one bringing the drugs into the country, but of course she didn't know that. You put the boxes in the van but on the way to the apartment you removed the heroin and resealed the boxes. The boxes on the trolleys were empty. And once inside the apartment out of sight of the surveillance camera you simply flattened the boxes and hid them under the wardrobe." He turned to Inspector Kwok. "You may arrest Mr. Yin now," he said. "The mystery is solved."

Inspector Kwok had been staring at Mr. Yin with her mouth wide open and she jumped when Inspector Zhang spoke. She took out her handcuffs, fastened them to Mr. Yin's wrists, and took him out.

Sergeant Lee was scribbling in her notebook.

"What are you writing, Sergeant Lee?" asked Inspector Zhang.

"Everything," she said. She looked up from the notebook. "You knew he was guilty before you even brought him here, didn't you? Before you even found the boxes."

Inspector Zhang smiled. "Yes, that's true. I did."

"How?" asked Sergeant Lee.

Inspector Zhang tapped the side of his head. "By using ze little grey cells," he said, in his best Hercule Poirot impersonation.

"Something he said at the warehouse?"

"Before then," said Inspector Zhang. "When I watched the surveillance video footage at New Phoenix Park, I knew he was our man."

"But all we saw was him delivering the boxes and leaving," said Sergeant Lee. "Nothing else happened."

"He unlocked the door," said Inspector Zhang.

Sergeant Lee's frown deepened.

"It was his first time at the apartment," said Inspector Zhang. "But he knew that the key had to be turned twice to open the door. He unlocked the door without any hesitation, but how could he have known that it was a security lock and required two turns of the key?"

"He couldn't," said Sergeant Lee. "Unless he had already been to the apartment."

"Exactly," said Inspector Zhang. "You saw the problems that Inspector Kwok had when she tried to unlock the door the first time. But Mr. Yin had no such problems. Because he had already been to the apartment."

"You solved the case, so why didn't you arrest Mr. Yin? Why did you let Inspector Kwok arrest him?"

"It is her case," said Inspector Zhang. "I was only brought in to assist."

"You have saved her career," said Sergeant Lee. "She will take the credit."

"I solved the mystery, that is all that matters to me," said Inspector Zhang.

"You are a wonderful detective, Inspector Zhang."

Inspector Zhang smiled but said nothing.

Later that night, Inspector Zhang's wife served him fish head bee hoon, a creamy vermicelli noodle soup with chunks of fried fish head, one of his favourite dishes. They were sitting at the dining table and the television was on, with the sound down low. Mrs. Zhang poured red wine into her husband's glass and he smiled his thanks. On the television, a beaming Senior Assistant Commissioner was standing next to Inspector Kwok who was being interviewed by a reporter from Channel News Asia. Behind them were the ten cardboard boxes that had been opened to reveal the drugs inside. Mr. Yin had obviously given the drugs to the police, probably hoping to escape the death penalty.

"Isn't that the case you were working on?" she asked.

"Yes," said Inspector Zhang, watching as Inspector Kwok flashed the reporter a beaming smile. "Yes it is."

"So why aren't they interviewing you?"

Inspector Zhang took a sip of his wine. "I suppose I'm not handsome enough for television," he said.

"You're much more handsome than the Senior Assistant Commissioner," said Mrs. Zhang.

"The eye of the beholder," said Inspector Zhang.

Mrs. Zhang watched as the reporter continued to interview Inspector Kwok. "She's very pretty," she said.

"Yes, she is."

"Is she a good detective?"

Inspector Zhang looked a little pained. "She will do very well in the Singapore Police Force," he said. "She is destined for great things."

"But she is not a good detective?"

"My own Sergeant Lee is better," said Inspector Zhang.

"But not as pretty."

Inspector Zhang raised his wine glass to her. "No, my dear. Not as pretty. And neither of them hold a candle to you."

"Is there something going on between the Senior Assistant Commissioner and the pretty inspector?" asked Mrs. Zhang quietly.

"Why do you ask?"

"Just they way they stand together, the way that he keeps looking at her and once I saw him rub his wedding ring as if it was troubling him."

Inspector Zhang chuckled softly. "My dear, you would make a great detective," he said, reaching for his chopsticks and spoon.

6.

INSPECTOR ZHANG AND THE PERFECT ALIBI

Sergeant Lee frowned as she looked up from her pocket notebook. She had been scribbling in it for at least two minutes and now, as she read through her notes, her confusion began to show. "So he did not leave the cell?" she asked.

"How could he?" asked Inspector Zhang. "The walls are solid, the windows are glass blocks, and the CCTV footage shows that no one entered or left the cell from six o'clock in the evening until he was given his breakfast at seven-thirty."

They were standing in the corridor that led to the holding cells in the Jurong West Police Headquarters. They had spent half an hour going over every inch of one of the cells, tapping on the walls, floor and ceiling. Everything was as it should be. Prior to checking the cell they had gone through the CCTV footage of the corridor to confirm what the duty officer had told them – that nobody had gone near the cell all night, other than at midnight when there had been a change of shifts.

"But while he was in the cell, his fingerprints appeared on the knife that was used to kill Miss Chau and he managed to bite her on the arm," said Sergeant Lee. She was wearing a dark green jacket over a pale green skirt and had tied her hair back into a ponytail making her look much younger than her twenty-four years.

"You have summed up the facts most succinctly," said Inspector Zhang. A smile played across his lips.

"Inspector Zhang, if Mr. Yip was in the cell all night, how could he have killed Miss Chau?"

"How indeed?" said Inspector Zhang.

"Inspector Zhang, this is an impossible case," said Sergeant Lee and she sighed in exasperation.

Inspector Zhang could see that his sergeant was using all her restraint to stop herself from stamping her foot and his smile widened. "But Sergeant Lee, it is the impossible cases that are the most fun, don't you think?" he said. "Almost every murder in Singapore is solved within hours. Isn't it refreshing to have a case that exercises ze little grey cells?" It was his very best Hercule Poirot impression and he made a point of twiddling an imaginary moustache.

"Sherlock Holmes?" said Sergeant Lee hopefully.

"Hercule Poirot," said Inspector Zhang. "The famous Belgian detective, created by the wonderful Agatha Christie. She was an English lady who wrote more than ninety books and is renowned as the best-selling novelist of all time. More than four billion copies of her books have been sold. Can you imagine that, Sergeant Lee? Four billion books?"

"That is an awful lot of books," admitted Sergeant Lee. "But how would Hercule Poirot solve such a case?"

Inspector Zhang nodded thoughtfully." He would interview all the witnesses and the suspects, then he would compare what everyone had told him and he would look for inconsistencies. Then he would gather everyone together in the drawing room and reveal the culprit."

"A drawing room?"

"The main social area in a country house or hotel," said Inspector Zhang. "But the room isn't important."

"But in this case there are no witnesses," said Sergeant Lee. "And our one suspect has a perfect alibi."

"Exactly," said Inspector Zhang. "So if our one suspect has a perfect alibi, we have no choice other than to find another suspect."

Sergeant Lee's eyes opened wide. "A twin brother!" she said excitedly. "Mr. Yip has a twin brother with identical fingerprints and teeth. The twin brother killed Miss Chau while he was in the cell." She nodded enthusiastically. "Have I solved the case, Inspector Zhang? Have I used ze little grey cells?"

"Perhaps," said Inspector Zhang. "You should check with the Registry of Births and Deaths. But first we need to speak with Mr. Yip and then we must visit the crime scene." The crime scene was the townhouse where Miss Sindy Chau had lived until her untimely death. It was on a small gated estate two miles from Changi Airport. Miss Chau worked as a flight attendant with Singapore Airlines. She had been due to fly to London on Monday and when she hadn't turned up for work a colleague had gone around to her house and discovered her dead in the kitchen.

Inspector Zhang hadn't been the first detective to handle the case, but twenty-fours after the body had been discovered he had been summoned to police headquarters. The Deputy Commissioner had kept him waiting for half an hour and had appeared flustered when Inspector Zhang was finally ushered into his office. "We have a problem, Inspector Zhang. A problem that requires your particular skills."

Inspector Zhang said nothing. He removed his spectacles and methodically polished them with his pale blue handkerchief.

"You have impressed us all with your deductive skills, the way you seem to have a knack for getting to the heart of seemingly impossible situations." The Deputy Commissioner sat back in his high-backed leather chair and steepled his pudgy fingers under his chin. The Deputy Commissioner had put on a lot of weight in recent months and his expanding waistline strained at his tunic and the top button of his shirt threatened to pop off at any moment. "The reason I've called you in is that we have what initially appeared to be a simple case which has in fact become an impossible situation. And unless we resolve this impossible situation promptly, we run the risk of having the Singapore Police Force appearing to be a laughing stock."

Inspector Zhang put his spectacles back on. "I am, of course, at your disposal," he said.

The Deputy Commissioner leaned forward, opened a manila file and took out an eight by ten colour photograph. He slid it across the desk to Inspector Zhang. "Miss Sindy Chau was murdered in her home two days ago," he said. "The pathologist put her death in the early hours of Monday morning."

Inspector Zhang picked up the photograph. A young woman lay face up on what appeared to be a kitchen floor, blood pooling around her head. He looked closer and saw a gaping wound in the woman's throat. Close to the woman's left hand was a bloody kitchen knife. She was wearing a pink nightgown.

"There was a broken window which suggested an intruder," said the Deputy Commissioner. "It looked as if she had heard a noise and come downstairs where the burglar grabbed a knife. There was a struggle, during which the attacker bit Miss Chau on the arm, and then she received a fatal wound. The attacker then fled."

"Leaving the knife behind, I see," said Inspector Zhang.

"The knife came from a set owned by Miss Chau," said the Deputy Commissioner. "The attacker must have grabbed it when he was disturbed. We assume Miss Chau found him in the kitchen and he panicked and killed her." He took the photograph back and slid it into the file. "You should take this," he said, passing the file to Inspector Zhang. "At first we thought the case to be a very simple one," she said. "We do not have a major burglary problem in Singapore, and we know most of the criminals who specialise in such crimes. The forensics team discovered fingerprints on the knife and they proved to belong to a well-known burglar. Yip Kam-ming. Our detectives went to arrest Mr. Yip, and that is when the situation became impossible. Mr. Yip had been in police custody since Saturday evening. At the time Miss Chau was murdered he was in a police cell at Jurong West Police Headquarters."

"On what charge?" asked Inspector Zhang.

"He assaulted a police officer," said the Deputy Commissioner. "Neighbours had complained about Mr. Yip playing music late at night and when two officers went around to his apartment to talk to him, he lashed out. He broke the nose of a sergeant and was arrested for assault. "

"And he was not granted bail?"

"He remained belligerent and was remanded in custody in order that he could be put before a Judge first thing on Monday morning."

Inspector Zhang nodded thoughtfully. "Miss Chau was bitten, you said?"

"On her arm. There is a photograph in the file. It appears that she grabbed for the knife with her left hand and tried to push him away with her right hand. He bit her close to the elbow."

"And comparisons were made to Mr. Yip's teeth?"

"Our detectives visited Mr. Yip's dentist this morning and the dental records he has are a perfect match to the bite on Miss Chau's arm."

"That is interesting," said Inspector Zhang.

The Deputy Commissioner frowned. "It is more than interesting, Inspector," he said sternly. "It calls into question the standards of our CID investigators and casts doubt on our forensic dentistry department. Our forensic experts are certain Mr. Yip bit Miss Chau during the course of the robbery. But Mr. Yip was supposedly in our custody at that time. So either Mr. Yip managed to get out of his cell or our forensic scientists have made an error. Either way, it looks bad for the Singapore Police Force."

"And that we cannot allow to happen," said Inspector Zhang.

The Deputy Commissioner leaned forward, his eyes narrowed as if he suspected that Inspector Zhang was being sarcastic. But the inspector was nodding seriously and the Deputy Commissioner realised that Inspector Zhang was not being ironic or sarcastic. He was merely expressing an honest opinion. "Indeed," he said. "That is why we need your particular skills. You have something of a reputation for solving mysteries, and that is what we have here. If Mr. Yip managed to get out of a locked cell to commit this murder, we need to know how he did it. And if he did indeed remain in his cell, we need to know who killed Miss Chau."

"I am on the case, Sir," said Inspector Zhang.

Sergeant Lee drove them to the Jurong West Police Headquarters in her three-year-old Toyota. She was a good driver, calm and unflustered, and kept well below the speed limit, which Inspector Zhang appreciated. Even though Singaporean motorists were among the best in the world, there were still almost two hundred deaths on the island state's roads every year.

The first thing he did was to speak to the Custody Officer who had booked Mr. Yip into the cells. He was a sergeant in his late forties with a lazy eye which was so off-putting that Inspector Zhang tried to avoid looking at the man's face as much as possible. Sergeant Kwok was a worried man who clearly believed he was going to be somehow blamed for what had happened, and the more questions Inspector Zhang asked, the more nervous he became. At one point he produced a large white handkerchief and mopped the sweat from his brow. "He was in the cell the whole night, Inspector, I am sure of that."

"Were you on duty all the time?" asked Inspector Zhang.

"I was on the afternoon shift; I started work at 4pm and finished at midnight."

"So you processed him and placed him in the cell?"

Sergeant Kwok nodded. "He was brought in at just before six o'clock. Mr. Yip has been here several times in the past so he knew the procedure and he was compliant."

"He was happy to be kept overnight?"

"Not happy. But cooperative."

"And how often was he seen in the cell?"

"He was given food at seven thirty, and his tray was removed at eight. I left at midnight."

"Who took over from you?"

"Sergeant James Song."

"Do you have his phone number? I will need to talk to him."

Sergeant Kwok consulted a notebook and gave the number to Sergeant Lee. She wrote it down and repeated it back to him to check that she had written it down correctly. Inspector Zhang nodded his approval at her thoroughness.

"Did Sergeant Song check on the cells when he relieved you?" asked Inspector Zhang.

"Of course. Look Inspector, can you tell me what time this murder was committed. The one that Mr. Yip was supposed to have done."

"According the file, the time of death has been put at between one o'clock and two o'clock in the morning."

Sergeant Kwok smiled with relief. "Then it was not my responsibility," he said.

"No one is looking to apportion blame," said Inspector Zhang.

"Of course, of course. But as I finished my shift at midnight, Mr. Yip was not in my charge." He folded his arms. "You should speak to Sergeant Song. The responsibility was his."

"I will do that, of course," said Inspector Zhang. "And can you tell me how many people were in the holding cells overnight?"

"Four," said Sergeant Kwok. "Mr. Yip and three others."

"And did anyone leave the cells while you were on duty?"

Sergeant Kwok shook his head. "They did not."

Inspector Zhang smiled. "Excellent," he said. "So now I need to do three things. I need to see the CCTV footage of the custody suite from the time Mr. Yip was brought in to the time his cell door was opened. I need to examine the cell he was held in. And then I need to talk to Mr. Yip himself. I assume he is still here?"

The sergeant nodded. "Oh yes," he said. "He won't be going anywhere until this has been resolved. And the Deputy Commissioner has made it clear that he has to be under observation at all times."

Inspector Zhang and Sergeant Lee were shown to an interview room. It was equipped with two CCTV cameras and a voice recording system, but Inspector Zhang did not feel it necessary to record the interview. All he wanted was information at this stage.

He and Sergeant Lee sat down on one side of a grey metal table and a few minutes later a uniformed constable showed Mr. Yip into the room. Inspector Zhang knew from the file he'd read that Mr. Yip was fifty-five, but the inspector felt that he looked a good ten years older. He was bald and his arms and hands were marked with liver spots and his face was weather-beaten and wrinkled. He was wearing the clothes he'd had on when he was arrested – a stained vest, baggy shorts and flip-flops. Inspector Zhang waved at the seat opposite him. "Please sit down," he said.

Mr. Yip did as he was told while the uniformed officer closed the door and then stood with his back to it.

"You can wait outside," said Inspector Zhang but the officer shook his head.

"I am under orders to keep him under constant observation," said the officer.

"Even when I go to the toilet," complained Mr. Yip.

Sergeant Lee took the police file out of her bag and placed it on the table, then took out her notepad and pen and began taking notes.

"I am Inspector Zhang," said the inspector. He nodded at his assistant. "And this is Sergeant Lee. Have you been informed that you are now a suspect in a murder investigation?"

Mr. Yip nodded. "I didn't kill anyone, Inspector Zhang. I don't hurt people. That's not what I do."

"You are entitled to have a lawyer present, but at this stage I am just trying to find out what happened. You have not yet been charged with murder and this conversation will not be recorded."

"I don't need a lawyer. I didn't do anything," said Mr. Yip.

"Excellent," said Inspector Zhang. "Now, it is fair to say that you are a thief?"

"I am a burglar, Inspector Zhang. And a good one."

Inspector Zhang smiled. "If that were true, you would not have served three sentences in Changi Prison. And how many lashings have you received over the years?"

Mr. Yip looked down at the table and winced at the memory of the beatings that he had received. "Almost a hundred," he said quietly.

"Eighty-six, according to your file," said Inspector Zhang. Singapore was one of the few countries that still believed in corporal punishment, in particular the use of a rattan cane. "Of course now that you are aged over fifty, caning is not an issue," said Inspector Zhang. "But the lashings and sentences you received do suggest you might have been better seeking an alternative career."

Judicial caning was introduced to Singapore and Malaysia during the British colonial period and was still used for many offences under the Criminal Procedure Code including robbery, rape, illegal money-lending, hostage-taking, drug-trafficking and house-breaking. In fact, over the years, the Singapore Government had increased the number of crimes that could be punished by caning and had raised the minimum of strokes. There were strict rules about the way that the caning was carried out, including the stipulation that the person being punished had to be male, above the age of eighteen and below the age of fifty, and no one should receive more than twenty-four strokes at any one time. The criminal had to be certified medically fit by a medical officer and the law decreed that the cane should not exceed half an inch in diameter and not be longer than 1.2 metres. The cane was soaked in water to make it heavier and more flexible, and was wiped down with antiseptic before use to prevent infections. If the offender was under eighteen then the maximum number of strokes was just ten and a lighter cane was used. For some reason that Inspector Zhang had never understood, a criminal who had been sentenced to death could not be caned.

"Mr. Zhang, I am a burglar, I am not denying that. But you've seen my file. Have I ever hurt anyone before?"

"You hit the police officer who came around to your apartment on Saturday evening."

"That was different. He assaulted me and I was defending myself. He wanted to enter my apartment and I said he couldn't without a warrant. But that's not the point, Inspector Zhang. The point is that in all the years I have been a thief I have only ever broken into empty homes. I would never break into a house if there was someone there."

"Perhaps you did not know that Miss Chau was at home. Perhaps she surprised you, which is why you killed her."

"But I was in the cell when she was murdered. If I was in the cell, how could I have killed her?"

"Your fingerprints were on the knife."

"That doesn't mean I killed her. Maybe I had touched the knife at some other time."

"And there was a bite mark on her arm, a bite mark that matches your teeth."

Mr. Yip shook his head. "That is impossible," he said, emphatically.

"Did you know Miss Chau? Miss Sindy Chau?"

Mr. Yip frowned. "I don't think so."

"She was a flight attendant with Singapore Airlines."

"So?"

"I think you know why that is significant, Mr. Yip. At your last trial you confessed to robberies at the homes of more than a dozen employees of Singapore Airlines, specifically pilots and flight attendants. The prosecution alleged you were receiving help from someone within the airline who was tipping you off regarding the flight rosters. So more often than not you knew when the person would be away and also if they were married or not."

Mr. Yip grinned. "It was a perfect scheme," he said. "I knew the homes were empty and I had all the time in the world to get in and out. The only reason I got caught was because one of the pilots had installed a silent alarm in his villa." Mr. Yip leaned across the table, licking his lips. "But don't you see, Inspector Zhang, that proves exactly what I've told you. I would never break into a house that was occupied. I wouldn't have to. I'd have known exactly when Miss Chau was due to fly out and I would have waited until she was out of the country."

"Unfortunately Miss Chau's shift was changed at short notice. The flight she was due to leave on was cancelled because of engine problems. Your contact probably didn't know about the shift change."

"Inspector Zhang, I swear I did not kill Miss Chau. Even if I had been there and she'd seen me, I wouldn't have killed her. That's not in my nature." He leaned across the table. "Between you and me, the person who was giving me the information left the company months ago."

"I will need that person's name," said Inspector Zhang.

"Why?"

"Because I will need them to confirm what you have just told me."

Mr. Yip shook his head and sat back in his chair. "I can't do that, inspector."

"Honour among thieves?"

"I just can't," said Mr. Yip. "It wouldn't be right."

"Then how are we to believe you aren't still receiving information about Singapore Airlines employees?"

"You have my word, Inspector Zhang."

Inspector Zhang shook his head slowly. "I'm afraid that won't be good enough," he said. "This is a murder investigation and when people are accused of murder they tend not to tell the truth." He looked over at Sergeant Lee, who was writing in her notepad. I think we have done all we can do here," he said. "Now we need to look at the crime scene."

"What about me; can I go?" asked Mr. Yip.

Inspector Zhang stood up and shook his head. "I'm afraid not, Mr. Yip. At the moment you are still the prime suspect in the murder of Sindy Chau. And once we have worked out how you got out of your cell, you will be charged with that offence."

Mr. Yip moaned and put his head in his hands. "This is a nightmare," he said.

Sergeant Lee gathered up the file and followed Inspector Zhang out of the interview room. They headed outside and got into Sergeant Lee's car. The address of Miss Chau's house was in the file and it took less than half an hour to get there.

They had to show their warrant cards to the security guard at the gate to the cluster of townhouses and he told them which way to go. There was no mistaking the crime scene as the door was criss-crossed with blue and white police tape. Sergeant Lee had the key to the front door and she let them in. "The kitchen, I believe," said Inspector Zhang. He walked down the hallway into a kitchen with a terracotta tiled floor and top of the range appliances. There were dark patches on several of the tiles by the sink which Inspector Zhang realised were dried blood.

"Can you pass me one of the scenes of crime photographs?" he asked, and Sergeant Lee passed one over. Inspector Zhang compared the bloodstains with the photograph and he shuddered. "So young to have died like this," he said. He looked at the photograph again. "I do not see any defensive marks on her hand."

"There was the bite mark," said Sergeant Lee.

"But no cuts from the knife. The investigating officers thought she had grabbed for the knife with her left hand."

Sergeant Lee looked through the file, pulled out the post mortem report and quickly read through it. "You are right, there were no defensive cuts," she said.

"Which is strange," said Inspector Zhang. He handed back the photograph and went over to examine the French windows that led to the rear patio. One of the panels had been broken and there were still shards of glass on the floor. The remaining glass panels and the door handles inside and outside had been dusted for fingerprints.

"Were Mr. Yip's fingerprints found on the door or the glass?" he asked.

Sergeant Lee pulled out the forensic team's report and studied it before shaking her head. There were no prints, she said. "Other than Miss Chau's."

"But his fingerprints were on the kitchen knife?"

Sergeant Lee nodded. "That is correct."

Inspector Zhang frowned. "So we are to believe that Mr. Yip managed to break into the house without leaving any prints, but when he stabbed Miss Chau he held the knife with his bare hand?"

"That is strange, isn't it?" said Sergeant Lee.

"Strange indeed," said Inspector Zhang. "It would mean he wore gloves when he broke in and then removed them to kill Miss Chau. That makes no sense at all." He sighed. "Well, I think we need to search the house thoroughly, from the top to the bottom."

They started in Miss Chau's bedroom and bathroom, then searched the spare bedroom, a guest bathroom, the sitting room, and a small dining room. It took more than an hour, after which Inspector Zhang and Sergeant Lee went back to the kitchen. Inspector Zhang looked at the wooden block that held the kitchen knives. There was one empty space, presumably belonging to the knife that had killed Miss Chau. He shook his head sadly. "So what do you think of the house, Sergeant Lee?" he asked.

"It is neat and tidy."

"An expensive property, do you think?"

"Oh yes, I couldn't afford it," she said.

"And neither could I," said Inspector Zhang. "Perhaps she rents. We should check that."

"I will," said Sergeant Lee. "But even if she rented it, could a flight attendant afford it? And only one bedroom is used so she did not share."

"You think she lived alone?"

Sergeant Lee frowned. "There were only her clothes in the bedroom," she said. She waved at the photographs on the wall. "The pictures are family pictures of her and her parents; I don't see any pictures of her with a boyfriend. Why Sergeant Lee, do you think someone else lives here? If that was the case, why haven't they come forward?"

"A good question," said Sergeant Lee. "Did you notice there were two toothbrushes in her bathroom? Two brushes in two glasses? And no toothbrushes in the guest bathroom."

"I didn't," she said. "I'm sorry."

Inspector Zhang waved away her apology. "And there were two types of shampoo. One a more masculine anti-dandruff brand. That suggests to me that a man stays here, at least some of the time."

"But he leaves no clothes here?"

"Exactly," said Inspector Zhang. "Which suggests what?"

Sergeant Lee's eyes widened. "She has a boyfriend."

"But why are there no photographs of him?" asked Inspector Zhang. He knew the answer but he wanted his sergeant to work it out for herself.

She nodded enthusiastically. "Because he is married."

"Exactly," said Inspector Zhang. "He either told her not to keep photographs of him, or he removed them."

"You think her boyfriend might have killed her?"

"It is possible, Sergeant Lee. It is very possible."

"But how does that explain Mr. Yip's fingerprints on the knife?" she asked.

"It doesn't," admitted Inspector Zhang. "Not yet, anyway." He rubbed his chin thoughtfully. "And of course it doesn't explain the bite on her arm. It is the bite that worries me the most."

"Dental forensics is not an exact science," said Sergeant Lee. "Though when accompanied by the fingerprint evidence, it does look bad for Mr. Yip."

"It would if he did not have the perfect alibi," said Inspector Zhang. "Do you know how the match was made between the bite and Mr. Yip's teeth?"

Sergeant Lee flicked through her notebook until she found the relevant page. "Mr. Yip was identified first from the fingerprints on the knife that killed Miss Chau. The investigating officer then obtained Mr. Yip's dental records from his dentist and they were sent to the Forensic Management Branch who made the comparison."

"That is most interesting," said Inspector Zhang. "So no comparison has been made between Mr. Yip's actual teeth and the bite mark?"

Sergeant Lee frowned and brushed a stray lock of hair behind her ear. "Why is that significant?" she asked.

"It might not be," said Inspector Zhang. "To find out, we must speak to the dentist."

The dentist was a Dr. Henry Hu and his surgery was in the busy Orchard Road, a prime tourist area lined with up-market shopping malls and prestigious office buildings. Sergeant Lee drove them in her car and parked in the underground car park. They rode up to the sixth floor in the lift. The door was mirrored and Inspector Zhang adjusted his tie as he looked at his reflection. It was a dark blue tie with small white magnifying glasses on it. His wife had bought it as a novelty Christmas present, but truth be told, Inspector Zhang was quite proud of it and wore it often.

"I really don't like going to the dentist," said Sergeant Lee.

"We are there to ask questions, not to have our teeth checked," said Inspector Zhang. "There is nothing to worry about."

"I know, I'm just nervous," she said. "I have been like this ever since I was a child. Actually that's why my teeth are in such good condition now, I was so scared of going to the dentist that I brushed and flossed three times a day." She flashed him a beaming smile and he had to admit her teeth were flawless. Inspector Zhang's teeth were not in such good condition. Four of his back teeth had been replaced with gold ones when he was in his forties. And he had more than a dozen fillings. He had always had a sweet tooth as a child and his love of sugar had caught up with him in middle age.

Inspector Zhang and Sergeant Lee both showed their warrant cards to the receptionist, a fierce looking Chinese lady with hair like spun glass who stared at the cards intently as if trying to memorise the information on them, then asked them to take a seat. She hurried off down a corridor and when she returned she explained that Dr. Hu was with a patient but could see them in fifteen minutes.

"We shall wait," said Inspector Zhang.

Sergeant Lee busied herself on her BlackBerry while Inspector Zhang picked up a copy of the Straits Times and began to methodically read his way through it. He tried to read every article in the Times each day, not because he enjoyed reading the paper but because he never knew in advance what information was going to be useful in the pursuance of his profession.

He had just reached the letters page when a man in a white coat walked into reception. He was in his early forties, short and with a pair of gold-rimmed spectacles perched on the end of his nose. He nodded curtly at Inspector Zhang and walked over. "I am Dr. Hu," he said. "You wanted to speak to me?" He had a mobile phone in a leather holster on his right hip.

Inspector Zhang got to his feet and fished out his warrant card. He showed it to Dr. Hu. "I am Inspector Zhang of the Singapore Police

Force, and this is my colleague, Sergeant Lee." Sergeant Lee showed her warrant card, but stood slightly behind Inspector Zhang as if she was trying to keep him between her and the dentist. "I would like to ask you some questions about your patient, Mr. Yip."

"Ah yes, the burglar," said Dr. Hu. "How did the dental records I sent compare with the bite?"

"You weren't told?" asked Inspector Zhang.

Dr. Hu shook his head. "I was just asked to supply Mr. Yip's dental records so a comparison could be made," he said.

"And you were told about the case?"

"Just that there had been a murder and that Mr. Yip was a suspect." He smiled. "It was a very unusual occurrence," he said. "Like something off a TV show."

"No, it is very real," said Inspector Zhang. There was a young couple sitting close by who were obviously listening to the conversation. "Is there somewhere private we can talk?"

"I have a meeting room we can use," said Dr. Hu. He took them along the corridor and opened a door. It was a small room with a polished teak table and four plastic chairs. Dr. Hu ushered them in, closed the door, and they all sat down. Dr. Hu looked at his watch. "I have a patient waiting," he said. "I hope this won't take too long."

"We just have a few questions, Dr. Hu. Mr. Yip's dental records were up to date, were they?"

"In what sense?"

"The records you supplied matched the bite marks on a murder victim. So I need to know if those records are an accurate depiction of his teeth."

"Of course they are."

"When was the last time you treated Mr. Yip?"

"A month ago. Well, we started treatment a month ago and we finished two weeks ago. The last X-rays were taken then. "

"What treatment did Mr. Yip need?"

"He had a rotten molar," said Dr. Hu. "He needed root canal work and then I fitted a crown."

"His teeth are not in good condition?"

Dr. Hu shook his head. "Too much sugar," he said. "And an ineffective brushing technique. He will need more crowns in the future, I'm sure." He scratched his chin. "Though I suppose if he is sent to prison, I won't be able to continue as his dentist, will I?"

"I think the prisons have their own medical staff," said Inspector Zhang. "What sort of patient was he?"

"A very nervous one," said Dr. Hu. "I had to give him nitrous oxide while I did the root canal. Some patients can manage with an injection, but Mr. Yip has a thing about injections." He smiled thinly. "Which is ironic considering he stabbed a young woman to death."

"Indeed," said Inspector Zhang. "Now can you tell me where the records were kept?"

"In the reception area, in filing cabinets. They are also fully computerised. The files in the cabinets are more of a back-up, these days."

"So were the detectives who called given an actual file or a computer file?"

"A computer file," said Dr. Hu. "They were supplied on a thumb drive."

Inspector Zhang nodded thoughtfully. "Is it possible the records could have been tampered with?"

Dr. Hu frowned. "I'm not sure I understand what you mean, inspector."

"I need to know if there is any way the records you supplied were not in fact the records of Mr. Yip. Is that possible?"

"I don't see how."

"Could someone have gained access to your computer and changed Mr. Yip's records?"

"Absolutely not."

"You seem very sure, Dr. Hu."

The dentist nodded. "I am. The only person who is able to access the records on the computer is myself. And it is password protected."

"So your staff cannot access the records?"

"They can access them. They can read the files and look at the X-rays and photographs but they cannot make any changes. Only I can do that. As I just said, the files are password protected." He interlinked his fingers and leaned forward. "Is something wrong, inspector? I assumed the case was - what do you call it -open and shut?"

"It has become somewhat complicated," said Inspector Zhang.

"In what way?"

"I'm afraid I'm not at liberty to divulge any details of the case," said Inspector Zhang.

"But Mr. Yip did kill that girl, didn't he?"

"That is what we are trying to ascertain," said Inspector Zhang. He stood up. "There is no need for us to take up any more of your time," he said.

"I am more than happy to help the police in any way I can," said Dr. Hu. He stood up and held out his hand. Inspector Zhang looked at the hand for several seconds, and then shook it.

"Do you validate?" asked Sergeant Lee.

"Validate?" asked Dr. Hu.

Sergeant Lee held out her car parking ticket. "We parked downstairs," she said.

"My receptionist can handle that for you," said Dr. Hu. "I am afraid I do have a patient waiting."

The receptionist stamped Sergeant Lee's car park receipt which allowed them to park the car free of charge. They went downstairs. "What do we do now, Sir?" asked Sergeant Lee as they walked towards her car.

"What you think we should do, Sergeant?"

"I still think we should be looking for a twin brother," said Sergeant Lee. "That is the only explanation."

"Then you should follow up that line of inquiry."

"I have already put in a call to the Registry of Births and Deaths."

"Excellent," said Inspector Zhang. "But now I think we need to speak with the officer who arrested Mr. Yip."

"Really?"

"Really," said Inspector Zhang. "It seems to me the crucial question we need answered is whether or not Mr. Yip wanted to be arrested that night."

The sergeant frowned, opened her mouth to ask a question, then changed her mind.

The constable who had arrested Mr. Yip was an Indian in his early thirties, dark-skinned with a thick moustache. He was slightly overweight and made a soft wheezing sound when he breathed out through his nose. Inspector Zhang and Sergeant Lee arranged to meet him on his beat, standing outside a public housing block. "I'm sorry to take you away from your work, Constable Patel," said Inspector Zhang. "I just need to ask you a few questions about your arrest of Mr. Yip on Sunday night."

"Is there a problem, inspector?" asked Constable Patel. "Has he made a complaint?"

"Not at all, Constable. So far as I am aware, everything about the arrest was as it should have been."

Constable Patel looked relieved. "So how can I help you, Inspector?"

Sergeant Lee's mobile phone rang and she walked away to take the call. "The night you arrested Mr. Yip, you had gone around to his apartment because of a noise complaint?"

The constable nodded. "The neighbour who lived below Mr. Yip complained about music being played too loudly. Do you mind if I look at my notebook?"

"Of course, please do," said Inspector Zhang.

The Constable fished his notebook out of his tunic pocket, licked a finger and began flicking through the pages. "I went around with a colleague at four o'clock in the afternoon."

"That seems early for a noise complaint."

"The neighbour had guests around, playing Mah Jong. The music was so loud they could not concentrate on their game. We went up to speak to Mr. Yip. He had been drinking but he agreed to turn the music down. He did, and we went down to talk to the neighbours again and all was well. But we were called out again at five thirty. The music was so loud the glasses were vibrating in the neighbour's flat. We went back to see Mr. Yip and this time he was clearly drunk. We asked him to turn the volume down and he refused. We tried to get into his apartment and he became abusive and violent. We arrested him and took him to Jurong West Police Headquarters." He closed his notebook. "The Duty Officer decided to remand him in custody; basically he was too drunk to be bailed. My understanding was he was to appear in court on Monday morning."

"The matter has become somewhat more serious," said Inspector Zhang. "Now please tell me again how Mr. Yip came to be arrested."

Constable Patel shrugged. "I asked him to turn the volume down. He refused. I told him I would turn it down myself and I tried to get by him. He pushed me in the chest and told me I could not enter his apartment without a warrant. I said that as he was causing a nuisance I was entitled to, and when I tried to enter a second time he gripped my arm and pushed me out into the hallway. At that point my colleague and I handcuffed him and I arrested him for assault."

"Did you at any point form the impression he wanted to be taken into custody?"

The constable shook his head. "He was very angry and it took both of us to get him into the back of the van."

"And do you have any idea why he didn't turn the music down after your first visit?"

"I think he'd had more to drink, inspector. He was a lot less reasonable the second time we went to his apartment."

Inspector Zhang smiled and nodded. "Thank you for your time, Constable. I have everything I need."

"And I'm not in trouble?"

"You behaved impeccably, Constable."

"Thank you, Sir." The Constable saluted and walked away.

Sergeant Lee returned, slipping her BlackBerry into her bag. "It is bad news, Inspector Zhang," she said.

"Oh dear, "said the inspector. "What is the problem?"

"Mr. Yip does not have a twin brother," she said. "He has a sister who is three years older and two brothers who are both younger."

"That is indeed a pity," said Inspector Zhang. "Have you considered a clone?"

Sergeant Lee's mouth opened in surprise. "A clone?" she said. "Do you think that's what happened? You think Mr. Yip used a clone to commit the murder?"

Inspector Zhang raised his hand. "I apologise, Sergeant Lee, I was being flippant. My little joke." He shook his head. "No, I think in this case Mr. Yip is the innocent party. The worst thing he did on Sunday night was to assault a police officer, and that was because he was drunk. He is not a killer."

"Then who killed Miss Chau?" asked Sergeant Lee.

"There is only one person who could possibly have murdered her," said Inspector Zhang. "But in order to prove it we must talk to the detectives who collected the dental records from Dr. Hu, and then we must examine Miss Chau's belongings."

Two hours later Inspector Zhang and Sergeant Lee arrived at the home of Dr. Hu. He lived in a penthouse apartment in the Marina Bay Residences, one of the most expensive buildings in Singapore. The apartments formed part of a $5 billion hotel and casino development that was opened in 2010 and which had spectacular views over the harbour. It was just after eight o'clock in the evening. Inspector Zhang was tired and he could have left the visit until the following day, but he knew he wouldn't be able to sleep until he had closed the case.

There were two security guards at the reception desk, men in their fifties who looked as if they were former soldiers. He showed them his warrant card. "I am here to see Dr. Hu, but he is not expecting us. I would like to go up unannounced."

One of the security guards escorted Inspector Zhang and Sergeant Lee to the lifts and they rode up to the top floor. Inspector Zhang rang the bell and after a few seconds Dr. Hu opened the front door. He frowned when he saw the officers on his doorstep. "Is something wrong?" he asked. He was wearing a dinner jacket and had an untied black bow tie around his neck. His mobile phone was in a leather holster on his belt.

"We would like a word with you, Dr. Hu," said Inspector Zhang.

"And it couldn't wait until tomorrow?"

"I'm afraid not."

"I am just on my way out," said Dr. Hu. "My wife is hosting a dinner at the Imperial Treasure restaurant."

"I'm afraid it is rather important," said Inspector Zhang.

Dr. Hu looked at his watch. "Five minutes," he said tersely. "Then I really must go."

He stepped aside to allow Inspector Zhang into the apartment, then closed the door behind them. "I really must fix my tie," said Dr. Hu, and he hurried off to his bedroom before the inspector could say anything.

Inspector Zhang wandered around the huge room with its floor to ceiling windows that overlooked the harbour. There was a huge chandelier hanging from the ceiling and furniture that would have looked at home in the Palace of Versailles. There were gilt-framed oil paintings on the wall and ornate marble statues of leaping dolphins and mermaids on a cabinet. The sitting room alone was twice the size of the apartment where Inspector Zhang lived with his wife.

"This apartment is lovely," said Inspector Zhang. "I don't think I have ever been in such a spectacular apartment."

"It's beautiful," agreed Sergeant Lee. "But I don't like being so high in the air."

"My wife would love it," said Inspector Zhang. "She always asks for a high floor when we stay at hotels. But, personally, I prefer being close to the ground."

Dr. Hu reappeared from the bedroom, his bowtie neatly tied. He looked at his watch again. It was gold with diamonds around the face. "Now, how can I help you," he said. "Because I really must be going."

"I was just saying to my assistant what a wonderful apartment this is."

"Thank you," said Dr. Hu, flustered by the unexpected compliment.

"My mother always wanted me to be a dentist," said Inspector Zhang, looking around. "I am starting to think perhaps she was right."

"What do you mean, Inspector?" asked Dr. Hu.

Inspector Zhang waved a hand around the room. "Just that on an inspector's salary I couldn't afford to buy more than a few square metres of an apartment like this. Now, if I had been a dentist..." He shrugged. "As they say, hindsight is a wonderful thing."

Dr. Hu chuckled. "Ah, I understand. No, Inspector, it is not my salary as a dentist that pays for this lovely home. My wife is the one with money. Her father runs a shipping company and he has been doing very well in recent years."

"I wondered if you were married," said Inspector Zhang. "I noticed you do not wear a wedding band."

"Dentists tend not to wear rings," said Dr. Hu. "They would get in the way and they also harbour germs. Our hands are often in people's mouths so hygiene is paramount. A ring might pierce a surgical glove, for instance." He held up his left hand. "So, no rings."

"Of course," said Inspector Zhang. "Though I suppose that not wearing a wedding ring also helped you meet Miss Chau."

"I'm sorry?"

"The first time you met she wouldn't have seen a ring and wouldn't have known you were married. Or was it that she knew but didn't care?"

"Inspector, what are you talking about?"

"Miss Chau. Sindy Chau. I am assuming she was threatening to spoil the arrangement you had and that's why you killed her."

Sergeant Lee's jaw dropped and she lowered her pen and notebook.

"That is ridiculous," said Dr. Hu.

"On the contrary," said Inspector Zhang. "There is absolutely nothing ridiculous about murder."

"But you have the murderer in custody," said Dr. Hu. "You told me so when you came to my surgery."

"And that was your downfall, because Mr. Yip was in custody when he was supposed to be killing Miss Chau. Your plan was almost perfect, Dr. Hu. But the only thing you could not control was the fact that Mr. Yip would lose his temper with the policeman who asked him to turn down the volume of his music."

"Music?"

"You knew Mr. Yip lived alone. So you assumed that if you killed Miss Chau late at night and framed Mr. Yip, he would not have an alibi other than to say he was home alone."

"I did not even know Miss Chau. Why would I want to kill her?"

"You had the oldest reason of all, Dr. Hu. But I have to admire your creativity. If Mr. Yip had not been arrested, you would have gotten away with it."

Dr. Hu threw up his hands in exasperation. "How dare you come to my home and make allegations like this," he said. "I insist you leave. I shall be complaining to your superiors."

"So you are not interested in how you gave yourself away?" asked Inspector Zhang.

Dr. Hu's eyes narrowed. "What are you talking about?"

"When we came to see you in your surgery, do you remember? We wanted to talk to you about the comparison between the bite on Miss Chau's arm and the dental records you had."

"And they were a perfect match; your own forensic people told you that. All I did was to supply the records; I did not make the comparison. Mr. Yip bit Miss Chau on the arm; that is irrefutable."

"No, Dr. Hu, it is not. Mr. Yip did not bite Miss Chau. In fact he never met her. He certainly did not burgle her house nor did he kill her. Someone else did. But it wasn't until you gave yourself away that I began to consider you as a suspect."

Dr. Hu sneered at the inspector. "Gave myself away? You are talking nonsense. Now please leave." He gestured at the door impatiently.

"Do you remember what you said to us, Dr. Hu? When we talked about Mr. Yip, you said how you didn't think he was the sort of man who would stab an innocent woman."

"Because he had always seemed to be a perfectly nice man whenever I saw him. I did not know he was a criminal, let alone a criminal capable of murder."

"I am sure you knew exactly the sort of man Mr. Yip is," said Inspector Zhang. "It was vital to your plan that he was a known house-breaker."

"My plan? What plan are you talking about?"

Inspector Zhang ignored the dentist's question. "Dr. Hu, how did you know that Miss Chau had been stabbed?"

"What?"

"When we saw you in your surgery you said Mr. Yip had stabbed an innocent woman. But no one had told you she had been stabbed. The cause of death had not been released at that stage."

Dr. Hu frowned. "Someone must have told me. The detectives who collected the records from me, perhaps."

Inspector Zhang turned to Sergeant Lee. "My sergeant has spoken to the detectives and they confirmed they did no such thing. Isn't that right, Sergeant?"

"I spoke to both of them myself," she said. She flicked through her notebook. "They said they told you it was a murder investigation but gave you no details of the case. They did not tell you the name of the victim, nor the manner in which she died."

"They are wrong," said Dr. Hu. "They made a mistake when they told me and now they are lying to cover it up."

"I think you will find in a case like this a court is more likely to believe two detectives with more than twenty years' experience with the Singapore Police Force between them than a murderer who is desperate to save himself."

"How dare you call me a murderer," said Dr. Hu angrily.

"That is what you are, Dr. Hu," said Inspector Zhang calmly.

"You have no proof."

Inspector Zhang reached into his jacket pocket and took out a mobile phone. "I do have this," he said. "This is Sindy Chau's phone. She wasn't a patient, you said? In fact you said you never met her?"

"That's right. You can check with my surgery. I have never treated her."

"Miss Chau doesn't have you listed by name on her phone," said Inspector Zhang. "I assume you told her not to, in the same way you insisted on her having no photographs in her house, the house you were paying for. Of course the lease was paid through a company but I doubt that we will find it difficult to connect you to it."

"Ridiculous," said Dr. Hu.

"Miss Chau doesn't have you listed in her phone contacts but she does have a listing for Dentist," said Inspector Zhang. "So let's see what happens when I press it. I assume it will go through to whichever surgery she uses."

Inspector Zhang pressed the call button and the colour seemed to drain from Dr. Hu's face. After a few seconds there was a musical ringtone from the phone attached to Dr. Hu's belt.

Inspector Zhang's face broke into a smile. "It sounds like someone is calling you, Dr. Hu," he said. "Perhaps you should answer that."

"You don't understand," said Dr. Hu. "She was threatening to tell my wife. She said she was fed up with being just a mistress, and if I didn't choose her then I'd lose her and I'd lose my wife."

"On the contrary, I understand everything, Dr. Hu. You did not wish to lose the lifestyle that came from your wealthy wife. So you decided the way to keep it would be to dispose of your mistress. You had read about Mr. Yip's criminal career in the newspapers and realised he would be the perfect fall guy. He was a difficult patient which meant he would require a full anaesthetic for the root canal work. You took a knife from Miss Chau's kitchen and while he was unconscious you placed it in his hand to get his fingerprints on it."

The phone was continuing to ring, so Inspector Zhang cancelled the call and put it back into his pocket.

"But you realised the knife alone might not be enough to convict Mr. Yip, so you decided to increase the stakes. You took a cast of Mr. Yip's teeth to ensure his new tooth was a perfect fit. I believe you used the cast to make a set of false teeth that matched Mr. Yip's perfectly. While you were at Miss Chau's house, you killed her with the knife then used the teeth you had made to bite her arm. Then you faked the break-in and left. I did not ask you if you had an alibi for the night that Miss Chau was murdered but I am sure you do not. At least, not an alibi as good as the one that Mr. Yip has."

Dr. Hu's shoulders slumped. He dropped down onto a sofa like a marionette whose strings had been cut, put his head in his hands and began to sob quietly.

"It was almost the perfect crime, Dr. Hu. You very nearly got away with it." Inspector Zhang turned to Sergeant Lee, who was scribbling frantically into her notebook. He had a sly smile on his face and he waited until she looked up from her notebook before speaking. "So tell me, Sergeant Lee, how did it feel to have a case that we could really get our teeth into?" he asked.

Sergeant Lee smiled, then went back to writing in her notebook, knowing Inspector Zhang was not expecting a reply.

"Please come with us now, Dr. Hu," said Inspector Zhang. "Though perhaps you would like the opportunity to change into something more suitable for a prison cell."

7.

INSPECTOR ZHANG AND THE ISLAND OF THE DEAD

'Do you think it will rain again?' asked Sergeant Lee, peering out of the window at the street below and then up at the darkening sky.

'It is the monsoon season so there is a high probability of rain,' said Inspector Zhang. They were in the Major Crimes Division office in New Bridge Road police headquarters building and they had just received a call to attend a murder scene on Sentosa Island. Sentosa was one of Singapore's major tourist attractions with long sandy beaches, two golf courses, a number of top hotels and the Universal Studios theme park. There were also several very upmarket housing developments where Singapore's wealthier residents could enjoy a house with a garden, a rarity in crowded Singapore where most people lived in cramped apartments.

'Shall I bring an umbrella, do you think?' asked Sergeant Lee. She had her hair clipped up at the back and was wearing a pale blue suit.

'Better safe than sorry,' said Inspector Zhang.

They took the elevator down to the ground floor. They had decided to use Inspector Zhang's car and he drove south out of the police station car park. It was early evening but the worst of the rush hour traffic had gone. 'So remind me what we have, Sergeant,' said the inspector.

Sergeant Lee studied her notebook. 'The victim is Dr Samuel Kwan. His house was broken into and Dr Kwan was stabbed. His wife, Mrs Elsie Kwan, discovered the body.' She looked up from her notebook. 'I suppose I should say widow. Not wife. Now that he is dead.'

'Wife or widow is fine,' said Inspector Zhang.

'Widow is, I think, more appropriate,' said Sergeant Lee. 'Anyway, the police have already secured the area.'

'There have been a number of break-ins on Sentosa Island,' said the inspector. 'But always late at night and no one has been hurt previously.'

'Perhaps Dr Kwan disturbed the burglar,' said Sergeant Lee.

Inspector Zhang looked at her over the top of his spectacles. 'And perhaps we should at least wait until we have examined the crime scene before we jump to conclusions,' he said.

Sergeant Lee's cheeks flushed and she averted her eyes.

'Do you know how Sentosa Island got its name?' asked Inspector Zhang.

'The name means peace and tranquillity in Malay,' said the sergeant.

'Indeed it does,' said the inspector. 'It was given the name in 1972, I suppose as a way of attracting tourists. Prior to that it was known as Palu Belakang Mati – which literally means Island Of Death from Behind.' He smiled. 'That name was obviously not so tourist-friendly. It was also referred to as the Dead Island or the Island of the Dead.'

'Why such a dark name?' asked Sergeant Lee.

'No one is sure,' said the inspector as he joined the traffic heading over the causeway that led to the island. 'There was definitely murder and piracy in the island's past. But there are some Malay legends that say there are warrior spirits laid to rest on the island. There were also a lot of deaths in the past thought to be a result of swamp fever though it later proved to be malaria. The government's first malaria research station was located on the island.'

They drove on to Sentosa and Sergeant Lee gave the inspector directions to the estate where Dr Kwan's house was located. There were several dozen large houses built on a smaller island surrounded by tributaries that led to the sea. Most of the homes had expensive yachts and cruisers moored at private jetties jutting from their properties. Even from a distance it was clear which was Dr Kwan's house – there were two police cars, a forensics van and an ambulance parked outside and the area had been cordoned off with blue and white police tape. Inspector Zhang pulled up behind one of the police cars. As he climbed out of the car he saw the tower blocks of the city state's business district in the distance, dotted with lights. There were three cars parked on the driveway in front of the house: a Mercedes sports car, a Porsche Cayenne SUV and a white Lexus.

A uniformed officer was standing on the other side of the police tape. Inspector Zhang flashed the man his ID. 'Who is the senior officer?' he asked.

'That would be Sergeant Wu,' said the officer. He lifted up the tape so that the two detectives could duck under it.

'Where is he?'

'She is in the house with Mrs Kwan,' said the officer.

Inspector Zhang and Sergeant Lee walked towards the front door of the house. 'Jenny Wu, I went to the Police Academy with her,' said Sergeant Lee.

'She seems to have done a good job of securing the house,' said Inspector Zhang. They reached the front door just as Sergeant Wu emerged. She had short hair and an upturned nose on the end of which were perched a pair of wire-framed spectacles. Her eyes widened and she smiled when she saw Sergeant Lee. 'Carolyn, how are you?' she asked.

'I'm fine,' said Sergeant Lee.

'I haven't seen you for more than a year.'

Sergeant Wu looked as if she was about to continue the conversation so Inspector Zhang gave a quiet cough. 'I'm here with Inspector Zhang,' said Sergeant Lee, hurriedly. 'From Major Crimes.'

'Of course, of course,' said Sergeant Wu. She turned to Inspector Zhang. 'Sergeant Wu, Sir. We have secured the crime scene. The victim is a Dr Kwan. He appears to have been stabbed. The body was discovered by his wife and a Dr Mayang. The only other person in the house was the Filipino maid.'

'Where is Mrs Kwan?'

'In the sitting room,' said Sergeant Wu.

159

'I think I should introduce myself first, then examine the crime scene,' said the inspector. He gestured at the front door. 'Please lead the way.'

Sergeant Wu headed into the house and the two detectives followed.

The hallway was clad in expensive marble and above their heads was a huge gold and crystal chandelier. There were ornate golden dragons either side of a doorway that led into a sitting room that had a large window overlooking a waterway at the rear of the house.

Two middle-aged women were sitting on an overstuffed sofa. Behind them were a series of framed calligraphy paintings. Calligraphy was an occasional hobby of the inspector's and he recognised the quality of the work. One of the women was Chinese. She was small and had a bird-like face, with a sharp nose and pinched mouth and had her hands clasped together in her lap. She was holding a red-spotted handkerchief and fiddling with her wedding ring as she stared off into the middle distance. Her clothes were clearly expensive. Inspector Zhang was no expert on women's fashion but he recognised a Chanel suit when he saw one. And he had been around enough shoe shops with Mrs Zhang to know that Mrs Kwan's footwear was very expensive indeed.

The other woman was Malaysian, wearing a dark green suit. There was a black medical bag at her feet. Her shoes didn't seem as expensive as Mrs Kwan's, so far as the inspector could tell.

'This is Mrs Kwan,' said Sergeant Wu, gesturing at the woman in the Chanel suit. 'And this is her friend, Dr Mayang.'

The two women looked at Inspector Zhang with blank faces. Neither moved to get up. On the coffee table in front of them was a bottle of red wine and two glasses, and a stainless steel tray dotted with snacks.

'I am Inspector Zhang and this is my colleague, Sergeant Lee,' he said. He directed his gaze at Mrs Kwan. 'Can I first say how sorry I am for your loss?'

She gave him a small nod and continued to fiddle with her wedding ring.

'I understood that you discovered the deceased?'

Mrs Kwan nodded. 'We heard glass breaking. Then a scream. A terrible scream. We went to the study but the door was locked. We went around to the rear of the house and saw that a window had been broken and the door opened. And my husband had been stabbed.'

'Again, I am very sorry for your loss,' said the inspector. 'But the door was locked, you said? From the inside?'

Mrs Kwan nodded. 'It was my husband's habit to lock the door while he listened to music on his headphones,' she said. 'He didn't want to be disturbed. It was his nightly habit for our maid to take him a cup of hot green tea and he would lock the door and listen to his music before retiring to bed.'

The inspector nodded sympathetically. 'And did you see anyone? Anyone who might have done it?'

Mrs Kwan shook her head and so did Dr Mayang.

Inspector Zhang nodded at the bag at Dr Mayang's feet. 'I notice that you have your medical bag with you.'

The doctor smiled. 'I always have my bag with me,' she said. 'Sadly there was nothing I could do to help Dr Kwan.'

'Why was that?'

'He had been stabbed through the heart. He bled to death very quickly.' She looked over at Mrs Kwan. 'I'm sorry, Elsie,' she said.

Inspector Zhang nodded at Sergeant Wu. 'Perhaps you would be good enough to show us the room where it happened.'

Sergeant Wu took the detectives back into the hallway. She pointed at one of the doors. 'This is the door to the study,' she said.

'It is still locked?'

'I thought it best to touch nothing until the forensic team arrived,' she said.

'Very wise,' said Inspector Zhang. He tried the door handle but the door was clearly locked.

Two forensic investigators appeared at the main entrance. They were wearing white hooded overalls and had paper covers on their shoes. They were both men in their mid-thirties. One of them recognised Inspector Zhang and smiled. 'You were here quickly, Inspector,' he said.

'The traffic was light, Mr Yuen,' said Inspector Zhang. He gestured at the door to the sitting room. 'I notice that Mrs Kwan, the wife of the victim, has what appears to be blood on her hands and on her suit. Could I suggest that samples are taken immediately.'

'Of course,' said the forensic investigator. He nodded at his colleague. 'Can you do that, Ronnie, I'll go with the inspector.'

The second forensic investigator disappeared into the sitting room.

Sergeant Wu took them through a large kitchen and out of a back door that led to the garden. 'This is the way that Mrs Kwan and Dr Mayang went after they heard the sounds of the break-in,' she said.

There was a large terrace overlooking the waterway, a hot-tub and a swimming pool. Floodlights on the roof illuminated the terrace and there was a line of fluorescent lights along the waterway making it as light as day.

'This is a spectacular house,' said Inspector Zhang. 'How much do you think a house like this would cost?'

'At least twenty million dollars,' said Sergeant Wu. She pointed towards a large yacht that was moored on a private jetty on the edge of the property. 'The yacht also belongs to Dr Kwan.'

'So Dr Kwan was clearly a very wealthy man.'

'He had a chain of plastic surgery clinics, here in Singapore but in the Middle East, too. He had an unusual speciality.'

'Did he? Perhaps you would care to enlighten me.'

The officer moved so that she was standing with her back to Sergeant Lee and lowered her voice. 'He makes women virgins again.'

Inspector Zhang frowned. 'He does what?'

The officer moved her head closer to the inspector. 'Women who have had sex, he can make it seem as if they are still virgins. He does a lot of work in the Middle East. Muslims want their wives to be virgins, you see.'

The inspector nodded. 'Well it must pay well,' he said. 'I could not afford a house like this if I worked for a hundred years.' He looked over at the bridge that linked the housing development to Sentosa Island. 'How quickly did your men get here?'

'We sealed off the island within ten minutes of getting the call but it seems the intruder had already left,' said Sergeant Wu. 'That suggests he was in a car or on a motorbike.'

'He could have left in a boat,' said Inspector Zhang. 'When you say island, do you mean this small island or the main Sentosa Island?'

'The housing compound,' said Sergeant Wu. 'Obviously we couldn't seal off the entire island, there is just too much traffic.'

Inspector Zhang turned back to look at the house. 'Do you know if the doctor had any enemies, anyone who might wish him ill?'

'Not that we know of,' said Sergeant Wu. 'Though he was in the process of being divorced by Mrs Kwan.'

Inspector Zhang raised his eyebrows. 'Really? She didn't mention that.'

'It's been quite ugly, by all accounts. He had hired a top legal firm and was making it very difficult for his wife. That was why she was still in the house, she had nowhere else to go.'

'They have been married for a long time?'

'More than twenty years,' said Sergeant Wu. 'She used to be his nurse. Mrs Kwan discovered that Dr Kwan had been having an affair and had started divorce proceedings.'

Inspector Zhang smiled thinly. 'I shall obviously have to have another word with Mrs Kwan,' he said.

Sergeant Wu took him along to the terrace to a set of French windows. Sergeant Lee and the forensics investigator followed. The doors opened outwards. One was still closed, but the other, with a broken pane, had been opened.

'So Mrs Kwan and Dr Mayang came along here and discovered the broken window?'

'Yes. And the maid was with them. Mrs Kwan went inside.'

'She was presumably distraught?'

'Yes, of course. She rushed over to her husband and held him.'

'That would explain the blood on her hands,' said the inspector.

'Inspector Zhang, would you put these on please?' said the forensics investigator. He was holding out a pair of paper shoe covers.

'Of course,' said Inspector Zhang. He slipped on the shoe covers. The two sergeants did the same.

Inspector Zhang leaned into the study and examined the broken glass on the floor of the study. There were raindrops, too, from the evening's earlier rain. He knelt down and peered at the broken glass, then gently prodded a small piece with his finger. It stuck to his flesh and he had to shake it free. He nudged another tiny shard of glass and it too stuck to his finger.

'Inspector, I'm sorry but I must insist that if you are going to touch evidence you should wear gloves.' Inspector Zhang looked up to see Mr Yuen looking down at him and offering a pair of blue latex gloves.

Inspector Zhang flicked the shard of glass from his finger and straightened up. 'Quite right,' he said. He took the gloves and put them on, then pointed at the glass and raindrops. 'Be careful to step over this,' he said to Sergeant Lee. He stepped into the room. At first he didn't see the body of Dr Kwan, but as he walked across the parquet flooring he saw a winged leather armchair with its back to the window. Dr Kwan was sprawled in the chair. He was wearing a white silk shirt and baggy black linen trousers, with ornate Chinese silk slippers on his feet. He had a pair of Bose noise-cancelling headphones over his ears. The plug had been pulled out of its socket on the stereo. Close to his right hand, on a small teak table, was a red and gold beaker on a matching saucer and next to it a CD case. He picked up the beaker and sniffed it cautiously. It was almost empty and had contained green tea.

As Inspector Zhang walked carefully around the chair he saw a black-handled knife had been thrust into the man's chest. Blood had gushed around the blade and soaked into the shirt.

'One stab wound,' he mused. He peered carefully at Dr Kwan's hands. 'And no defensive wounds.'

'It looks as if Dr Kwan had his back to the French windows so he did not see the attacker break in,' said Sergeant Wu. 'And with the headphones on, he would not have heard the glass breaking.'

Inspector Zhang nodded. 'Was anything taken?'

'Mrs Kwan says no,' said Sergeant Wu. 'Dr Kwan had an extensive collection of coins and banknotes which he keeps in the display cases over there.' She pointed at the wall by the door. There were two large mahogany and glass cases filled with coins and framed banknotes. 'As you can see, they have not been interfered with. The burglar probably panicked, killed Dr Kwan and then ran off.'

Inspector Zhang frowned. 'Have you been involved in any other robberies in Sentosa?' he asked.

'Several,' she said.

'Does this appear similar in any way?'

'Often with houses like this, access is gained through the French windows. But break-ins usually take place at night. Our advice is that householders have alarm systems fitted. There is an alarm system here, but of course it was not switched on because the Kwans were moving around downstairs.'

Inspector Zhang looked around the room, then walked back to the French windows, taking care not to tread on any of the broken glass. 'When the intruder broke in, they would not have seen that Dr Kwan was sitting in the chair. That is certainly true. And wearing the headphones meant he would not have heard the glass break.' He walked slowly towards the chair and then stopped. 'From here I can see that Dr Kwan is in the chair. But Dr Kwan would not be able to see me. At this point, surely, I would just turn and walk away.' He looked across at the forensic investigator. 'What can you tell me about the knife, Mr Yuen?' he asked.

The investigator walked around the chair and peered at the handle. 'It appears to be a kitchen knife,' he said. 'I think it best to leave it in position until the autopsy. But yes, from the handle I would say that it looks like a kitchen knife. The blade would be perhaps six inches long, more than long enough to pierce the heart.'

Inspector Zhang nodded. 'That is what I thought. But what sort of burglar brings a kitchen knife with him?'

'For protection, perhaps?' said Sergeant Wu. 'In case he was disturbed?'

'In my experience, most burglars who are caught in the act simply run away. They don't attack.'

Sergeant Wu nodded. 'That is true,' she said.

'So we have to ask ourselves why the burglar brought a kitchen knife with him,' continued Inspector Zhang. 'And why he stabbed Dr Kwan when there was clearly no need to do so. Having broken in without being seen or heard, he could have simply left once he had seen that the room was occupied.'

'Panic?' said Sergeant Lee.

'Possibly,' said Inspector Zhang.

'Also, he would have heard Mrs Kwan shouting from the hallway,' said Sergeant Lee. 'Perhaps he thought the house was unoccupied and once he realised it wasn't, he ran.'

'But surely he would have seen the three cars parked outside? That alone should have told him the house was occupied. What sort of burglar doesn't take a careful look at the house he is about to burglarise?'

Sergeant Lee scratched her head but didn't say anything.

Inspector Zhang walked over to the door and examined it. There was a brass bolt at the top of the door and he slid it back. 'I think it is time to talk to Mrs Kwan and Dr Mayang again,' he said. He pulled open the door and stepped into the hallway. The two sergeants followed him while the forensic investigator got to work in the study.

The two women looked up as Inspector Zhang walked into the sitting room. A male uniformed officer was standing just inside the door, his hands clasped behind his back.

'Once again I am very sorry for your loss, Mrs Kwan,' he said.

Mrs Kwan nodded and forced a smile. 'Thank you.'

'You did not tell me that you and Dr Kwan were in the process of divorcing.'

'I didn't see that was any of your business,' said Mrs Kwan. 'My husband was killed by an intruder. Our personal situation has nothing to do with that.' She pointed at the forensic investigator who was bending over his case. 'And why did you tell him to take my handkerchief?'

'I noticed there were spots of blood on it,' said Inspector Zhang. 'And on your suit, too.'

'Of course there was. I touched the knife when I checked on my husband. I used the handkerchief to wipe it off me.'

'Then the handkerchief is evidence, Mrs Kwan. I am sure you can understand that. But what I don't understand is why, if you were divorcing, you are still living in the same house?'

Mrs Kwan gave him a long, hard look before replying. 'My husband was a very difficult man,' she said, her voice barely more than a whisper. 'He had been having an affair for the past three years but he was refusing to give me what was rightfully mine.'

'I don't understand,' said the inspector.

'I am entitled to half the marital assets. Our house, our business, the yacht, our investments, his coin collection, his pension fund. But he was refusing to give me anything. That's why I was forced to live under the same roof as him, despite the shame he brought on me.'

'What shame would that be?' asked Inspector Zhang,

'I really do not see what business that is of yours, Inspector,' said Mrs Kwan tersely.

'This is a murder investigation,' said Inspector Zhang. 'I have the authority to ask any questions that I see fit, and I have the power to insist that you come to the police station if you don't provide satisfactory answers to those questions.' He blinked at her but then smiled like a kindly uncle. 'The sooner you answer my questions, Mrs Kwan, the sooner I can leave.'

Mrs Kwan took a deep breath to compose herself 'When my husband and I married he had just one small clinic. He had one nurse, and that was me. We worked seven days a week to build the clinic and then open another and another. I wanted children but he said to wait until we were on a firmer financial footing. Then when we had all the money we needed he still always had a reason why the time wasn't right for us to have a child.' She took another deep breath and Inspector Zhang saw that there were tears in her eyes. 'Last year I discovered that my husband had been keeping a mistress. It turned out that she had been a nurse in our clinic in Dubai. The icing on the cake was that they have a child. A two-year-old daughter.'

Inspector Zhang nodded sympathetically. 'That being the case, why did you not leave?'

'Because my lawyer told me that if I left the marital home voluntarily that could be considered desertion.'

'And your husband did not consider moving out to be with the mother of his child?'

Mrs Kwan shook her head. 'He was more concerned that he kept the house. He had already moved most of our money into offshore trusts and he was making it difficult for me to get a lawyer.'

'And how exactly was he doing that?'

She shook her head. 'I don't know. All I know is that every time I went to see a lawyer they would agree to take my case, but within a week they would come up with some excuse for not taking me on as a client. I'm sure my husband was behind it, but I could never prove it. The only lawyer I could get is frankly not up to the job.'

Inspector Zhang nodded thoughtfully. 'It appears that nothing was stolen. Is it possible that your husband had enemies? Someone who would want to hurt him?'

'Other than me, you mean?' She smiled tightly. 'If my husband treated others the way he treated me then yes, I'm sure he had a lot of enemies.'

'Inspector, I really think you are being a tad insensitive with Mrs Kwan,' said Dr Mayang. 'Her husband has been brutally murdered. And she was sitting next to me on this very sofa when it happened.'

'I do understand your concerns,' said the inspector. 'I would like to suggest that Mrs Kwan speaks with Sergeant Lee in the kitchen while I speak with you.'

'Is that really necessary?' asked Mrs Kwan, archly.

It was, very much so, thought Inspector Zhang, but he simply smiled and nodded. 'It will make things easier and we will take up less of your time,' he said. In fact it was important to get the two witnesses apart when they told their stories so that their individual versions could be compared.

Mrs Kwan stood up, clearly unhappily. 'Very well then,' she said. 'It will at least give me the chance to prepare some Jasmine tea. Would you like some?''

'That would be lovely,' said Inspector Zhang.

'I was talking to Dr Mayang,' said Mrs Kwan. 'I do not expect that you will be here long enough to be drinking tea.'

'I would love some tea, thank you,' said Dr Mayang.

Mrs Kwan walked out of the room, followed by Sergeant Lee.

Sergeant Wu nodded at Inspector Zhang. 'I shall be outside, Inspector. No doubt the media will be here soon.' She left the room. The forensic investigator went to join his colleague in the study.

Inspector Zhang sat down on the sofa next to Dr Mayang. 'So what time did you arrive at the house, Dr Mayang?'

'At six o'clock.'

'Precisely six o'clock?'

The doctor smiled. 'I am always on time, Inspector. I am a very punctual person.'

'And Mrs Kwan was expecting you?'

'We had arranged for me to call around at six. She had wanted to see me earlier but I had a patient to see in my surgery so six o'clock was the earliest I could get here.'

'And was it raining?'

Dr Mayang frowned. 'It stopped while I was driving, I think.' She narrowed her eyes and then nodded. 'Yes, it stopped before I got here. I know because I had an umbrella and I didn't need it when I got out of the car.'

'And what was the purpose of your visit?'

'The purpose?'

'Was it a professional visit, or a social one? I see you have your medical bag with you.'

The doctor smiled. 'Ah, I see what you mean. Mrs Kwan has been my patient for many years. But she is also a friend. And before that, many years ago, she worked for me. She had just qualified as a nurse and I gave her her first job.'

'But your visit today?

'A social visit, Inspector. A chance to chat and drink some wine.'

'On those occasions that your visits are professional, what is the nature of your consultations?'

The doctor smiled. 'I'm afraid I can't tell you that, inspector. Doctor-patient privilege. I'm sure you understand.'

Inspector Zhang removed his glasses and carefully polished them with a large blue handkerchief. 'Of course,' he said. 'So please tell me what happened this evening.'

'I arrived here at about six o'clock,' she said. 'Mrs Kwan opened a bottle of wine and we drank and chatted. She is having a difficult time, with the divorce and everything. Then we heard the sound of the window breaking. It was followed a few seconds later by a loud scream. Mrs Kwan rushed across the hallway but the door to the study was locked. She banged on the door but nobody answered.'

'You were with Mrs Kwan in the hallway?'

'Yes. She was very distraught. She rushed to the kitchen and shouted for the maid.'

'For what reason?'

'For what reason? I don't understand.'

'Did she want the maid to do anything?'

Dr Mayang shook her head. 'I don't think so. I think perhaps she just wanted people around her when she went outside. She took us out of the kitchen door and around the back of the house. As soon as we got near the study we could see that the window had been broken. Mrs Kwan rushed inside and began screaming that her husband was dead.'

'Was the door open when you first approached it?'

'I'm not sure.'

'Please try to remember, Dr Mayang. It is important.'

The doctor nodded slowly. 'It was ajar, I think.' She frowned and then put up a hand to her face. 'No, she said. 'It was closed. I remember that Mrs Kwan had to turn the handle to open it.' She nodded, more confidently this time. 'Yes, I'm sure, it was shut.'

'And where were you and the maid at the point that Mrs Kwan went inside?'

'We were on the terrace.'

'You didn't go inside?'

'We did, yes. But she rushed ahead. She was quite frantic.'

'Who followed Mrs Kwan inside first? You or the maid?'

'The maid first. Then I followed.'

'And what did you see?'

'Mrs Kwan was bent over her husband. I couldn't see that at first, of course. The chair was facing away from us so I just saw the chair and her. Then she stood up and looked at me and said that he was dead. I hurried over and took a look for myself.'

'And was he dead?'

'He was dying,' said Dr Mayang. 'I felt a very faint pulse initially and there was a slight movement of his chest, but he was covered in blood.'

'You didn't touch the knife?'

'Of course not,' she said. 'Removing the knife would have only hastened the blood loss.'

'What was Mrs Kwan doing at this point?'

'She was shouting at the maid to call for an ambulance. But I could see that was a waste of time. Mr Kwan took his last breath and then there was no pulse.'

'He died while you were there?'

The doctor nodded. 'Most definitely.'

'And did you see anyone else, while you were on the terrace? Anyone running away, for instance? Or anyone who shouldn't have been there?'

'I don't think so,' she said. 'But to be honest I wasn't looking. Once we saw the broken window, that was all we were looking at.'

Sergeant Lee appeared at the doorway. 'Mrs Kwan has tea for Dr Mayang,' she said.

'That is fine, I have finished my interview with Dr Mayang,' said Inspector Zhang.

Sergeant Lee stepped to the side and Mrs Kwan walked into the room, carrying a tray of tea things. She put the tray on a side table and Inspector Zhang stood up so that she could sit down next to her friend.

'Are we finished?' asked Mrs Kwan as she sat down.

'Soon,' said Inspector Zhang. He smiled at Sergeant Lee. 'Sergeant, I need you to do something for me as a matter of urgency. Would you contact the Meteorological Society and obtain from them the times of today's rainfall.'

'It rained for about half an hour, not long before we left the station.'

The inspector flashed her a kindly smile. 'I need the precise times, please.'

'Of course, Inspector,' said Sergeant Lee. She fished her mobile phone from her handbag as she left the room.

'Is this going to be much longer?' asked Mrs Kwan.

'I just have a few more questions,' said Inspector Zhang.

Mrs Kwan looked at her wristwatch. 'I really can not spare you more than a few minutes,' she said.

'I'm sure that will be more than enough,' he said. 'Now, Dr Mayang has quite rightly not given me any information about her professional relationship with you.'

'Doctor patient privilege,' said the doctor, nodding.

'The Singapore Medical Council, if I remember correctly, states in its Ethical Code and Ethical Guidelines, that information obtained in confidence or in the course of attending to the patient should not be disclosed without a patient's consent.'

'That is quite correct, inspector,' said the doctor.

'That being said, I would like to ask you, Mrs Kwan, if the medical problems you have had have been associated with your divorce.'

She threw up her hands. 'It has been a nightmare, Inspector Zhang. A living hell.'

'One that Dr Mayang has been able to offer you some help, I suppose?'

'My nerves are in a tangle,' said Mrs Kwan. 'I barely sleep these days. My blood pressure has been through the roof. I think that was always his plan, to put me under such stress that I would simply die.'

Inspector Zhang nodded sympathetically. 'So Dr Mayang prescribed you tablets for your blood pressure?'

Mrs Kwan nodded.

'And for your nerves? An anti-depressant perhaps?'

'They have been a life-saver,' said Mrs Kwan.

'And for those sleepless nights? No doubt she prescribed you sleeping tablets?'

'They are the only way that I can get a good night's sleep,' said Mrs Kwan. 'Without them I just lie in my bed, my mind in a turmoil.'

'It can't have been easy, living under the same roof with a man you wanted to divorce.'

'I had no choice, I knew that if I ever left I would never see my house again,' said Mrs Kwan. 'But this has been my home for almost twenty years? Why should I leave?'

'You had separate bedrooms?'

Mrs Kwan nodded. 'We did. And during the day I confined myself to this room and he stayed in the study.'

'You rarely spoke?'

'There was no need,' said Mrs Kwan. 'If I needed to tell him anything I passed a letter to our maid.'

'Chanel?'

'Yes, Chanel. If my husband wanted to say something to me then he would give a note to Chanel. But mainly he communicated through his lawyers and they would write to me. But really, Inspector Zhang, he never had anything of importance to say to me on a daily basis. He hated me. I had never wronged him yet he hated me with a vengeance.'

'Why did he hate you, do you think?'

'I don't think, I know. Because I wanted what was rightfully mine. I wanted the house, and I wanted half the business. He wasn't prepared to give me either.'

'So Chanel, the maid, she served you both?'

Mrs Kwan nodded. 'She is our maid and also our cook. She prepared meals for both of us.'

'But you never ate together?'

Mrs Kwan laughed but here was a hard edge to her voice. 'Of course not. He could not bear to be in the same room as me.'

'She prepared your meals at the same time?'

Mrs Kwan frowned. 'I don't understand the question.'

'Did Chanel cook one meal and serve it to you separately? Or did she make individual meals?'

'Individual meals. We each told her what we wanted and when we wanted it.'

'And Chanel. Where is she now?'

Mrs Kwan nodded at the door. 'She has a room off the kitchen. She stays there when she is not working.'

'If you don't mind, I would like a word with her.'

'She didn't see the burglar, I'm sure of that,' said Mrs Kwan. 'She was in the kitchen when we heard the break in.' She looked across at Dr Mayang. 'That's right, isn't it?'

The doctor nodded in agreement.

'Who exactly was the last person to see your husband alive?' asked Inspector Zhang.

'That would have been Chanel. She took him in his cup of tea. He always drank a cup of hot Japanese green tea in the evening. She took him his tea at about five o'clock, I think.'

'And what about his evening meal?'

'My husband always ate early. He would have eaten at about four-thirty. You would have to ask Chanel, I really take no interest in my husband's eating habits.' She looked at her watch again and made a tutting sound.

'I need to have a conversation with her,' said Inspector Zhang. 'I would be grateful if you and Dr Mayang would remain here for a while longer.'

'I really must protest,' said Mrs Kwan tersely. 'It is most improper that I am being kept a prisoner in my own home.'

'I won't keep you for much longer,' said the inspector. He found the maid sitting in a small windowless room at the back of the kitchen. She was in her mid-thirties with nut brown skin and glossy black hair tied back in a ponytail. There was a small wooden cross on the wall above her tiny bed and below it were taped half a dozen photographs of two small children, a boy aged nine or ten and a girl a couple of years younger.

She had left the door open. Inspector Zhang could understand why, the room was hardly much bigger than the kitchen table, certainly smaller than any prison cell he'd ever seen. She looked up as he appeared at the door and began to get to her feet. She was wearing a white apron over a simple print dress and flat shoes that appeared to be made of plastic. She started to stand up but Inspector Zhang smiled and waved for her to remain sitting. He showed her his police identification. 'My name is Inspector Zhang and I just need to ask you a few questions,' he said.

'Am I in trouble?' she said. 'I cannot lose this job, Inspector, my children need the money I send home every month.' Her lower lip was trembling and she pulled a handkerchief from her apron and dabbed at her eyes.

Inspector Zhang smiled and shook his head. 'Of course you're not in trouble,' he said. 'I just have some questions, that's all. Can you tell me what happened earlier today?'

'About Dr Kwan, you mean?'

Inspector Zhang nodded. 'Yes,' he said. 'I understand you were the last person to see Dr Kwan alive?'

She nodded and dabbed at her eyes again. 'I served him beef noodles in the study at half past four. Then at five o'clock I took him his tea. He always drank tea in the evening as he listened to his music.'

'So you went into the study?'

She nodded tearfully.

'The door was locked, was it?'

'No, he always waited until I took him his tea before he began listening to his music. I would give him his tea and then he would lock the door.'

'So Mrs Kwan never made tea for her husband?'

Chanel shook her head. 'She didn't do anything for him. And he didn't do anything for her. They never even spoke to each other.'

'And where was Mrs Kwan while you were making Dr Kwan's tea?'

The maid frowned as she struggled to remember. 'I think she was in the kitchen.' She nodded. 'Yes, she was getting the glasses and wine ready for her visitor. It was red wine and she opened the bottle. She always opened red wine at least an hour before she drank it. She said red wine needs to breathe. Is that true, do you know?'

Inspector Zhang smiled. 'I think it is,' he said. 'Allowing air to come into contact with the wine makes it taste better.'

'That's what Mrs Kwan said.'

'So she was here with you in the kitchen?'

176

'Yes. She said she was expecting Dr Mayang and asked that I prepare some snacks once I had given Dr Kwan his tea.'

'What sort of snacks?'

'Cheese, crackers. Some spring rolls. Dr Mayang loves my spring rolls.'

'And you prepared the snacks after you had served Dr Kwan his tea?'

The maid nodded.

'What happened when you gave Dr Kwan his tea?' asked Inspector Zhang.

'I knocked on the door. He said to come in. I put the tea down on the table by his chair.'

'So you served him his tea and went back to the kitchen?'

'Yes, inspector.'

'And where was Mrs Kwan at his point?'

'She had gone to the sitting room.'

'And what did you do next?'

'I prepared the snacks as Mrs Kwan had asked.'

'How long did that take you?'

'About half an hour.'

'And during that time, Mrs Kwan was in the sitting room?'

'I think so,' said the maid.

'And what time did Dr Mayang arrive?'

'At just after six o'clock,' she said. 'I'm really not sure exactly.'

'You let Mrs Mayang in?'

The maid nodded. 'Yes. And I served the wine and the snacks and then came back here, to my room.'

'Your room is quite some distance from the sitting room,' said the inspector. 'How does Mrs Kwan summon you if you are needed?'

The maid smiled and pointed at a small metal box above the door. 'That is a bell, Sir. Mrs Kwan presses a button and it rings.'

'The button is in the sitting room?'

'It's a wireless system, Inspector. Mrs Kwan and Dr Kwan carry small beepers and when they press them the bell rings. Mrs Kwan's bell is like a real bell and Dr Kwan's is like a buzzer so I know who is ringing me and I go looking for them.'

'And you were in here when the window broke?'

The maid picked up a leather-bound book. 'I was reading my Bible,' she said.

'You didn't hear the window break? Or the scream?'

She put the Bible down on a small stool next to her bed. 'No,' she said.

'But you heard Mrs Kwan shouting?'

The maid frowned as she tried to remember. 'I don't think I heard her in the hallway but I heard her shouting when she came into the kitchen,' she said eventually.

'Mrs Kwan came here? You didn't go out to see what was happening?'

'Yes. She wanted to know where I was. She said that something had happened to Dr Kwan.'

'She said that? She said something had happened to her husband?'

The maid frowned again. 'I'm not sure,' she said. 'Maybe she said she had heard glass breaking. I'm sorry. It was all very frantic.'

'I'm sure it was,' said the inspector. 'So what happened then?'

'Mrs Kwan told me to go with her. She took me and Dr Mayang out of the kitchen door and out into the garden. That was when we saw that the window had been broken. We could see Dr Kwan in his chair. Mrs Kwan rushed over to him and then she screamed that he was dead.'

'You saw Dr Kwan in his chair? Are you sure? Think carefully, Chanel.'

178

The maid frowned and then shook her head. 'No, of course, we couldn't see anything from the terrace. It was only when we went inside that we saw the body.'

'And were the French windows open? Or closed?'

'Closed. Definitely closed.'

'And did you see anyone else in the garden?'

The maid shook her head and dabbed at her eyes again.

'And who called the police?'

'Dr Mayang. She used her mobile phone.'

'Did you call for an ambulance?'

The maid frowned. 'No. No, I didn't.'

'I thought that Mrs Kwan told you to call for an ambulance?'

The maid nodded quickly. 'Oh yes, sir, she did. But then Dr Mayang said that an ambulance wouldn't be necessary.'

'Had Dr and Mrs Kwan being arguing at all?' asked the inspector. 'Had they been fighting over the past day or two?'

'They didn't argue,' she said. 'They didn't speak. You know they were divorcing?'

Inspector Zhang nodded. 'Yes, I heard that.'

'I don't understand how couples can divorce,' she said. 'You marry for life, for better or worse, until death do you part.' She took a deep breath and then sighed. 'My husband died five years ago. Cancer.'

'I'm sorry to hear that,' said the inspector.

'Now I have to work in Singapore to make money for my children,' she said. 'I need this job, Inspector. Mrs Kwan won't sack me, will she?'

'I don't see why she would,' said Inspector Zhang. He stood up and thanked her before heading back to the sitting room. Sergeant Lee was waiting for him in the hallway. 'What did the Meteorological Society say?' he asked her

The sergeant looked at her notebook. 'There were two showers,' she said. 'The first started at two-forty-six and finished at three-

179

thirteen. The second shower started at five-fifteen this evening and finished at five-forty-two.'

'And that was all? Just the two showers?'

'Just the two,' she said.

The inspector smiled. 'Then we have our murderer,' he whispered.

'We do?' asked the sergeant.

The inspector's smile widened. 'Oh yes, most definitely,' he said.

He walked across the room to the sofa where the two women were sitting.

'Are we done yet?' asked Mrs Kwan, pointedly looking at her watch.

'Almost,' said Inspector Zhang.

Sergeant Lee came into the room, putting her notepad into her handbag.

'I really must insist that you leave us now, Inspector,' said Mrs Kwan. 'There are funeral arrangements to be arranged, I have to talk to the people who run our clinics. My husband's death is going to cause a lot of problems.'

'I'm sure that's true,' said the inspector. 'Perhaps you would be good enough to join me in your husband's study.'

Mrs Kwan and Dr Mayang both got to their feet but Inspector Zhang waved a hand at the doctor. 'There's no need for us to bother you, Dr Mayang,' he said. The doctor sat back on the sofa.

The forensic investigator was kneeling down in front of the body and he looked up as the inspector walked in.

'Have you dusted the handle of the knife for fingerprints, Mr Yuen?' asked Inspector Zhang.

'I have, but it's clean,' said the investigator. 'The killer must have been wearing gloves.'

'I think not,' said the inspector. He walked over to the side table next to Dr Kwan's chair and picked up a CD case. It was Jazz, a collection of songs by Ella Fitzgerald. 'Your husband was a fan of Jazz?' he asked Mrs Kwan.

Mrs Kwan nodded. 'I hated it. That was why he used his headphones.'

'That was considerate of him,' said Inspector Zhang.

'It had nothing to do with consideration,' said Mrs Kwan. 'He used to play his music at full volume all evening until the Judge told him to stop. Now if he plays music through the speakers he has to appear in court.'

Inspector Zhang opened the CD case. There was a CD inside. 'Ah, so he wasn't listening to Ella Fitzgerald. That's interesting.'

Mrs Kwan's face tightened.

'I wonder what he was listening to?' said the inspector. He put the case back on the side table. He walked over to the stereo system and ran his finger along a row of CDs. 'They all seem to be in place,' he said. 'The Ella Fitzgerald is the only case out. So I wonder what the good doctor was listening to?'

He turned to look at Mrs Kwan. Her face was ashen and she was fiddling with her wedding ring. 'Inspector Zhang, please…' she said.

'It would be better if you confessed now and at least showed some remorse,' said the inspector. 'The longer you allow this to go on, the worse it will be for you.'

Dr Mayang appeared in the doorway. 'What is going on?' she asked. The uniformed officer was standing behind her, his arms folded.

'I am about to arrest Mrs Kwan for the murder of her husband,' said Inspector Zhang.

'That is nonsense,' said the doctor. 'I was with her when her husband was attacked. We were both in the sitting room when we heard the glass smash and him scream.'

'Both those statements are true,' said the inspector. 'But that does not make her less of a murderer.' He frowned. 'Or murderess, I suppose I should say.'

'Inspector Zhang, it would have been physically impossible for Mrs Kwan to have been in two places at the same time.' She looked over at Mrs Kwan. 'Don't worry, Elsie, I shall be a witness for you. This is ridiculous.'

Tears were welling up in Mrs Kwan's eyes.

'Yes, you will indeed be a witness, Dr Mayang,' said Inspector Zhang. 'A witness to Mrs Kwan murdering her husband.'

'How can you say that, Inspector Zhang? Mrs Kwan was with me in the sitting room when her husband was killed.'

'That is what she wanted you to think, Dr Mayang. In fact Mrs Kwan went to a great deal of trouble to make it seem that she was drinking wine with you when her husband died. But that's not what actually happened. Is it, Mrs Kwan?'

Mrs Kwan said nothing.

'Very well,' said Inspector Zhang. 'There were two things I immediately noticed about the stereo,' he said to Dr Mayang. He pointed at the headphones which were still on Dr Kwan's head. 'The headphones were unplugged.'

'The plug could have come out during the struggle,' said Dr Mayang.

'Except there was no struggle,' said Inspector Zhang. 'Dr Kwan died where he sat, killed with one blow to the heart. There were no defensive wounds, so there was no struggle.'

Dr Mayang frowned as she stared at the headphone cable on the wooden floor.

'The second thing I noticed was that the volume dial was turned full on.' He pointed at the dial. 'That seemed unusual as it would have been deafening through the headphones. Until of course I realised that Dr Kwan wasn't in fact listening to music when he was killed.' He pressed the eject button on the CD player and there was a click and a whirr before the CD was ejected. Inspector Zhang took it out and held it up for them all to see. 'This is not a commercial music CD,' he said. 'It is a data storage CD. And I am certain that it contains no music at all.' He re-inserted the CD and pressed play. 'I am also certain that most of the CD is blank. The first forty-five minutes or so, at least.'

He used the fast-forward function to skip through the early section of the CD, then pressed the play button. 'If I am correct, there are only two things on this CD. Let us see.' He folded his arms and waited. Everyone in the room was now staring at the CD player.

The seconds ticked by and Inspector Zhang began to worry that he had been mistaken. But suddenly there was a loud crash through the speakers that made them all flinch. Three seconds later there was a blood-curdling scream. Inspector Zhang smiled and pressed the stop button.

Mrs Kwan slumped to the floor and Dr Mayang hurried over to her. The doctor helped Mrs Kwan over to a sofa and she sat there, sobbing.

'I don't understand,' said Dr Mayang.

'It is simple enough,' said Inspector Zhang. 'When you and Mrs Kwan were in the sitting room drinking wine and eating snacks, you did not hear the window break or Dr Kwan scream. You heard a recording, played at full volume over the stereo.'

'But what was Dr Kwan doing?" asked Dr Mayang.

'He was asleep,' said Inspector Zhang.

'Asleep?'

'Mrs Kwan had drugged her husband,' said Inspector Zhang. 'Probably using the sleeping tablets that you had prescribed for her. I am assuming she put them into the tea that the maid took to Mr Kwan. Then, when she was sure that he was drugged, she went around to the garden and broke the window. To make sure that she wasn't heard, I believe she used some sticky plastic to stick on the glass before she broke it. The only sound would be a dull crack, She then pulled the glass pieces off the plastic and placed them on the floor. I believe that she then pulled the headphones out of the stereo, turned the volume to maximum and placed the CD that she had made earlier into the CD player.'

'How did she make the CD?' asked Dr Mayang.

'It is not difficult,' said Inspector Zhang. 'The sound files can be downloaded from the internet and then burned onto a CD. The important thing was the timing. She had to time the sound effects so that they would be heard at the exact moment you and she were in the sitting room.'

Dr Mayang stared at Mrs Kwan in horror. 'Elsie, is this true?'

'You don't understand,' sobbed Mrs Kwan. 'I had no choice. He was killing me. My nerves, you know the state my nerves are in. I couldn't go on. I couldn't. I had to do something.'

'So you killed him,' said Inspector Zhang. 'You came around to the French windows and went inside while Dr Mayang and the maid remained on the terrace. You hurried over to Dr Kwan, bent over him, and you plunged the knife into his heart. You concealed the knife in one of the pockets of your suit, and you held it with your handkerchief so that your fingerprints would not be on the handle. You were a nurse, you knew exactly how to inflict a fatal wound. Then Dr Mayang came over in time to see Dr Kwan take his last breath. Dr Mayang was able to confirm that Dr Kwan had been only recently stabbed. Of course Dr Mayang assumed that the killer had only just fled, little did she know that the murderer was Mrs Kwan herself.'

He nodded at the uniformed officer. He went over to Mrs Kwan, took her arm, and led her out of the study. Dr Mayang followed.

'What made you first suspect that the break-in was staged?' asked Sergeant Lee. 'Everything suggested that someone had broken in from the outside.'

'Indeed,' said the Inspector. 'The glass was inside the house, as it should have been. But when I touched it, I noticed that some pieces stuck to my fingers.'

Sergeant Lee nodded. 'Yes, I remember that.'

'That made me think, how could the glass have become sticky? Then I realised that there was something on the glass that had made it sticky. Some sort of adhesive. Perhaps from some sort of plastic sheeting that had been applied to the window before it had been broken.'

'But why would anyone do that?'

'So that the glass could be broken silently,' said Inspector Zhang. 'Then the pieces of glass could be picked off the plastic and placed on the floor. But the question then was how could she do that with Dr

Kwan in the room. That's when I realised that Dr Kwan must have been drugged. And of course Mrs Kwan used to be a nurse so she would have known exactly how much medication to give him.'

Sergeant Lee frowned. 'But why didn't Mrs Kwan kill her husband then? She could have simply discovered the body later.'

'Because it was important that the doctor was there to testify that the body has only just been killed, that Mr Kwan had been stabbed while Mrs Kwan was drinking wine with Dr Mayang. And that brings me on to the rain. I asked you to check the time that the rain started and finished today. Do you recall?'

'Of course,' said the sergeant. She flicked through her notepad. 'The second rain shower started at five-fifteen this evening and finished at five-forty-two.' She looked up from her notepad. 'It was a brief shower.'

'Indeed it was,' said Inspector Zhang. 'Just twenty-seven minutes in fact. And you remember that the wooden floor was wet from the rain that had come in from the broken window?'

Sergeant Lee nodded.

'And what time was the body discovered?'

Sergeant Lee studied her notebook carefully before answering. 'Twenty past six,' she said. Her eyes widened. 'Of course,' she said.

Inspector Zhang beamed, pleased that she had worked it out for herself. He waited for her to continue.

'The rain had stopped before Dr Mayang heard the sound of breaking glass.'

'Exactly,' said Inspector Zhang.

'The body was discovered at twenty minutes past six, so they heard the window breaking shortly before that,' said Sergeant Lee. 'A minute or two at most. But it wasn't raining then. The rain had stopped. So it would have been impossible for rain to have blown into the room.' She was speaking so quickly in her excitement that the words were almost running into each other. 'But there were raindrops on the wooden floor which meant that the window had to have been broken sometime before the rain had stopped at five forty-two.' She snapped her notebook shut. She smiled over at the inspector. 'Well one

185

thing is for sure, Inspector Zhang. I shall never complain about the Monsoon season again.'

'Indeed,' said the inspector. 'It really is the case that every cloud has a silver lining.'

8.

INSPECTOR ZHANG GOES TO HARROGATE

Inspector Zhang climbed out of the taxi and held the door open for his wife. "It's lovely," said Mrs Zhang. "As pretty as the picture in the brochure." They were standing outside The Mallard Hotel in Harrogate. They had taken the train up from London and caught the taxi at the station. The driver was a man in his sixties with a flat cap and an accent that Inspector Zhang had great trouble understanding. The driver went to the boot and took out their suitcases, pocketed Inspector Zhang's ten pound note and drove off.

"I can't believe we're really here," said Inspector Zhang. The hotel was built of local Yorkshire stone and covered with ivy; two three-storey wings either side of a columned entrance.

"It's like a dream, isn't it?" said his wife. Inspector Zhang nodded in agreement. The hotel was truly beautiful and unlike anything in their native Singapore.

"It is the best birthday present ever," said Inspector Zhang. "I can't believe you arranged it all without me knowing. I didn't realise what a secretive wife I have."

"I wanted to do something special for you," said Mrs Zhang, "something you would never forget."

Inspector Zhang smiled at her. "Well you've achieved your objective," he said.

"Oh my goodness, what's that?" said Mrs Zhang, pointing to the driveway.

Inspector Zhang turned to look. There was a white painted outline of a body on the Tarmac. He chuckled. "It's a mystery writers' convention," he said. 'It's a joke."

"I'm not sure the outline of a dead body is a laughing matter," said Mrs Zhang.

"I doubt that there are many real murders here in Harrogate," said Inspector Zhang, picking up their cases. They walked up the stairs to the reception where an efficient young woman in a black suit checked them in. On the opposite side of the room three tables had been lined up and several young women were standing behind them wearing black t-shirts with the words "Harrogate Mystery Writers' Convention".

On the walls were posters of best-selling mystery writers, and Inspector Zhang recognised many of the names including Val McDermid, Peter Robinson, and Jo Nesbo. The convention was a coming together of some of the best mystery writers in the world and Inspector Zhang had always dreamed of one day attending. His wife had booked Business Class tickets on Singapore Airlines, hotels in London and Harrogate, and gotten him tickets to the convention without once letting slip what she had done. She had presented the tickets to him on his birthday a week earlier and he had almost fallen off his chair at the breakfast table. He looked over at his wife and for the thousandth time felt the urge to hug her and tell her how much he loved her. She caught him smiling at her. "What?" she said.

"I just want to thank you for the best birthday present I have ever been given," he said.

She blushed and averted her eyes. He was about to take her in his arms when the receptionist handed him his room key and pointed at the staircase. Inspector Zhang thanked her, slid the key into his pocket and picked up the suitcases. "I should register now, before we go up," he said, and he carried the cases over to a table above which was a large poster that read "Welcome To The Harrogate Mystery Writers' Convention". A blonde woman with lipstick Inspector Zhang thought was a little too red took the tickets from him, asked them to sign their names on a list on a clipboard, and handed over two nametags and two large black carrier bags. "The nametags allow you admittance to all our events," she said. "Except for the murder mystery lunch tomorrow."

"Oh that's all right, we have tickets for that," said Mrs Zhang.

Inspector Zhang gave the nametags and the bags to his wife, picked up the cases and together they went upstairs. Their room was in the left wing of the hotel, overlooking the lawns at the front. Inspector Zhang put down the cases and looked around the room thoughtfully. 'It is quaint,' he said. "Just as I imagined."

"It's lovely," said Mrs Zhang. She put the two carrier bags on the bed and went through to the bathroom. "Oh my goodness, come and look at this," she said. Inspector Zhang joined her in the large, airy bathroom. Against the wall was a massive cast iron bath with clawed legs and above it, hanging from the ceiling, was a large shower head the size of a dinner plate. A shower curtain hung from a stainless steel rail. It could be drawn all the way around the bath to stop water spraying over the tiled floor. "Have you ever seen a bath like that?" said Mrs Zhang. "It must be a hundred years old."

"It is a copy, I'm sure," said Inspector Zhang. "But it is impressive."

Mrs Zhang went back into the bedroom and emptied one of the carrier bags. There were half a dozen books, a brochure for the convention, a map of Harrogate, a bar of chocolate, and a pair of black handcuffs." She laughed and held up the handcuffs. "What on earth are these for?"

"They're handcuffs."

"I can see that," she said. "Why are they giving us handcuffs?"

Inspector Zhang took them from her and examined a small label on one of the cuffs. "It's a promotional device," he said, "publicising a book." He raised his eyebrows. "Held To Ransom by Sean Hyde. I didn't realise he had a new book out."

"It's here," said Mrs Zhang, holding up one of the hardbacks.

Inspector Zhang took it from her and flicked through it. "Excellent," he said. "This can be my bedtime reading."

"Well I hope we haven't come all this way just so you can read in bed," said Mrs Zhang coyly.

Inspector Zhang chuckled and looked at her over the top of his spectacles. Mrs Zhang looked away, a little flustered, and picked up the convention brochure. "Oh, he's talking on the next panel," she said.

"Mr Hyde?"

Mrs Zhang nodded and gave him the brochure. "You should go," she said. She nodded at the book he was holding. "You should get him to sign it for you."

"Aren't you coming?"

"I'm tired," she said. "I think the jet-lag is catching up on me. I'll have a bath and a nap and then I'll be ready for the evening events."

Inspector Zhang kissed his wife on the cheek and headed downstairs. Most of the convention events took place in the ballroom of the hotel. Two girls in convention t-shirts were closing the doors as he arrived but they smiled and allowed him to slip inside. There were more than a thousand people sitting in rows facing a stage on which there were already five people seated in armchairs.

Inspector Zhang spotted an empty chair about ten rows from the front and he made his way to it. Just as he sat down, the man sitting in the middle chair on the stage began his introduction. He was a well known local TV presenter and the panel was to discuss the changing face of publishing, especially the way in which eBooks had taken a larger share of the market. Sean Hyde was on the panel, along with a horror writer Inspector Zhang had never heard of. His name was Sebastian Battersby and he had a purple and green mohawk haircut that gave him the look of a peacock.

There was an agent on the panel, a jovial man in his fifties, and a middle-aged woman who represented a major publishing firm.

Inspector Zhang wasn't a fan of eBooks. He had toyed with the idea of buying a Kindle but had decided against it. He loved the feel of books, and their smell. He liked to be able to sit and look at his overflowing bookshelves though he appreciated the convenience of a device that allowed him to have hundreds of books available at the press of a button.

Inspector Zhang was a big fan of Sean Hyde's mysteries, but he hadn't realised he was also a very successful eBook publisher. He had sold almost a million eBooks that year, a fact which the rest of the panel clearly resented. The key to his success, according to the TV presenter, was that he sold his eBooks cheaply – much cheaper than a regular paperback – and marketed and promoted them aggressively.

The discussion very quickly turned into a spirited argument, with the three other panellists arguing that Mr Hyde was devaluing books by selling them so cheaply. Mr Hyde argued his case well, suggesting that agents and publishers needed to adapt to the new technologies that were revolutionising publishing and that writers like Mr Battersby had to understand that publishing was now all about the readers and that writers had to supply well-written books at the right price. Badly-written over-priced books were doomed to fail, said Mr Hyde, at which Mr Battersby sat back, folded his arms and glared at Mr Hyde with undisguised hostility.

"You're killing publishing for everyone, you bastard!"

Everyone turned to see who had shouted the abuse. A middle-aged man in green cargo pants and a blue polo-shirt was walking towards the stage, his arm outstretched as he pointed at Mr Hyde.

"You're a liar, you're a cheat, you sell crap to people who are too stupid to know what they're buying." The man whirled around and shouted at the audience. "Can't you see what he's doing? He wants everyone to get their books for free. He's killing publishing, killing it for everyone."

Mr Hyde stood up and held up his hands. "I have to apologise for the interruption, ladies and gentlemen. Mr Dumbleton here is my resident stalker. When he isn't screaming abuse at me in public he's hounding me on Twitter and various blogs."

"Your books are shit!" shouted the man. "People only buy them because they're cheap!" Two young men in convention t-shirts walked up behind him. One of them reached for Dumbleton's arm but he shook him away, his face contorted into a savage snarl.

"People have a choice," said Mr Hyde. "They can get my eBooks for less than the price of a cup of coffee, or they can pay seven quid for one of your awful paperbacks. The fact that you sell so few shows that they are choosing not to buy yours. That's not my fault. You need to write better books."

"I'm a better writer than you'll ever be!" shouted Mr Dumbleton.

"If that's true, why did you sell fewer than a thousand books last year?" said Mr Hyde calmly. "For every paperback you sell, I sell a thousand eBooks. "

Mr Dumbleton jabbed his finger at Mr Hyde. "I'll kill you, Hyde! I swear to God I'll kill you!"

The two convention workers put their hands on Dumbleton's shoulders. "Don't touch me!" he yelled, then turned and stormed out of the hall.

Mr Hyde sat down and smiled at the TV presenter. "Now where were we before we were so rudely interrupted?" he said. The audience burst into applause.

The rest of the session went smoothly, though it was clear that the rest of the panel resented Mr Hyde's views on the future of publishing. When the session came to a close, the TV presenter thanked everyone and announced that Mr Hyde and Mr Battersby would be signing copies in the temporary bookshop that had been set up in a room outside along the corridor.

There was a long queue of people waiting to get their books signed and Inspector Zhang joined it. Most people seemed to want Mr Hyde's signature and Sebastian Battersby was sitting back in his chair, toying with his unused pen.

It took Inspector Zhang fifteen minutes to reach the front of the queue. He held out his book and Mr Hyde smiled up at him. "Who shall I make it out to?" asked Mr Hyde.

"To Inspector Zhang. I am a huge fan. I have been for years."

"That's good to hear, Inspector Zhang. So you are a policeman? From Hong Kong?"

"From Singapore. I am a Detective Inspector with the Singapore Police Force."

Mr Hyde signed the book with a flourish and handed it back. "And you came all the way to Harrogate for the conference?"

"I am a huge fan of mysteries, I have been ever since I was a child," said Inspector Zhang.

"Well you're certainly in the right job," said Mr Hyde.

"Sadly not," said Inspector Zhang. "There are very few mysteries in Singapore. That's not to say low crime means no crime, but generally there are few surprises." He took, the book from Mr Hyde and thanked him. "I have to ask, what happened at the panel, does that sort of thing happen a lot?"

"Archibald Dumbleton, the idiot who screamed at me? He's a bit of a stalker, I'm afraid. It's not the first time he's threatened me," said Mr Hyde.

"Why is he so angry at you?"

Mr Hyde shrugged. "He's a spectacularly unsuccessful writer," he said. "The advent of eBooks has changed the business of publishing. Some writers are adapting and some are struggling. Dumbleton is struggling. I sold a million eBooks last year. Dumbleton sold fewer than three thousand paperbacks. With sales that low it's only a matter of time before his publisher drops him. He knows that so he's taking his resentment out on me."

"And he's said he wants to kill you before?'

"That's the first time he's made a death threat, but he's made all sorts of allegations online. He's called me a paedophile, a cyber-bully, a fraud. He tweets about me several dozen times a day, he's written to my publisher, my agent, my accountant. He's published personal details about my home and my family on-line." Mr Hyde shrugged. "I think he's got mental problems."

"What about talking to the police?"

Mr Hyde chuckled. "I don't know what the police are like in Singapore, but here in the UK bullied best-selling authors are a low priority."

"Bullshit!" hissed Sebastian Battersby. "You're killing publishing and you're taking us all down with you." Mr Battersby's face was contorted with anger and his hands had bunched into fists.

Mr Hyde turned to look at him. "You're just bitter because your sales are as bad as his."

"And whose fault is that?" said Mr Battersby. "You're devaluing books. Once people expect to pay less than a quid for a book how are we supposed to earn a living?"

"By selling more books," said Mr Hyde. "By writing better books instead of the crap you're writing now."

"My books aren't crap!" shouted Mr Battersby, slamming his hands down so hard on the table that Inspector Zhang flinched and took a step backwards.

"Come on now, Sebastian, your sales figures speak for themselves. You write horror schlock and the Great British public isn't buying it. They wouldn't read your stuff if you gave it away."

"Bullshit!"

"So you said. The simple fact is you've got no future as an author, your publisher knows that and so do you. It's time you started looking for another line of work."

Mr Battersby stood up, his eyes blazing. He raised his pen, holding it like a dagger, as if he was about to plunge it into Mr Hyde's eye.

Mr Hyde looked up at Mr Battersby and smiled tightly. "What are you going to do, Sebastian? Stab me? In front of a room full of witnesses? This isn't a cheap horror novel. This is the real world. And despite all the murders in your books, you're a wimp at heart."

Mr Battersby sneered at Mr Hyde, his hand trembling, and for a moment Inspector Zhang thought he really was about to stab the author. Then he grunted, threw the pen on the floor and stormed out.

Mr Hyde smiled up at Inspector Zhang. "Sticks and stones," he said. "Sometimes writers start to think they're characters in their own story."

"He is very angry."

"He's losing his livelihood. For years the key to being a professional writer was having a publisher. Those writers lucky enough to be selected by the publishers made money. But with eBooks a writer can sell direct to his readers. Now anyone can challenge the exclusive little club that Battersby and Dumbleton belonged to and that scares them." He pointed with his pen at the growing line of people waiting to have their books autographed. "Anyway, I have books to sign. It's been a pleasure talking to you, Inspector Zhang. Enjoy the conference."

Inspector Zhang thanked him and went back to reception. He saw Mr Battersby and Mr Dumbleton standing outside the hotel, smoking cigarettes, deep in conversation.

He went upstairs. Mrs Zhang was lying on the bed but she opened her eyes when he walked in. "How did it go?"

"Interesting," he said, slipping off his shoes. He held up the book. "Mr Hyde signed it for me."

"How lovely," she said.

"I thought we could have lunch and then see a few of the afternoon panels together. Val McDermid is speaking and I'd love to see her." He took off his jacket, draped it over the back of a chair, and lay down next to his wife. "But first, I think I should thank you for my wonderful birthday present."

He slipped his arms around her and kissed her on the back of her neck. She giggled and pressed herself against him.

Later, Inspector Zhang had lunch with his wife and then they spent the afternoon listening to some of the best mystery writers in the world talking about their craft. They had dinner together and then spent an enjoyable evening in the hotel bar talking to mystery novel enthusiasts.

Inspector Zhang and his wife were up early the following morning. They had breakfast, took a short walk around the town, and attended three panels discussing various aspects of mystery writing. By the time they broke for lunch Inspector Zhang had another six signed copies from authors he'd long admired.

Lunch was a special event, billed as a Murder Mystery Meal. There were twenty tables, each hosted by a writer, and during the meal actors were to play the part of various characters involved in a murder. At the end of the meal each table was to decide who the killer was, and there would be prizes for the winners.

The writer hosting Inspector Zhang's table was a young woman from Scotland who had written a historical murder mystery. There were free copies of her book for everybody. As he took his place at the table, Inspector Zhang saw Sebastian Battersby at the neighbouring table, and on the other side of the room, close to the main table, he saw Archibald Dumbleton. There was no sign of Mr Hyde.

There were eight people on each table, including the writer. On Inspector Zhang's left were two middle-aged sisters, and sitting next to Mrs Zhang was an elderly headmaster from Taunton. Opposite Inspector Zhang were a young couple in their twenties, a young man with shoulder-length blond hair and his girlfriend who had a crew cut and wide shoulders.

The starter was smoked salmon, and as the plates were being cleared away the master of ceremonies introduced the four characters who were the suspects in a murder that had just occurred in a greenhouse on the hotel grounds.

There was Professor Green, a sixty-something balding man in a tweed jacket; Doctor Miller, who was staying at the hotel with his wife;. Miss Susan Smith who was one of a dozen writers attending a creative writing course at the hotel, and Dick Reynolds, a convict who had recently been released from prison where he had written a best-selling gangster novel.

The master of ceremonies explained that the body of an agent had been found in the greenhouse, to which there were cries of "shame!" and a ripple of laughter. The agent had been stabbed with a shard of glass, and the four characters were all suspects. The four suspects then took turns to explain who they were, and where they had been at the time of the murder.

Most of the diners at Inspector Zhang's table scribbled notes on their menus, but he just sat and listened with a quiet smile on his face. "Isn't this fun?" asked his wife.

Inspector Zhang nodded. "It is very amusing," he agreed.

The main course was roast chicken with vegetables and a yellowish sauce that Inspector Zhang found quite pleasant. Once the plates were removed another actor stood up and revealed himself to be a forensic analyst. He then proceeded to go over the physical evidence in the case, including the fingerprints found on the glass shard used to kill the agent, footprints in a flowerbed outside the greenhouse, and an analysis of blood on a handkerchief that had been found in Miss Smith's handbag.

As the actor was coming to the end of his presentation, a chambermaid pushed open the doors and hurried across the room, clearly distraught. She rushed over to a tall man in a dark suit who Inspector Zhang recognised as the hotel manager. The manager was standing close to Inspector Zhang's table and as the worried woman spoke to him he heard the words "dead body" and "hanging".

The manager put his am around the woman's shoulder and walked with her to the door. Inspector Zhang stood up. "What's wrong?" asked his wife.

"Somebody has died," he said.

"Yes, dear, I know. And we have to find out who the killer is."

Inspector Zhang gestured at the manager and the chambermaid. "No, I think there has been a death in the hotel. I won't be long." He hurried out of the room and caught up with the manager and the chambermaid at the bottom of the stairs. "Is there a problem?" he asked the manager.

"Nothing for you to worry about, Sir," said the manager. He was in his forties, tall and with a suntan that looked as if it was from a bottle rather than the sun.

"I am a police officer," said Inspector Zhang. "If there has been a death there are certain procedures that need to be followed."

"You work here in Harrogate?" asked the manager.

Inspector Zhang shook his head. "I am from Singapore but I am sure the procedure is the same. The local police must be called and the body must not be touched. Can you tell me what has happened?"

"He's hanged himself, that's what's happened," said the chambermaid.

"I'm just going to check the room now," said the manager.

"That is fine, but the body mustn't be touched."

The manager went over to the reception desk and told the receptionist to call the police, then he headed up the stairs with the chambermaid and Inspector Zhang in tow.

"I heard a thump when I was in the corridor, but I didn't think anything of it," said the chambermaid. "Then when I opened the door to clean the room, he was there. Dead. Hanging, he was. It was horrible."

There were a dozen people standing in the corridor, peering into the room.

"Excuse me please," said the manager, pushing his way through.

Inspector Zhang followed him into the room. The chambermaid stood in the doorway as if she couldn't bring herself to step over the threshold.

The body was hanging from the bathroom door and Inspector Zhang realised with a jolt that it was Mr Hyde. There was a rope looped around his neck that went over the top of the door. He was wearing grey trousers and a white shirt and there was a damp patch on the front of his trousers from where the bladder had emptied.

To the left of the door was an upturned chair that Mr Hyde had obviously been standing on.

"Suicide," said the manager, shaking his head. "Don't people realise the trouble they cause when they kill themselves in a hotel?"

"I'm sure that's the last thing on their minds," said Inspector Zhang. He peered around the bathroom door. The other end of the rope was tied around the door handle.

"I mean, if someone wanted to kill themselves, why not do it at home?"

Inspector Zhang ignored the manager and stared at the body. There was no doubt Mr Hyde was dead so there was no rush to get the body down. There was something not right about the way the man's hands were stuck behind his back and Inspector Zhang gently moved the body to get a better look. The man's wrists were handcuffed with what appeared to be a pair of cuffs that had been in the convention's welcome bag.

Inspector Zhang felt a nudge against his shoulder and he turned to see a middle-aged women peering at the body. "I've never seen a dead body before," she said.

"Madam, please, I must ask you to move away," said Inspector Zhang. He turned to see that there were now more than a dozen people crowding into the room. He raised his hand. "Everyone needs to get out of this room immediately," he said. "This is a potential crime scene."

"This is clearly a suicide," said the manager. "How can it be a crime scene?"

"It is a sudden and unexpected death. It is up to the local police to decide whether it is suicide, and until that decision has been made this room remains a crime scene."

The manager opened his mouth as if he was about to argue with the inspector, but then he seemed to accept the logic of his argument. He held up his hands and addressed the twelve or so people in the room. "Ladies and gentlemen, could you please make your way back into the corridor." No one paid him any attention, so he repeated his request in a louder voice. He held his arms out and ushered the onlookers from the room.

"Why is he staying?" asked a young man with shoulder-length hair and a Mexican-style moustache.

"He's a policeman," said the manager.

"He's Chinese."

"I am Singaporean," said Inspector Zhang. "It is important that you leave as there could be evidence on the floor."

"Please ladies and gentlemen, can you all move outside," shouted the manager, with more authority in his voice this time. The onlookers gradually did as they were told. When the last one left the room, the manager followed and pulled the door closed behind him.

Inspector Zhang heard the manager asking everyone to go downstairs where they would be given free coffee and tea. He looked around the room and noticed a crumpled handkerchief lying on the floor by the desk. He knelt down beside it and took a pen from his jacket pocket. He used it to carefully move the handkerchief.

The door opened and the manager reappeared. "They've gone downstairs," he said. He walked over and peered down at the handkerchief. "What's that?" he asked, reaching for it.

Inspector Zhang pushed his hand away. "That is evidence and it must stay where it is," he said. The manager apologised as Inspector Zhang straightened up "Perhaps you could wait downstairs and bring up the local police when they arrive," said the inspector.

"What about you?" asked the manager. "Should you be in here?"

"I am familiar with the procedure necessary to maintain the integrity of a crime scene,' said Inspector Zhang, "and some evidence can degrade quickly. For instance the handkerchief was damp in places and flecked with what appears to be saliva. That could well have dried by the time the police arrive."

The manager nodded. "You think the handkerchief was in his mouth?"

"Perhaps," said Inspector Zhang. "But DNA analysis will tell us for sure. Now please, if you will..." He motioned at the door. The manager left and closed the door behind him.

Inspector Zhang went over to the upturned chair and carefully examined it. Then for the next fifteen minutes he walked slowly around the room looking for a note or any indication of why Mr Hyde might have taken his own life. He reached the window that overlooked the front of the hotel. A nondescript grey saloon had just parked and two men were climbing out. They had the same world-weary look of detectives the world over, men who were used to seeing the bad in people, who expected to be lied to and who were rarely disappointed. One of them slammed the driver's door and looked up at the hotel. He was in his fifties, probably about the same age as Inspector Zhang. But whereas Inspector Zhang had a full head of hair that was only starting to grey at the temples, the British detective was almost bald. He was wearing a grey suit the jacket of which flapped in the wind. His colleague was younger and taller, but also losing his hair. He appeared to be wearing the better suit, a dark blue pin-stripe. As Inspector Zhang watched, the two men walked towards the hotel entrance.

Inspector Zhang went over to the bathroom door and squeezed past the body, taking care not to touch it. He looked around the bathroom, then went back to the bedroom and opened the door. The two detectives were standing there with the manager behind them.

The detective in the grey suit frowned at Inspector Zhang. "Who the hell are you and what are you doing in this room?"

"I am Inspector Zhang of the Singapore Police Force," said Inspector Zhang. He took out his wallet and showed them his warrant card, but the detective ignored it.

"What are you doing here?" repeated the detective.

"Inspector Zhang said he wanted to make sure that evidence wasn't disturbed," explained the manager, wringing his hands.

"It is important to preserve the crime scene," said Inspector Zhang.

"Crime scene? I was told Mr Hyde had killed himself," said the detective.

"That is certainly what it looks like," said Inspector Zhang, opening the door wide. The two English detectives walked into the room and looked at the body hanging from the bathroom door. "But one can never be too careful when one has a sudden death."

"You haven't touched anything?" asked the detective.

Inspector Zhang shook his head. "Of course not."

The detective nodded as if he wasn't sure Inspector Zhang was telling the truth. "I'm Chief Inspector Hawthorne," he said. He nodded at the younger detective. "This is Sergeant Bolton."

Inspector Zhang shook hands with the two men. "Have you had a chance to talk to the chambermaid?" asked Inspector Zhang. "She discovered the body."

The two detectives looked at the manager. He nodded. "Maria. She's down in the housekeeping office. She's a bit shocked, obviously. She was in the corridor outside the room and remembers hearing a thump, probably the chair falling over. But there was no other sound so she thought nothing of it."

"What time would that have been?" asked the Chief Inspector.

"She went in to clear the room at two-fifteen. She said she heard the thumping sound a few minutes before that."

Chief Inspector Hawthorne walked over to the bathroom door and looked up at the body.

"His name is Sean Hyde, he's one of the writers who was appearing at the conference," said Inspector Zhang. He saw that the sergeant was about to tread on the handkerchief and he hurried over to him. "Be careful please, Sergeant. I think that handkerchief was in Mr Hyde's mouth at some point."

The chief inspector walked over and looked down at the handkerchief. "Are you sure?" he said, taking a pair of blue latex gloves from his pocket.

"It was damp, and screwed up," said Inspector Zhang.

The chief inspector took a polythene evidence bag from his pocket, picked up the handkerchief and placed it inside. He went back to the bathroom door and carefully pushed it open so he could examine the end of the rope that was tied to the handle.

"There is no note," said Inspector Zhang.

"Suicides don't always leave notes," said the chief inspector. He walked out of the bathroom and examined the chair. Then he turned to look at the body. He frowned, then peered behind the body. "Handcuffs?" he said.

"Handcuffs?" repeated the sergeant, looking up from his notebook.

"They were given to everyone attending the convention," said Inspector Zhang. "A promotional gimmick. I have a pair myself."

"So he stood on the chair, put the noose around his neck, handcuffed himself and then rocked the chair until he fell. Suicide."

"I am not so sure," said Inspector Zhang.

"Why not?' asked the chief inspector. "Mr Hyde was in the room alone when he died. It can only have been suicide."

"He was certainly alone in the room," said Inspector Zhang. "But that doesn't mean it was definitely suicide."

The chief inspector frowned. "I don't follow you, Inspector Zhang."

The Singaporean detective shrugged. "There are suicides that look like murder, and murders that appear to be suicide," he said.

The sergeant laughed. "You're saying he was murdered? Just because you are at a mystery writers convention doesn't mean this is a mystery to be solved."

"I'm merely suggesting things are not always as they seem," said Inspector Zhang. "As I said, there is no note. That is always a red flag for me."

"Not all suicides leave notes," repeated the chief inspector.

"But most do," said Inspector Zhang. "And it seems to me that a man who made his living from words would take the opportunity for one final page. Also, when I spoke with Mr Hyde yesterday he didn't strike me as the type to kill himself."

"The type?" queried the chief inspector.

"He didn't seem the least bit depressed," said Inspector Zhang. "In fact when he was on the panel he told us all the plot of the new book he was working on. He certainly wasn't suicidal at that point."

"So if he didn't kill himself, who did?" asked the chief inspector.

"There are several suspects," said Inspector Zhang. "Indeed, there was one man who threatened to kill Mr Hyde in front of a room full of witnesses."

The sergeant looked up from his notebook. "Really? Who?"

"Another writer called Archibald Dumbleton. Frankly I think he might be unbalanced. He interrupted one of the panel discussions, accused Mr Hyde of all sorts of things and then threatened to kill him."

"Is this Mr Dumbleton still here?" asked the chief inspector.

"I saw him downstairs at the Murder Mystery lunch," said Inspector Zhang.

"And you said there were other suspects, Inspector Chang?" asked the chief inspector.

"It is Zhang," said Inspector Zhang. "Not necessarily suspects, but there were certainly others who were unhappy with Mr Hyde. He appeared to have inspired considerable jealousy and hostility in quite a few people."

"Oh really? And how did he manage that?"

"I gather that Mr Hyde had been very successful at publishing cheap eBooks. Several members of the audience seemed to think he was selling them too cheap, and others disagreed strongly with his views on marketing."

"Anyone in particular come to mind?" asked the chief inspector.

"There was an author on the panel with Mr Hyde. A Mr Sebastian Battersby, I think his name was. He had one of those punk rocker haircuts. He was very aggressive and at one point I thought he was going to strike Mr Hyde with his pen."

The sergeant chuckled. "They do say it's mightier than the sword," he said.

The chief inspector flashed him a warning look and the smile disappeared from the sergeant's face. "Why was that?" the chief inspector asked Inspector Zhang. "What were they fighting about?"

"Mr Hyde pointed out how few books Mr Battersby was selling and suggested he wasn't likely to get a new deal from his publisher. Mr Battersby took offence to that. But it couldn't have been Mr Battersby, he was at the table next to mine at lunch and I didn't see him leave at any point."

"Anyone else?"

"There was an agent on the panel. I forget what his name was. But Mr Hyde told him that agents didn't have much of a future and they got into quite a heated argument."

"So basically this Mr Hyde wasn't exactly winning friends and influencing people?"

Inspector Zhang frowned, not understanding the reference.

"He was making enemies, that's what you're saying," said the chief inspector.

"I think so. Yes."

"But do you really think any of these people were angry enough to kill Mr Hyde?"

"Who knows what drives a person to kill?" said Inspector Zhang. "Sometimes it can be the slightest thing."

The sergeant put away his notebook and folded his arms.

"The thing is Inspector Zhang, we have what looks like a suicide and no real motive for it to be anything other than that," said the chief inspector.

"The handcuffs worry me," said Inspector Zhang. "Why would he handcuff himself?"

"To make sure that he couldn't help himself?" said the sergeant. "He could have handcuffed his own hands behind his back then kicked away the chair, knowing that with his hands cuffed it would be a sure thing."

"Have you ever known someone to kill themselves in such a manner? Handcuffing themselves first?"

"I've seen a man cut his wrists and hang himself," said the sergeant.

Inspector Zhang nodded thoughtfully, then looked across at Chief Inspector Hawthorne. "And what about the handkerchief?" he said, nodding at the evidence bag in the detective's hand. "Why would he put that in his mouth and then spit it out?"

"We don't know for sure it was in his mouth," said Chief Inspector Hawthorne. "We'll have to wait for the DNA results and the way the lab is backed up that could be a week or more?"

"Backed up?" repeated Inspector Zhang. In Singapore all forensic tests were completed within twenty-four hours, and usually the results came back on the same day.

"They're busy. Even if I put a rush on it, it'll take a week or so. But here's the thing, Inspector Zhang. If Mr Hyde did indeed have the handkerchief in his mouth, why did he spit it out?"

"I have been asking myself the very same question." Inspector Zhang shrugged. "I do not know."

"And if it was in his mouth, why didn't he call for help once he had spat it out?" He looked over at the manager. "Did the chambermaid hear anything?"

The manager shook his head. "No shouting. Just a thump, she said. Probably the chair falling over."

"But no shouts?"

"No. Nothing like that."

"And did she see anyone entering or leaving the room?"

"I asked her that and she said no, no one," said the manager.

The chief inspector looked at Inspector Zhang and shrugged. "So Mr Hyde was alone in the room, and at no point did he cry out for help."

"I agree, it is a mystery," said Inspector Zhang.

"In Singapore you might describe it as a mystery, but here in England we call it suicide, plain and simple."

"If you say so, chief inspector."

Chief Inspector Hawthorne sighed and shook his head. "It isn't a matter of what I say, it's about looking at the facts," he said. "I don't know how you go about things in Singapore but in England we base our conclusions on facts and not feelings. And the facts in this case are that the door was closed, as was the window. No one left the room by the door and the window is locked. The window and the door are the only way into the room, therefore Mr Hyde was alone when he died. If he was alone, then it can only have been suicide."

Inspector Zhang shrugged but said nothing.

The chief inspector held up the evidence bag. "Whether or not Mr Hyde's DNA is on this handkerchief doesn't change anything. Nor does the fact that there was no note."

"I understand," said Inspector Zhang. "But bearing in mind the threats made by Mr Dumbleton yesterday, I wonder if it might be worth interviewing him."

"Do you now?"

Inspector Zhang smiled, took a red handkerchief from his pocket, removed his spectacles and began to polish them. "I am being a nuisance, I understand that. And I know I am simply a visitor to your country."

"I appreciate your professionalism," said the chief inspector. "And your enthusiasm. But sometimes things are exactly as they seem."

"I wonder if I might ask you to grant me the professional courtesy of at least asking Mr Dumbleton a few questions," said Inspector Zhang.

"I'm not sure that's appropriate," said the chief inspector.

"Considering the threats that Mr Dumbleton made, he must surely be considered a suspect. And I was a witness to those threats."

The chief inspector rubbed his chin and sighed. "I suppose it couldn't hurt," he said. "But as an observer only, is that clear?"

"As crystal," said Inspector Zhang. He put his glasses back on and smiled amiably.

"Then let's go and talk to him. You said he was at a lunch?"

"The Murder Mystery Meal. In the banqueting hall on the ground floor."

The chief inspector opened the door. There were still half a dozen people in the corridor. "Please, will you all go downstairs," he said. "There is nothing here to see." He turned to his sergeant. "You'd better stay here until the doctor arrives," he said. The sergeant closed the door, stood with his back to it and folded his arms.

The chief inspector went downstairs with Inspector Zhang and the manager. When they got to the ballroom they found it was almost empty, though Mrs Zhang was still sitting at her table. She waved and came over to him.

"What happened?" asked Inspector Zhang. "Where is everyone?"

"When they heard that Mr Hyde had killed himself, they decided to bring the lunch to an end," she said. "He had a lot of friends here and everyone was a bit shocked."

The chief inspector turned to the manager. "See if you can find out where Mr Dumbleton is now," he said. The manager nodded and hurried off to reception.

"Is it true, did Mr Hyde kill himself?" asked Mrs Zhang.

"It seems that way," said the chief inspector.

"I'm sorry, this is my wife," said Inspector Zhang.

The chief inspector shook her hand. "A pleasure to meet you, Mrs Zhang. My name is Chief Inspector Hawthorne."

"I'm sure my husband will be a big help in your investigation," she said. "He is the best detective in Singapore."

Before the chief inspector could reply, the manager returned. "Mr Dumbleton is in his room."

"Let's go and have a word, then," said the chief inspector. He and Inspector Zhang followed the manager up to the top floor and along the corridor to Mr Dumbleton's room. Chief Inspector Hawthorne knocked on the door and after a few seconds Dumbleton opened it. The chief inspector showed Dumbleton his warrant card and he let them into his room. The manager waited in the corridor and Inspector Zhang left the door ajar.

"You have heard that Mr Hyde died in his room earlier this afternoon?" asked the chief inspector.

Dumbleton nodded. "Hanged himself, didn't he?"

"Can you tell me where you were at about two o'clock?"

"I was at the murder mystery lunch," said Dumbleton.

"At which table?" asked Inspector Zhang.

Chief Inspector Hawthorne flashed him a withering look and Inspector Zhang held up his hands.

"If you could tell us the table number and anyone you know who was sitting with you," said the chief inspector.

"You think I had something to do with Hyde's death? It was suicide, wasn't it?"

"Please Mr Dumbleton, just tell us what table you were at."

"I forget," said Mr Dumbleton. "Twenty-two, I think. I was guest writer at the table and the rest were punters. There were a couple of middle-aged ladies, a married couple from Durham, a wannabe writer from Liverpool and a couple of pensioners. They were local, I think."

Inspector Zhang had wandered over to the bedside table. There were two yellow ear plugs sitting next to a clock radio. "Do you have trouble sleeping, Mr Dumbleton?' asked Inspector Zhang.

Mr Dumbleton frowned. "What?"

Inspector Zhang nodded at the ear plugs. "I see you use ear plugs. My wife also has trouble sleeping when she is away from home and she finds that ear plugs help."

"I've always been a bad sleeper," said Mr Dumbleton. He reached for his cigarettes but put them down when he saw the look of disapproval on the manager's face.

"You are a heavy smoker?" asked Inspector Zhang.

'Twenty a day," said Mr Dumbleton. "It's my one vice."

"During the murder mystery lunch, did you leave the room for a cigarette?'

Mr Dumbleton shook his head. "I was going to when coffee was served, but we never got the coffee because they found the body."

"So did you leave the room at all?" asked Inspector Zhang.

"I don't think so," said Mr Dumbleton.

"Are you certain of that? If you did I'm sure the diners at your table would remember."

Mr Dumbleton looked over at the two British detectives. "Is he allowed to ask me these questions?"

"Actually he's not supposed to be asking any questions," said Chief Inspector Hawthorne. "But did you or did you not leave the room during the lunch?"

"I went for a pee," said Mr Dumbleton. "I wasn't gone more than a couple of minutes."

"Where was the bathroom?" asked the chief inspector.

"Out of the door and down the corridor to the left," said Mr Dumbleton.

"When?"

"Just after the main course. I finished my chicken and I went for a piss. But I didn't go upstairs, if that's what you're thinking."

"We're not thinking anything," said the chief inspector. "We're just trying to establish where everyone was."

"I thought Hyde killed himself."

"We have to investigate any unexpected death," said the chief inspector.

"Yeah, well good riddance is what I say," said Dumbleton.

"Why did you hate Mr Hyde so much?" asked Inspector Zhang.

"What?"

"This hatred you had for Mr Hyde, where does it come from?"

Mr Dumbleton glared at Inspector Zhang, his upper lip drawn back in a snarl. "What business is it of yours?"

"I'm just interested, that's all. Mr Hyde seemed a reasonably nice man, and while you might disagree with his views I don't see why that makes you so angry?"

Mr Dumbleton looked over at Chief Inspector Hawthorne. "Do I have to speak to him?"

"No, you don't."

"Then get him the hell out of my room," said Mr Dumbleton.

The chief inspector nodded at Inspector Zhang. "I think we've taken up enough of Mr Dumbleton's time," he said. He motioned at the door. Inspector Zhang smiled thinly and left the room. He waited in the corridor and a couple of minutes later the chief inspector joined him.

"He did it," said Inspector Zhang quietly. "He killed Mr Hyde."

"What makes you say that?"

"He is a sociopath. I can see it in his eyes. He hated Mr Hyde and he killed him."

"Mr Hyde was alone in the room when he died. Mr Dumbleton didn't have time to get upstairs to kill Mr Hyde and, even if he did, how did he get out of the room without being seen?"

"That is why I know it was him," said Inspector Zhang. "He is a crime writer, albeit not a successful one. He hated Mr Hyde and by killing him in a locked room mystery it adds to his feelings of superiority. It's his way of showing the world how clever he is."

"And where is your proof, Inspector Zhang?"

Inspector Zhang shrugged but didn't say anything.

"We need proof, Inspector Zhang. This isn't China, we don't throw people in jail because of a hunch."

Inspector Zhang frowned. "China?" he said. "Singapore isn't part of China. It never has been. The Republic of Singapore is a self-governed city state, it has nothing to do with China."

"Either way, we can't arrest Mr Dumbleton because you think he killed Mr Hyde."

"I understand," said Inspector Zhang.

"And really, it's time for you to go now," said the chief inspector. "We have to ask a few more questions and it's best that you're not with us."

"I understand," said Inspector Zhang. He shook hands with the policeman and then made his way down the stairs. His wife was waiting for him in reception, sitting in a green leather winged chair. She was holding a book and he squinted at the spine. It was Mr Hyde's book, the one that he had signed for Inspector Zhang. "I thought you didn't like mysteries," he said.

"I thought considering what has happened I'd give it a try," she said. "This is really rather good. I'm enjoying it. I have to say that it's a change to read a book by a good looking author. Most of the writers here do seem a little strange looking." She slipped it inside her handbag. "Anyway, how did it go with the English detectives?"

"I think they didn't appreciate me sticking my nose into their case," he said.

"They should be grateful for your help," she said. "Don't they realise what a wonderful detective you are?"

"They have their own way of doing things," he said. He told her what had happened in Mr Hyde's room. As he was finishing, Mr Dumbleton came down the stairs, holding his cigarettes. He glared at Inspector Zhang as he walked by and headed outside.

"I can never understand a person wanting to take their own life," said Mrs Zhang. "But I suppose Mr Hyde was mentally unbalanced."

"That is what the British detectives seem to think," said Inspector Zhang.

Mrs Zhang looked up at him, a slight frown on her face. "I know that tone," she said.

"Tone? What do you mean?"

"You don't think he took his own life, do you?"

"It doesn't matter what I think," said Inspector Zhang.

"It was a locked room, the door was locked and the window was closed. He was alone in the room."

Inspector Zhang nodded. "Everything you say is true. And I have no doubt that Mr Hyde was alone when he died." He held up his hands. "As the police kept saying to me, this is not my jurisdiction. I am a detective inspector with the Singapore Police Force. Here I am merely…" He shrugged. "A tourist."

The chief inspector came down the stairs followed by the hotel manager. "We have a doctor on the way to certify death and then we will have the body removed," said Chief Inspector Hawthorne. "We are going to talk to the chambermaid. But I doubt that she will tell us anything that makes us think this is anything other than a case of suicide."

"I understand," said Inspector Zhang.

"I just wanted to thank you for your interest in the case, and for securing the scene. But we now consider the case closed."

Inspector Zhang nodded but said nothing. As the chief inspector and the manager walked away, Mrs Zhang linked her arm through her husband's. "Tell me," she said.

"Tell you what?"

"Tell me what you think happened?"

Inspector Zhang sighed. Mrs Zhang fluttered her eyelashes prettily the way she always did when she wanted to twist him around her little finger and he laughed. "You know, you would make an excellent interrogator," he said.

"You're trying to change the subject," she said. "Tell me."

"Let's get some air," he said. They walked out of the reception area. Mr Dumbleton was standing outside the hotel, smoking a cigarette. Inspector Zhang nodded at the writer.

"You think I killed Mr Hyde, don't you?" asked Mr Dumbleton. He took a long drag on his cigarette then blew smoke directly at Inspector Zhang.

"Yes, I do," he said quietly.

"But you can't prove it, can you?"

"We shall see."

"Come on, Inspector. Hyde killed himself in a locked room. There was no one else there."

"Just like in all the best mystery stories," said Inspector Zhang.

"And you think that's what this is? A mystery to be solved? Well good luck with that, Inspector Zhang."

"He doesn't need luck," said Mrs Zhang, squeezing her husband's hand. "My husband solves cases with his brain. No one is better than him at solving mysteries."

"My dear, don't," said Inspector Zhang. He walked with her along the side of the hotel, away from Mr Dumbleton.

"But it's true," she chided him. She slipped her arm through his and gave him a gentle squeeze. "Now tell me, what happened in that room?"

Inspector Zhang chuckled at his wife's perseverance. "Everything you said was true," he said. "The door was closed and so was the window. But the important thing is the door wasn't locked and the bathroom window was open."

Mrs Zhang frowned. "I don't understand."

"There was a chain on the door but it wasn't on. So anyone in the room could have simply closed the door behind them when they left. Then the door is locked and someone on the outside has to use a key to get in. But that doesn't mean that Mr Hyde locked the door."

"But you said there was a maid in the corridor and she didn't hear anyone leave."

"That is true."

"But she heard the noise of the chair falling, you said. And she opened the door to discover the body."

"All true."

"So if Mr Hyde was murdered, she would have seen the killer if he had left through the door."

"Again, true."

They reached the corner of the hotel. Inspector Zhang looked up at the ivy-covered wall. He pointed at the window on the second floor. "That is the room where it happened," he said.

He turned the corner and pointed up at another window. "That is the bathroom. There is a large window and above it a much smaller window."

"Too small to climb through?"

"Much too small," said Inspector Zhang.

"And the other window was locked?"

They walked back to the front of the hotel. "Yes. But even if it wasn't, the killer couldn't have climbed down. He would have been seen." He reached up and patted the ivy. "Anyway, this is nowhere near strong enough to support a man's weight. Also, anyone climbing down would be clearly visible to anyone at the front of the hotel." He turned to look back at Mr Dumbleton, who was still smoking in front of the main entrance. "Where Mr Dumbleton is standing is where the smokers gather," said Inspector Zhang. 'If the killer made his escape down the ivy then he stood a very good chance of being seen. But as I said, the ivy is not strong enough."

"So there is a killer, you admit that much?" said Mrs Zhang.

Inspector Zhang chuckled. "Yes, my dear, I rather think there is."

"But if the killer did not leave through the door and he didn't leave through the window, how did he get out of the room once he had killed Mr Hyde."

"My dear, I believe that Mr Hyde was alone in the room when he died."

Mrs Zhang frowned. "So you do think he killed himself?"

"No, I am quite sure that Mr Hyde was murdered."

"You are confusing me now," said Mrs Zhang. She squeezed her husband's arm. "Come on, stop teasing me. How was Mr Hyde killed?"

"We know that, of course, he died by hanging. But I do not believe that he hanged himself."

"Someone pushed him off the chair?"

"Pulled, I think. But give me a minute or two to confirm my suspicions are correct." He looked over at Mr Dumbleton. He was watching them with narrowed eyes, the cigarette forgotten in his hands. "He is worried, you can see it in his eyes. There is something here that he does not want us to find, I'm sure of that."

He let go of his wife's hand and walked back around the side of the building. He looked up at the bathroom window, then at the ivy, and then he smiled to himself.

"I know that smile," said Mrs Zhang. "What have you seen?"

Mr Zhang chuckled but didn't say anything. He walked along the wall to a glass-panelled door and put his hand on the handle. He turned and pushed the door open. It led to a corridor. At the far end of the corridor was the reception area, and to his right were the bathrooms. Inspector Zhang closed the door and turned to smile at his wife.

"Mr Dumbleton was in the banqueting room at the murder mystery lunch, and he left only for a few minutes to visit the bathroom. That was when he killed Mr Hyde."

'But how? The maid would have seen him enter or leave the room."

"He didn't go into the room to kill Mr Hyde. He did it from here."

Mrs Zhang frowned. "From here? Now you're confusing me."

Inspector Zhang pushed away the ivy at the base of the wall. "He hasn't had time to remove the evidence. That's why he's outside. Whatever he used is still here."

"What could he have possibly used that would have made Mr Hyde kill himself?"

"String," said Inspector Zhang. "Or wire." He took a step to the side and brushed away a clump of ivy, then sat back on his heels. "Wire," he said.

215

Mrs Zhang looked over his shoulder. Half hidden by the ivy was a coil of green plastic-covered wire. Inspector Zhang pushed away more of the ivy to reveal a black fabric eye shade.

"What is that?" asked Mrs Zhang.

"An eye shade, like the one you wore on the plane," said Inspector Zhang. "Mr Dumbleton had difficulty sleeping. He used ear plugs. And I believe he used an eye shade, too. This eye shade." He took his fountain pen from his jacket and used it to gently turn the eye shade over to reveal the two Velcro strips that kept it in place. The green wire was looped around the eye shade at about the halfway point." Inspector Zhang nodded thoughtfully. "Now that was clever," he said.

"What's clever?" asked Mrs Zhang.

Inspector Zhang straightened up. "That was how he prevented Mr Hyde from calling for help," he said.

Mrs Zhang bent down to look at the eye shade. "How did it end up here?" she asked.

"Can't you see, it's tied to the wire?"

Mrs Zhang nodded. "I think I'm starting to understand."

Inspector Zhang smiled at his wife. "Why don't you tell me how he did it?"

"I'm not the detective," she said.

"I'd like you to try," said Inspector Zhang.

She squeezed his arm. "And I'd like you to try to iron your own shirts, but we both know that I do it better."

Inspector Zhang laughed and kissed her on the cheek. "Then I shall tell you what happened," he said. "Mr Dumbleton went to see Mr Hyde and somehow managed to get inside his room. This was long before the mystery murder lunch. Maybe after breakfast. I didn't see either of them at any of the morning sessions. Mr Dumbleton probably said he wanted to apologise, he'd have said whatever he had to in order to convince Mr Hyde to let him in. Once inside the room, he overpowered Mr Hyde. He handcuffed him and gagged him by stuffing a handkerchief in his mouth and keeping it in place with the eye mask. His plan was to wait until the murder mystery lunch was about to begin."

He took off his spectacles and began polishing them with his handkerchief. "Mr Dumbleton is a writer of mysteries, albeit not very good ones, and I think he had spent some time planning this, perhaps for a story. But yesterday, after his shouting match with Mr Hyde, he decided to put it into practice. He fixed a rope around the door, then put a chair under the noose. Then he forced Mr Hyde onto the chair and placed the noose around his neck. He then tightened the noose to restrict Mr Hyde's movement but not enough to cut off his air supply. It must have been a nightmare for Mr Hyde, not being able to move or to cry out."

Mrs Zhang shuddered. "That is horrible. Really horrible."

"Mr Dumbleton is a sociopath, I am sure he enjoyed making Mr Hyde suffer," said Inspector Zhang as he continued to work the handkerchief over the lenses of his glasses. "He took the wire and attached it to the eye shade, knotting it so that when the wire was pulled it would drag the eye shade away from Mr Hyde's face. Mr Dumbleton looped the wire around the leg of the chair. Then he passed both ends of the wire out of the bathroom window, allowing it to mix in with the ivy. Later, when he was outside, pulling on both ends of the wire would yank the eye shade away from Mr Hyde's mouth and then a fraction of a second later the loop would catch on the chair and pull it over. Mr Hyde would fall and be strangled. And Mr Dumbleton would simply pull one end of the wire through the window, bringing the eye shade with it. He had just enough time to coil up the wire and hide it here before returning to the banquet room. From start to finish it would have taken less than a minute."

"That's horrible," said Mrs Zhang. "Truly horrible."

The maid heard the chair tumble but Mr Hyde didn't have time to cry out. Later, when she opened the door to clean the room, she discovered the body. And by the time the alarm was given, Mr Dumbleton was eating his dessert. He had the perfect alibi, surrounded by several hundred mystery fans." He put his handkerchief away and replaced his spectacles. "That probably gave him a great deal of pleasure, to carry out the perfect murder in front of so many mystery fans. Sociopaths love to show the world how clever they are."

"But why would he kill Mr Hyde?"

"Jealousy," said Inspector Zhang.

"He killed a man for that?"

"Men have been killed for less, I'm afraid. But it's clear that Mr Dumbleton is unbalanced. A sociopath, or a psychopath perhaps. His mind does not function in the same way as yours or mine."

"He's mad?"

'We don't use words like that these days," said Inspector Zhang. "But yes, he is quite mad. I could see it in his eyes."

"And he killed Mr Hyde because he was jealous of his success?"

"That was the spark that ignited the fire, I think. But when his online campaign of harassment didn't achieve its objective, he became increasingly frustrated. The final straw, I think, was when he was publicly humiliated at the event where Mr Hyde was speaking. That is what pushed him over the edge."

"So he is a murderer, there is no doubt?"

"None at all," said Inspector Zhang. They walked together around the corner to the front of the hotel.

"But can you prove it?"

Inspector Zhang shrugged his shoulders. "I think the police here are as adept technically as we are in Singapore," he said. "I don't think that Mr Dumbleton would have worn gloves, or at least if he had done they would be here with the wire. That means his DNA is almost certainly on the wire. There should be marks on the window frame in the bathroom where the wire rubbed against it and I myself remember seeing marks on one of the chair legs. I am assuming that Mr Dumbleton did not come to Harrogate planning to kill Mr Hyde which means he almost certainly bought the wire locally. And if he used the sleeping mask himself, his DNA will be on it."

"Does that mean you will arrest him?" asked Mrs Zhang.

The inspector looked over at Mr Dumbleton. Mr Dumbleton smiled and nodded and raised his cigarette. The inspector nodded back. "I have no powers of arrest in England," he said. "And besides, a man as deranged as Mr Dumbleton can be dangerous. He might well lash out when cornered." The two English policemen walked out of the hotel. Chief Inspector Hawthorne looked at his watch and said something to Sergeant Bolton, then they began walking in Inspector Zhang's direction. "I will simply inform the local police of my findings and leave it up to them."

"So they will take the credit?"

"It is not about the credit, my dear," said Inspector Zhang. "It is never about the credit."

She squeezed his arm. "And you know what? We never did find out who the murderer was at the dinner."

"That? That was easy. It was the professor. He killed the victim with the shard of glass and then wiped the prints off with the victim's handkerchief. He then planted the handkerchief in Miss Smith's handbag when he sat down next to her in the library. He knew he would be alone in the greenhouse because he reset Mr Miller's alarm clock when he went to see him that morning. By resetting the clock by just one hour he knew Mr Miller would miss the appointment and the victim would be alone in the greenhouse."

"And what about the motive?"

Inspector Zhang nodded thoughtfully. "That was the difficult part. Because they were so keen to lead us astray, they gave strong motives to the three innocent parties. But Professor Green seemed to have no motive at all. In fact the real motive was only hinted at when he referred to the death of his partner, Mr Livingstone. Everyone assumed he was referring to a business partner but I think that he actually meant he and Mr Livingstone were lovers. Mr Livingstone, if you recall, killed himself after the victim took almost all the royalties from his first novel, the one that was a bestseller. I think that Professor Green killed the victim for revenge, one of the purest of motives."

"I have such a clever husband," said Mrs Zhang.

"And I have the best wife in the world," said Inspector Zhang. "Now, let me talk to the English detectives and then we shall go for a walk around this marvellous city."

THE END

Printed in Great Britain
by Amazon